The Sin Within

By

Thelmore H. McCaine

To Sallie Ruson
Enjoy life
from aunt
Thelmore Massey
Jan 27, 2010
and Back

ISBN: 0-7596-7273-3 (E-book)
ISBN: 0-7596-7274-1 (Paperback)

This book is printed on acid free paper.

1stBooks - rev. 05/05/03

The Sin Within is dedicated to Mr. John Eigel, who kept this book in my face for thirty-six years. Special thanks to GOD and to my Grand Daughter Tijuana Bradley and my son Craig McCaine.

Prologue

Jamestown, a landing of a white people in a strange land, a dream, a dream awaking, a dream of freedom and liberty come true.

Slavery, a landing of another people, a black people, in a strange land. "A dream, a dream alive with torment, forced to work hard at long lengths of time, most of the time in misery and pain—with no pay, sheer cruelty and agony." Slavery, the crack of the whip. Slavery, a way of life that changed the life of a people. Out of that change came a people—not a God-created people, but a man-laid people, the life of a people, not altogether in their ways. There was no time to talk of the old country from father to children. He lost the tongue he was born with; he learned what he knows of his beginning from books. Civilized through cruelty, brainwashing and violence—still filled with ignorance, somewhere he heard the words of the true living God. The Negro prayed and sang for deliverance. There was much praying, much singing and much 'Lord have mercy.'

"Our Father which are in heaven, hallowed be thy name. Thy kingdom come. Thy will be done on earth, as it is in heaven." Lord, I know you said, love thy enemy as thyself, love them that persecute you, bless them that misuse you. Ask, and it shall be given you. Seek, and you shall find. Knock, and it shall be opened unto you. Lord, if I ask this man for bread, he gives me a stone. If I ask for fish, he gives me a serpent. Lord I've got so many burdens down here. "Oh my Lord, my Lord, what shall I do? Lord the storm of life is ragging, stand by me." I pray and I pray. How long, O Lord, shall I bear this evil cross? Keep a-inch-ing along, a-inching, Jesus will come by and by. Nobody knows the trouble I've seen, nobody knows but Jesus. At last the Lord had the black man's soul and he was sure he believed.

Chapter 1

– Year 1963 –

It was long past their time of six-thirty, to leave for their employer's house about five stones throw from their own home. The two loyal Negro servants, Sam and Pursa McCloud, by this time six-thirty, would be in the Duncan kitchen. Pursa would be humming. Sam and Pursa would have had their coffee by 8:00 A.M. Pursa would be wailing away—'Jesus keep me near the cross.' Breakfast would be served by Sam to their employer, Andrew Duncan.

That morning seemed to be all out of sort. The two of them just couldn't get themselves together. It wasn't because they didn't sleep well. It wasn't because the night before Pursa and Sam fussed, and not because of the celebration either. It was because of tension and fear. All of the tension and fear started to grow from the time Andrew left, returned, and left again. This day he was coming home for a short stay.

The morning, of Andrew Duncan's homecoming, Pursa was piddling around their house pretending to dust, trying to delay going to the Duncan house. Pursa dusted those four rooms five times or more. Sam was in the bedroom looking in the big mirror over the dresser, trying to tie his tie. He tied one knot after another in that navy blue tie with red dots. None seemed just right. Sam wasn't in any hurry either to leave for the big house.

Andrew Duncan's homecoming was special. Sam and Pursa dressed in their Sunday best. Just the three of them were to celebrate this honored occasion—Andrew, Sam and Pursa. Pursa even baked a cake with white icing. On it, she wrote in red icing, "God Speed," to give Andrew courage to go on to be the man he always wanted to be.

Sam had on blue serge trousers and a white shirt. His dark face gleamed with the contrast of his collar. Pursa wore a light green, cool-looking cotton dress with little white stars. Oh, yes, Pursa had to have an apron. She wore a white very starched cotton apron. Sam always said if Pursa were to die before him, he would have an apron added to her burial clothes because she couldn't rest without one on. Pursa would wear an apron to church or to any affair, of that matter, if Sam didn't remind her, "You just don't wear aprons everywhere you go."

1

Pursa finally gave up pretending to dust. She flopped down in the old rocker in the living room and started to cry. Pursa cried so hard and loud that Sam rushed from the bedroom to see what was wrong with her.

"What's the matter Pursa baby, what is you crying for?" Sam said shaking with fright. The last time Sam heard Pursa crying so, was at Hattie Jones' funeral (one of her close friends) and that was some years ago.

Pursa replied, "Sam I just can't face him. You said he didn't even say he was really sorry, truly sorry for all the things he said and did...Hum, Hum, ...he should feel a might sorry. Mr. Andrew was always so kind and gentle!" Tears were streaming down her wrinkled face as she talked. "Sam do you think he was just nice 'cause we raised him that way? They always called him a nigger lover 'cause he treated colored folk with respect. I just don't understand this change in him. Lord what's wrong with that man?"

"Don't cry, Pursa baby, I don't understand this change in him neither and I don't want to go up there too, but we have to go up to the house. You make it like things worse than they are. Things ain't that bad. Come on, stop crying," Sam pleaded. Pursa wiped the tears away with her hand, but the tears kept raining down.

"Sam, I's just can't help it. I ain't going. I's too upset. He ain't the Mr. Duncan we know. I can't believe this our Mr. Duncan acting this way. He's been so good. Lord what troubling that man?"

"Now hush dat talk and stop crying. Pursa baby, since he done won, maybe he is in a good spirit. You surprise him with that cake you made and he'll tell us all bout the trip. We'll have a nice celebration. Everything will be all right," Sam said in a cheerful voice smiling putting his arm around Pursa's shoulder trying to comfort her.

Sam's consoling remarks didn't altogether make Pursa feel happy. His words prompted Pursa to fix her apron and blot up the tears, mourning to herself. "Lord have mercy, have mercy Jesus."

All this time, Trout, their Dalmatian pup of nine months, was waiting for them to leave for the big house. He looked from Sam to Pursa and wondered why they hadn't gone yet? He hadn't had his breakfast and he was hungry. He wondered too, why Pursa hadn't fed the mess of chickens they had out back. Trout cocked his head to one side, let out three barks, gave his tail a shove or two and waited for Sam to say, "Come on boy let's go." No word from Sam. He barked three more times, then looked from

2

Sam to Pursa. Neither said a word. To Trout, they just didn't have time for him this morning. Trout then took a long stretch, eased along side of the rocker, with sad eyes, and looked at the two of them talk.

"You know Sam, as I look back over the years, we ain't never had any mess like this. We never been stirred 'bout going up to the house. We ain't never had what you would call fusses, 'cause we all got along fine." Pursa's high-yellow face was dark and gloomy, she looked so unhappy. Sam stood in the middle of the living room floor in a glum sort of way, listening to Pursa talk. "We's never had to make any excuses for nothing, we's been one big happy family. Lord I's just don't understand this thing. Sam do you think the man done gone crazy?"

"Now Pursa, don't you start talking like dat. I know he done said and did lots of things that seems crazy but he's still our Mr. Duncan. He may be mad, but not crazy. Come on, let's get going 'cause we's late already."

"I ain't going Sam," Pursa said firmly. "Just because the goose done laid a golden egg-don't mean dat ain't no reason the goose won't still be mean as the devil. Now you's better be going. Tell him I's ailing this morning, 'cause I'll be up later on."

"I'll tell him something. Well, I guess I be moving along," Sam said reluctantly wishing Pursa would go with him. "Trout!" Sam called. Trout jumped up, whining and wagging his tail barking with joy. "Down boy, Down! You stay here and watch Pursa while I's go up to the house." Trout obeyed Sam and laid back down putting his sad face between his front legs. Pursa and Trout watched Sam close the screen door softly behind him, while he stepped out into the warm August morning air.

Sam started out alone. His face looked sadder than that of an old hound dog. Sam had gone through an awful trying experience. Pursa had been gone a month and she came back home only three weeks but the things she heard before she left and the things she heard when she got back upset her. Happenings that Sam told her being a woman and tender-hearted, made her all the more upset and fearful to go up to the big house. Around the Duncan place, they ain't never had bad happenings like this. It had the force of that like a wild fire.

At 80, Sam was as spry as a fox chasing a rabbit. That morning he kept his tall, hefty physique at a slow pace. He didn't notice the squirrel over yonder playing in the huge pecan tree or the many bees that buzzed around the beautiful yellow and pink mums that grew on either side of the path that led to the big house. He didn't hear the many songs of the mocking bird, which he so often imitated. That morning he didn't look up at the sky to see whether it was going to rain or shine. That morning he wouldn't say, "Mr. Andrew, the sun is going to shine mighty pretty but today we sho do need rain." He didn't observe any of these things on his way to the Duncan house. A little ways down the path, Sam turned and looked toward his house, wanting to go back, and wishing Pursa had come with him and in a distance he could hear Pursa singing "He's my rock, my sword, my shield; He's my wheel in the middle of the wheel. Oh my Lord, Oh my Lord, What shall I do?' "Lord", Sam said, "I wish that woman would stop that kind of singing." Shaking his head he continued up the path. He thought about his employer. How could a man change so? How could the changing times bring out so much evilness in a person overnight, Sam thought. Almost to the house, he stopped again. Looking at the old house, Sam took a minds' eye view of Spicewood Acres while many fond memories played with his mind.

Spicewood Acres was the name of the Duncan family estate. The white three story old place still stood in these modern times. The exterior of the old relic was well cared for with hunter green shutters enhancing the long windows, and a grand front porch with four tail graceful pillars on either sides. The lawn was greener than green, and it lay as if it were carpet. Here and there on the lawn were pink painted rustic iron benches and chairs placed neatly under the trees and in the garden. All around the grounds and around and about the house were beds of fanciful flowers; azaleas, zinnias, oleanders, camellias, poinsettia, asters and many beds of roses and other beautiful flowers. The fragrant honey-suckle was the great treat for the nose. When this greenery turned out her blossom, the fragrance made you take in a deep sniff to gather the perfume smell. On that somewhat busy highway, in front of the Duncan house, many a traveler slowed their cars just to take in the breathtaking scenery of the old plantation of the Duncan estate. Across the highway lay the latest in domiciles: the split-level, the ranch house, or someone's dream house was very unique indeed. But as you took a look at the old house, rain or shine, the huge structure stood out with pride saying, "at all times, I'm the fairest house in this land." To authenticate its grounds, the huge moss-draped oaks, about the front of the old place, brought out the picturesque look of the historic mansion.

The interior was reminiscent of the past. The high walls with some of the old masters paintings on them such as General Lee and Jackson and

4

some of the ancestors of Mr. and Mrs. Duncan's family, were lined with intricate moldings and decorative wallpaper. The six paneled, solid oak doors gave lead to a multitude of great rooms throughout; rooms adorned with antique pleasures, Oriental rugs, and imports of mahogany furniture. Some ways from the house was the family burial ground. Furthur down the backside of the house, lay a wooded area with two small lakes. Many Mongolia dotted in and out of the elms and maple and other trees and shrubs. About a mile from the house, land tapered off into the farm area.

After taking stock of the Duncan plantation, Sam moseyed on down the path where he reached the back door of the Duncan house. Instead of going in as usual, he just stood there trying to make up his mind whether to go in or not. Shaking his head in dismay, he took one more step, but something within him refused to go in. As Sam walked around the side of the house to the front, from the long window he could see Andrew Duncan sitting at the big desk with a paper in his hand. Andrew looked as though he were in a trance. He hadn't even seen Sam watching him. Sam stood there awhile looking at his employer, the man he loved as one of his own, the man he knew so well. Disheartened, Sam shook his head again and walked away from the window. Sam walked around the front yard a bit trying to think of something to say. What excuse could he give for them not being there to welcome him home? What real excuse could he give for Pursa? Couldn't he understand their feelings? What lie could he tell in place of the truth? He didn't want to hurt his feelings as bad as he hurt theirs. Seeming to look at the zinnia that smile in the August bright sun, Sam reasoned to himself about how things had changed around the place. As they say 'things ain't the way they used to be'. Looking toward the big old house again, remembering the place as it was in days gone by, gay as summer, a pinpoint smile came to his face and his eyes sparkled.

The Duncan's were a big splash in their day. He remembered the tasty hors d'oeuvres and the tantalizing drinks. Guests ranging anywhere from four to a hundred or more, not only from the south but from different parts of the country. The luncheons and teas were very clair de loom. Sometimes Pursa and other servants spent a couple of days in preparation for Duncan's elegant dinners and parties. The lace or linen tablecloths were spread on the tables. Crystal glassware, sparkling silver and delicate china were all in good taste. Many delicacy and rich dishes were served. The smell of bar-be-cue hunted his nose from the by-gone days of the big bar-be-cue. The sound of hounds drummed in his ears—a hunting we will

5

go to catch a fox, rabbit or raccoon. The conversation of these affairs were inspirational and the usual town's gossip. Mr. and Mrs. Duncan put on their real southern charm. The Duncan's were either going to some charming or high-sadditty affair or either giving one, but this was all gone now soon after the death of Andrew's father, Mase Thomas Duncan, who died in his prime. Mrs. Duncan lost interest in life and laid her social and charity activities aside and dismissed all of the servants except Sam and Pursa McCloud and their family. Pursa did the laundry, the cleaning and the cooking. Sam was the chauffer, the butler, and the groundskeeper. The children helped with these chores until they flew the coop. For some untold years they had been royal servants in the Duncan household. Life hadn't always been sweet, but as Sam's mind drifted back to the present, things seemed ever more unbearable now. His smile left and his face sunk into sadness. Looking down at the flowers, talking out loud to himself, "Sho been a long time since I gathered a bunch of you." Thinking flowers would show how he was missed and to say they were sorry they weren't there to greet him; they would be taken to show how proud he was of him for winning. Smiling, picking the pretty zinnias, he felt like a small boy with a well-chosen present. Walking back across the front lawn, he could see Andrew still sitting at the desk. He remembered when he came into the world, recollecting the words of Andrew's father, "Sam, it's a boy. He's going to make a fine man." With flowers in hand, opening the front door, Sam walked half way down the large entrance hall into the living room. On the left side of the entrance hall, he opened the large sliding doors to the study. The sound of the opening doors didn't disturb this man who sat in the big hand-carved chair. Andrew sat with the stillness like that of a store dummy. His eyes looked as if they were hypnotized on the piece of paper he held in his hand. On the desk lay a separate letter. Sam walked over, touched Andrew on the shoulder, smiling saying in his deep voice, "Mr. Duncan I brought you some flowers."

Springing from the chair, Andrew flung his arms around Sam's neck babbling, "Sam, oh Sam."

"What's the matter Mr. Duncan? What's the matter?" Sam said in a frightened voice.

Andrew had no answer. With his head on Sam's shoulder, Andrew sobbed like a child that had awakened out of a bad dream. Sam's almost black face broke out in a sweat; his stomach turned over. He had never seen this man in a state like this. Kind of collecting himself, Sam held the

6

flowers in one hand put his other arm around Andrew, patting him on his shoulder like he used to do when he was a child, to seemingly heal the hurt; Andrew quieted down.

"Now, now," old Sam said, "ain't nothing that bad." Still patting Andrew on the shoulder, "Tell old Sam what's wrong."

Andrew snatched himself from Sam shouting, "Get your black hands off me. Don't you pat me on my shoulder. I'm not a child anymore. Call Dr. Sliver! "Sam, I want to talk to you," Andrew said. As he was taking the letter from the desk, he took a pack of matches from the desk drawer, struck one, put it to the letter and watched it burn until it almost burned his fingers. It finished burning in the waste can. Sam started to sit on the old leather couch. "Here Sam, sit in my chair, maybe it will make you feel equal." Sam sat in the big chair with the flowers in his hands. Sam didn't know how to take this man whom he thought he knew so well. "You know Sam," Andrew said holding the note in his hand, "we southerners have a lot of pride." (Pointing the note at Sam). "Mind you not only the southern white but the American white man in general. We are truly proud of ourselves. The white man took this country that was just a wilderness and built a gigantic empire. This is a masterpiece of wonders." His voice was bold and plain. Sam wondered what was this all about. "I don't see what your people are crowing about. They are just like everyone else. There's the haves and have-nots."

"Yes sir" Sam said just to answer his remarks—but he still didn't know what he was talking about.

Andrew started pacing up and down the room. "The pilgrims came to this country for the cause, the Constitution is for the cause, the Gettysburg Address was about the cause, the Civil War was fought all for the cause, but we seem to really never get around to exercising these facts. For some, I guess we have to take the slow—but sure way—to get this monster out, his voice dropped in a wondering tone—out of our blood." The room filled with silence.

"Mr. Duncan, I don't really understand what you mean." Sam said breaking the silence.

Andrew walked slowly around the desk until he came face to face with Sam. Andrew, shouting in a loud angry voice with quivering tones, "You know damn well what I mean; you're not ignorant of what your people are doing and trying to do. You black bastards talk about equalization. If I get to be governor, (pointing to himself), I'm a good man. I'll do what I

7

promise. I'll keep this state in order. I'll keep you niggers out!" Old Sam said nothing. He was too shocked. He was glad Pursa didn't come. She would be hysterical by now. "Sam, just what do your people want? Didn't we give you freedom, jobs, homes, schools and your own neighborhoods and lots of other essential things any man needs to get going in this world? Not letting Sam answer his question-he went right on with his righteous sermon, still walking back and forth in front of Sam, lashing out again, "What will your people gain wanting to go to our schools and public and private places—just tell me that!" His voice was strong and direct expecting an answer from Sam.

"Mr. Duncan, I haven't thought about the problem one way or the other."

Andrew, looked at Sam in a somewhat sarcastic manner, "You mean to sit there and tell me that you haven't thought about this situation. Sam, I've never known you just tell a lie. I just can't believe you haven't given this thing—'integration'—a thought. Do you realize the white man is the one that keeps you people from acting like sub-humans? You are, and as long as the Negro remains in Mississippi, we will keep him in his place. Whoever heard of servants sitting down with his master and enjoying the luxury of his master; it just isn't done."

As Sam listened to Andrew talk, a small voice inside of him started singing, "Sometimes I feel like a motherless child a long way from home; sometimes I'm up, sometimes I'm down, sometimes I'm almost to the ground. Oh yes Lord, but Lord I ain't felt like this up or down." He was trying to let his feelings settle down thinking he was too old to think about such things. To change the subject, Sam looking down at the flowers, rose from the chair to give them to Andrew. Andrew forcefully pushed Sam back into the chair. Andrew's eyes were wild with rage—putting the note unconsciously in his pocket. "You listen to me", he yelled angrily pointing his finger in Sam's face, "Your people are still ignorant, irresponsible, troublemakers. The white man is the incomparable one! (Grabbing Sam by the collar) and shaking him, "You people have always called on the white man to take care of your wants and needs. Stay in your place. We don't want any jungle vultures like your people invading our world."

Sam sprang from the chair, pushing Andrew back, freeing himself. Sam was trembling, perspiration was running down his face, flowers falling to the floor, Sam grabbed Andrew by his arms with strength he didn't realize he had. "Listen Mr. Duncan," Sam said nervously, "If you don't stop acting up, me and Pursa have to leave." Andrew looked surprised. Sam let Andrew's arms free. "Mr. Duncan, we just can't stand this thing any longer; whatever is happening to you, we just have to leave. We just have to leave, that's all." Sam's words seemed to dissolve the tension and anger in him.

"Why Sam, you can't leave. You have been with the family ever since I can remember. I look up to you and love you as my own father. Why I couldn't do without you."

"Mr. Duncan, we don't want to leave this place. This is the only home we know. We love you as one of our own children. You always been like a son to me, but we can't stand the way you been acting."

"I'm sorry Sam. I just can't help the way I feel about this integration business."

"Me and Pursa don't bother about this thing. We do more looking at pictures in the paper than we read and what we listen to others say and what we hear on TV and radio, 'bout this integration business. Since all our children are grown and done left home, me and Pursa keep to ourselves. We just don't think 'bout this situation."

"Well maybe you haven't given this problem a thought," Andrew said with not much assurance in his voice, "but this does concern you too. It's the whole country's problem, whatever you believe in."

"Mr. Duncan, ain't me and Pursa been the same since this mess started?"

"Yes, you two have been the same, but you two should think about this problem."

"You know, Mr. Duncan, we could build up the same hate you have, but we ain't; we just ain't going to let this integration bother us. Our time is too short for that. But what troubles me is all these things you been doing and saying since you started campaigning. I can't believe it's you! This thing sure got your mind stirred up. I never believed this thing is in your heart. You musta got all this mess out of the garden somewhere. It sure ain't the good stuff; it must be the weeds."

"Sam I really hadn't given integration too much thought until I started running for governor. The more I campaigned, the more I thought, the angrier I became. Some damn fools want to change Mississippi just for political motives. Sometimes I wake up in the night thinking about this thing. I can't help or change what I believe."

9

"I think I know how you feel, but please stop taking it out on us," Sam pleaded.

"Sam I'm sorry. I hadn't realized that I've been that rude. I will try to keep my feelings to myself. For the life of me, I just can't see your peoples' side and I don't see some of those S-O-B's in Washington's point either. What are they trying to prove? I guess they think this is a little problem, but this is a big problem. It's bigger than the mind. It looks deep into the hearts of people. You can't tinker with integration like one does a toy."

"Mr. Duncan, you sure look all tuckered out."

"Sam, I am so tired; I'm so tired I could scream," Andrew said worriedly."

"Can I get you something?"

"No, I'd better wait for doc."

"You know we forgot all 'bout the celebration. Pursa baked a cake that says 'God Speed'. I picked these flowers, (Sam looked at the flowers on the floor) to show how proud we was of you winning the election. Congratulations," Sam said smiling.

"I'm sorry I took the joy out of my coming home. I really forgot all about the celebration. I was too riled up over this integration business. Where is Pursa?"

"Well, she thought you would be mean as a goose. She was afraid to come up."

"Have I been that much of a villain?"

"I's afraid you is."

As Sam gathered up the somewhat wilted zinnias, he still wondered what was all the crying about and too, he wondered about integration. Like Andrew said—this concerned him too. It is everybody's concern, whatever they believed. Sam scratched his head and dismissed his thinking. It was almost noon. Doc Sliver hadn't come. Sam had gone in the kitchen to fix Andrew a bite to eat. Sam thought a little food would quiet the anger. Sam brought in a tray with tomato juice, a roast beef sandwich, a small bowl of sliced peaches and a portion of the cake Pursa had made for the celebration. Andrew was sitting in the big chair looking the way he did this morning but this time it was more of a worried look. Sam wondered what was really troubling him. Maybe the big election was bothering him. Sam set the tray on the desk. "Mr. Andrew, now don't you fret 'bout that big election. Everything will be alright."

10

"It's not the election, Sam. I wish doc would hurry up. I need something to relax my mind and nerves." Andrew barely touched the food. Sam looked at the food on the tray that Andrew hardly touched saying in his festive concerned way, "Eating like a goldfish ain't doing you no good. Maybe if you would eat something, you might feel better."

"I'm not hungry!" Andrew shouted.

"I tell you what, Mr. Andrew, you go lie down in the spare bedroom down there. Try to get some rest. I'll go to the kitchen and fix up a tall cold drink that will make any man relax." Sam thought if he could get him a little woozy with a good stiff drink, he might go to sleep instead of staring like he's tried crazy.

Andrew did take Sam's advice about lying down. Instead of going to bed, he stretched out on the old couch in the study. Lying there trying to rest his mind, in come Trout out of somewhere. Trout jumped up on Andrew barking and whining his head off, wagging his tail to the tune of mighty glad to see you and welcome home, dog fashion, of course. Andrew sat up on the couch. Trout always brought a smile to his face. He patted Trout's head and stroked his back gently rubbing his face against Trout. "I see you're as frisky as ever. Glad to see me boy!" Trout whined a bit. "Good to see you too boy. I'm home for a little while and off again to the big race." Andrew stretched out on the couch again with Trout alongside.

Sam finally brought in the drink he thought would help ease Andrew's mind. While Andrew took a few sips, as Sam sat in the big chair watching him. Trout had scampered off to Sam continued to watch Andrew like a hawk and he tried to think about integration. He tried to remember some of the things the preacher had said about integration in church. His mind soon strayed away from his thoughts, looking at Andrew—he still didn't look right to Sam. Thinking he might go off again, Sam thought he'd better put his minds' eye on Andrew. "Mr. Duncan, do you feel any better?" Sam asked, with some doubt.

"I feel a little better. I just don't know what made me go off the way I did this morning. Maybe it's my nerves. Sam I'm pretty tired from all this campaigning. It's hard you know." While Andrew was explaining to Sam about politics, the doorbell rang. Old Sam answered the door. "Hi Dr. Sliver, come on in."

"How is Pursa?"

"Oh, she's fine, just a little upset; old I guess." Sam was trying to hint to doc the reason Pursa was upset.

"Sam, you bring Pursa in for a checkup. Now...on the other hand, well, who around here thinks their sick?" Doc said following behind Sam where Andrew was.

"I'm not sick Doc. I'm just run down, and real tired. What took you so long?"

"I'm a very busy man. I see patients in their homes as well as at my office. If you must know, I just delivered a baby. Take off your shirt."

"Doc, I don't need an examination. I'm just tired."

"Your heart sounds okay. Your blood pressure is a little high, but not too bad. You don't seem to have any fever, but you do look tired. I'm going to give you some pills to take. Take two now then take one three times a day. I'll have the pharmacist send over a few more. They will make you rest and settle your nerves. I think you should stay home a couple of weeks before you start campaigning again."

"Doc, I can't stay out of the race that long."

"From the looks of you, you need a month's rest. You've lost weight. You have bags under your eyes. A week's rest will do you good. You know me, Andrew. I don't pull any punches with my patients. Your committee can take over 'til you have rested."

"Alright Doc, I'll do as you say. I know you are right."

"Oh, by the way, congratulations! I hope you win the general election," Doc said with a smile on his somewhat fat, red face.

"Thanks Doc, I sure worked hard enough. The road ahead looks mighty rough. Thanks for coming and thanks again for your vote."

Doc wasn't interested in politics, only his patients—black or white. Doc picked up his little black bag to leave. Sam started to see him to the door. Sam still thought he should talk to Doc about how mean Andrew had been behaving. Andrew knew if Sam saw Doc to the door, Sam would spill to Doc how he acted this morning, not that Doc could care that much—but it would be a great embarrassment to Andrew. Andrew said quietly to Sam, "Sam get me a glass of water. I will see Doc to the door."

Andrew took the pills. He then settled down in the very comfortable spare bed downstairs. As he lay there, memories of the past invaded his mind. He thought of the primary election, his mother, and Lee and Doff Rainey.

Chapter 2

It was June 1963. The days were nice and hot. The Duncan truck farmers had put in their second crop for the year. Days were nearing for Andrew to tour the state for the primary election. His mother, Mrs. Lucy Ann Duncan, had gained a lot of courage seeing her son run for governor. It made her want to get out and meet people again. She began to hold her head up high like the high society lady she used to be. Andrew felt wonderful seeing his mother her old self again. One day, sitting in his study smiling to himself, he found some newfound joy. Winding his way out of the study into the living room, where his mother was, he stopped like a toy plane in front of her. She sat up in a dignified manner, and in a playful high voice she said, "What is it, son?" Putting out her tired, wrinkled hand.

He took her hand, speaking in his very distinguished southern voice, "Your ladyship, how would you like to go with your charming son touring the state, meeting people again, turning on that charm you have been hiding for years?"

A big smile covered her face, "My son, I would love that!"

Picking her up, swinging her around in a happy frame of mind, putting her down lightly. "Oh Mother, you make me feel so happy." She profoundly replied, "My son, I'm so happy for you. I hope your dreams come true."

"You know I always wanted to be governor. You remember all those speeches I used to make when I was just a little shaver?"

"How well do I remember. (Laughing) I know you remember the last speech you made."

Andrew laughed a little too. "I can't forget. That was the day that Pursa whaled the tar out of me. I can hear her now. You ain't running for no governor. You's too young. This is the last speech I want to hear around here. You hear me. I think that was the last time she ever spanked me." They both laughed heartily.

"Mother, I do hope my dream comes true. I wish Father were here. How he would love the glamour of campaigning. Why, with him out fighting with me, I would be the first republican governor here in Mississippi in years."

"Your Father has been dead for years. It would be so nice if he were alive." Her face looked grave; silence filled the room. Mrs. Duncan perked up with a smile. "I think you and your committee will do fine. You've always been ambitious. You have dealt with all kinds of people. You know what the people need and want. People seem to take to you."

"I pray many will marvel in me as you do and I trust I will get as many votes as your love for me. Mother, when I asked you to go campaigning with me, I forgot you aren't sixteen anymore. Campaigning is no easy task."

"I imagine campaigning is hard work but I think it will do me good to get out. Do you realize all I've done in the last twenty years is go up to the farm, help take care of the business, sit around here chatting with Sam, Pursa and you, whenever you come home. When your father died, I shut out almost everything and everybody out of my life. I don't know what the rest of the world looks like. The only person who comes around here is Doc Sliver and the only reason he comes, is cause he thinks he's sweet on me."

"Mother, I do think you ought to think about the tour before you give me an answer."

"You know, son, I don't know what your girlfriend looks like. When you entertain your friends, you take them to some restaurant because I refuse to have company in the house. This may be the best thing that ever happened to me."

"All well and true, but I do think you ought to give campaigning a good once over."

"Son, I'll campaign til all my power gives out. If I get tired, I can always come home."

"Alright, you're the boss. My lady friend is very nice. She lives about a mile down the highway in one of the new homes with her uncle and aunt. She's from Connecticut and she paints. She got tired of painting the old East and she decided to come down here and paint the old South. She's mighty pretty too. She has flaming red hair, green eyes, kind, tall, a little on the slim side."

"Son, a Yankee gal! She sounds like one of those movie stars!"

"She looks like one, but not the same personality traits."

"Let's have her over for dinner one night this week so I can kind of get acquainted with her. I'll have Pursa make something real scrumptious."

"I'm afraid you will have to meet Terence Honey Thompson when she gets back. She went home to take care of her sick mother."

"Well I am sorry to hear about her mother. We will get acquainted when she comes home or when we get back from campaigning. Terence Honey Thompson, hmm…that sounds kind of Hollywood to me but heck…dogs eat shoes…so what am I talking about? I don't know the girl." Andrew chuckled at his mother's remarks. It was all decided that Mrs. Duncan would go campaigning. Mrs. Duncan thought she would make herself ready for the biggest step in her son's life. She went out and brought herself a whole new wardrobe. Mrs. Duncan was so impressed with the fashions. It took her over two weeks to choose the clothes. She wanted to make an impression. When Sam drove her uptown to shop, she couldn't believe her eyes. She purred like a kitten at the sight of so many new homes, shops, food stores, and so many places to eat.

"They did a good job painting Braidwood up," Sam said, getting a kick out of her feeling so much joy in being her old self. "Look over there." Sam brought the car to a quick stop. The sign read 'Mr. Duncan, Attorney-at-Law.'

Everyone who knew Lucy Duncan was pleased to see her out of her cage. The lady at the beauty shop talked her into getting her long silver hair cut in the latest style. As Pursa put it, her new hairdo made her look ten years younger. She looked like a real glamour gal.

Chapter 3

When people read in the newspaper and by word of mouth that Andrew had chosen to run as one of the candidates for governor, many of Andrew's friends called and sent telegrams and letters wishing him well. One of his old friends, whom he hadn't seen or heard from in years, was Ms. Lee Rainey. Andrew, Lee and her husband grew up together in Braidwood's countryside. Lee wasn't a pretty woman, but was as attractive as a Picasso painting: a well-kept figure, long dark brown hair with big cow-like eyes. All of Lee's life, she had loved Andrew. But as life has its' turnabouts, instead Lee married Doff Rainey. Andrew went into law and farming. Doff took on real estate. He and Lee moved away while Andrew stayed in Braidwood with his mother. No matter how Lee tried to forget loving Andrew, her love for him wanted to blossom in her like monthly roses with sweet words of love on each petal and the dew filling the flower's wantonness. When she read in the paper that Andrew was running for governor, she sprang at the chance to talk with him. Time and time again, she would have loved to be in Andrew's arms. Out of the respect for her husband, she fought the feeling for years. Lee picked up the receiver, dialed the number she knew so well. Andrew answered. "Hi, Andrew, bet you can't guess who's calling?"

"No, I don't think I can."

"Lee, Honey," she said in a harmonious voice.

"Why Lee Honey, I haven't heard your voice in a long time. My, my. It's so good to hear from you." Andrew said smiling. "How is Doff and business?"

"Oh, Doff is fine. He's getting what they call the money spread fat around the middle. Business is good. How are things around the farm and your practice of the law?"

"Thank the good Lord, we have had wonderful crops for several years. You know there are so many wonder foods for crops. Shucks, that stuff makes vegetables look more and more like pictures every year."

"I still hate carrots. Remember you used to tell me if I ate those carrots they would make me beautiful. You brought them to me by the bunches and I would eat those things like a nut. You never knew how sick those carrots made me. You sure had me fooled."

"I don't know how much I fooled you, but you did turn out to be a looker. Those carrots turned you out to be prettier than a flower on a magnolia tree. You know, I have something to tell you that you never believed about carrots. We are working on a round carrot, one that will have more of a fruit flavor than a vegetable."

"You're kidding!"

"No, I am not. In the near future, you and a lots more people will be eating a most delicious carrot, pleasing to the taste like an orange or some other kind of fruit."

"Now that will be the day," she laughed heartily at the idea. "Andrew, you always wanted to be governor. You will be the greatest governor this state ever had. You always were a good Samaritan. Congratulations! Any time you need our help or advice, just call on us any time."

"Thanks Lee, I just might take you up on the advice, that's if I need to."

"Andrew Honey, when you get to Clearforest, you are invited to stay at our home, rest a day or two. And oh, I forgot to ask—how is your mother, Sam and Pursa? Your father's death took so much life out of your mother."

"If I feel that tired when we reach Clearforest, I'll take you up on the invite. Sam and Pursa are getting around like they're sixteen. God has blessed them with good health. Mother is bright-eyed and bushy-tailed. She's her old self again. I asked her to go campaigning with me. The idea seemed to perk her up."

"Don't you think campaigning is a bit too much for her at her age?"

"After I gave the idea second thought, I thought it was too much for her too. But she insisted on going. As she put it, if she gets tired, she can always come home."

"If she feels that way, she'll be alright." She reminded him of their childhood days when he used an old wooden box for a speaker platform and some of the phrases he used with them—"Vote for Andrew Duncan. I'll be the greatest governor Mississippi ever had. I'll give you all the peanuts and popcorn you can eat. You don't have to work six days, just three." They both broke out in laughter, at his childhood endeavors. "Andrew, I wish you all the luck in the world." They chatted about this and that, but Andrew ended the chit chat with "Lee, thanks a lot for calling. I've got to get on the run. Tell Doff hi. Keep your fingers crossed. Say a prayer. I'll need the luck."

17

"Give my regards to your mother, Sam and Pursa." When Lee put the phone on the cradle, she had a sly, shy smile of that of the Mona Lisa on her face that seemed to say—wouldn't you like to know what I'm smiling about?

As Andrew lay there in bed, he thought of some of the speeches he had made during the primary election. Sam had gotten a chair and sat outside the bedroom door where Andrew was, but not out of his sight. Sam thought he should still keep an eye on Andrew. While Sam sat watching, the things Andrew said speared his mind. "Sam this thing, integration, concerns you too." He too thought of the speeches Andrew had made and also of the things he had heard around town. But one question kept piercing Sam's mind…why do people need this thing integration? Of all the things he heard—the question of why or even why his people didn't need integration—didn't seem to fit in his mind. He knew it was something deeper but he just couldn't put his finger on it. Sam sat there scratching his head trying to break through his thoughts.

Chapter 4

Andrew was billed as one of Mississippi's most respected citizens - one of the most highly recognized citizens ever to run for governor. He had given time to his fellowman in many capacities—an attorney, a farmer, and a man of religion. He knew the wants of people and their needs and he well understood the integration problem. Andrew Duncan had campaigned long and hard against his opponent in the primary. He had won the honor to run for governor. For his first speech, all turned out in Braidwood and in other small towns: the good liver, the not so poor, the young, the old, the businessman, the laborer and the farmer. The Negroes came too, although they knew they weren't exactly wanted. There were only about one of fifty who could vote. Most were from the Ducan plant ranch (truck farm). They believed in Mr. Duncan. He would be their savior, another great emancipator. He would fight for their liberty and justice. He was a good man. He stood with the grace of Lincoln; his voice came loud and clear through the microphone. The tones of his voice were like that of a symphony orchestra. The winds, the strings, the woodwinds and the percussion of his speech played in the right spots and the rhythm of his voice held the crowd. He didn't even need to practice in speech-making. He had acquired that from summing up cases in court.

"Fellow citizens, you have gathered here this afternoon in hope of one who will stand up and fight for our great heritage which our forefathers fought a great war. We should lay hold to our basic principles, one who will keep the rights of our state and customs. I give myself to the people. I know the needs of the people in the state of Mississippi. Although I have done great works as attorney for the rich and the poor, what little I've done, I would do more if I were governor. Being a lawyer and a farmer traveling around the country, I find all our needs are basically about the same with some greater than others—decent jobs, fit housing, the best education, better prices for the farmers and their workers, decent and proper medical care for all our citizens." A hurrah of applause filled the air. "Federal aid for our schools and colleges. I'm a republican", he cried, "You need no democrat to fill your needs. All of you know me. My word is your security. If I have broken my word with anyone out there, raise your hand." There was only the sound of a few fans and deep silence. Not a hand was raised. Looking around at the crowd—smiling he said,

"In me you can keep this firm belief. It's important to increase the growth of our state. We need industry. You will want one who will keep corruption out of our government and not only with the gangsters but with that big inconspicuous creep they call integration!" The whites in the crowd went wild with cheers and applause. He waited til the crowd quieted down. Andrew took on another voice—that of a preacher speaking with loud, bold tones. "This thing called integration doesn't only lie in the south but in the hearts of all the American people. This tension is everywhere. The northerners say they are the do-gooders, and that we bare too much injustice to our niggers. Mind you, they aren't having a tea party with their niggers either." Wiping the sweat from his face, as he stood on the courthouse steps in Braidwood, a light cool breeze wandered through the crowd. The moss draped on the oaks swaying in the breeze. The breeze didn't help too much. People were everywhere on the Courthouse Hugh Lawn, on the sidewalk, in the street. The Negroes stood in the back; but as life goes, some black face will make it up front. Those little children's black faces just beamed. Whenever Andrew went to the farm, he always carried a box of penny peppermints or lollipops to give to the children. They loved him for this gesture. Although the heat remained relentless, Andrew went on with his righteous sermon. "This monster integration is putting its' fangs in the north's schools, housing, public and private places. Believe me, they aren't taking this thing like candy. It feels like a heart attack, just like it feels to us. It's a pain where it hurts the most. I tell you, if we let these cockroaches get started-they will be all over the place. We won't be able to breathe with them around. We ain't going to let them get started down here! We are going to kill that snake integration—here and now and its' tail ain't going to shake when the sun goes down. I mean it's going to be dead." The whites went wild with cheers. Andrew's face was red from the heat. He was wet with sweat from his head to his feet. His crisp shirt Pursa pressed was soaked and his trouser's hung off his 5'10" frame in misery. Regardless, his appearance didn't matter now; from the township's view, he was right. "I'll keep this state in order. Some men are guided by foolish opinions. Let our own minds be our guidebook. They say we are arrogant, that we southerners want to keep the Negro down, just for our folly. We want to be lords. We have given our Negroes what they worthy of. It is the laborer who is worthy of his hire. Now, there is no doubt in my mind what Negroes are striving for in this integration business—to degrade the virtuous white woman, to lower her dignity to that harlot, to sweet-talk, to harass her into being a whore to satisfy their evil weakness. Truly, the white woman is sweet and pleasant to the eye—who can find a more virtuous woman? Her price is far above rubies. Strength and honor are her clothing. Oh how lofty are the eyes of that of a black man. They tempted us in our hearts by asking equal rights for their lust. Our forefathers didn't fight for the love of death, but for what they believed—in our way of life based on our great heritage. I say to the Negro, this thing you call integration—put this evil from your hearts. The blacks in the crowd wanted to leave but they seemed to be charmed to listen like a snake charms a bird. Mr. Duncan looked up to the heavens and in a loud, trembling voice he said, "What is it the Negro wants, oh Lord?" He then looked down on the crowd. "We are for liberty and for a host of things that the blacks need. I beseech thee, O Lord, to look down on my black brother." Looking up to the heavens again, Andrew said in a very loud voice, "Oh God, please forgive them for they know not what they do." Looking down on the crowd again saying, "I thank you all for coming. Don't forget to vote for me, you hear."

Andrew had finished his furious speech. The blacks in the crowd stood there for a spell, not knowing what to say or do. They just looked at one another, then at him. Those who walked to hear this great man speak—went off to their homes in slow motion with their faces muddled. All of the Negroes well understood Andrew's speech. They looked as though they were hypnotized with disbelief. Sam and some of the other workers from the farm had prepared a tasteful bar-be-que. The bar-be-que didn't make them want to stay. All they wanted to do was to get away from this unbelieving tale. Hearing Andrew speak was like telling them there was no God. The blacks couldn't believe that was their Andrew Duncan speaking—the man who was so good to them; the man who paid them so well; the man who listened to their troubles. They thought of the nice barracks they lived in with all the conveniences of a modern home. For those who didn't live in the barracks, he built homes which were paid for on easy terms. The man you could call for a good job. Always in the same jolly mood, he made them feel that they were glad they were born. The Negroes from the Duncan farm going home that evening didn't talk among themselves about the speech. Going to the fields, the next morning, they were still too stunned to talk about the previous days events. By mid-afternoon, the speech was no longer a dream. Reality had speared their hearts in different ways. They argued and talked among themselves.

21

They had stopped the work in the fields and gathered together—the grownups and the children. Some of them thought it was just political talk. He never acted superior to them. He just didn't treat them that way. They began to think that it was just all a game, that he had to use the same tactics his opponents used if he wanted to win. It was all in the game. Things would be different if he won. Others argued differently. They said if he was the good man they thought he was, he would spit out the words that really stood for justice, the Constitution, Lincoln, John Brown, Frederick Douglass and the Great Challenge that brought so many people to this great land—not a selfish speech that was so undemocratic. The thing that really stung about the speech was the talk of sex and the black man's intentions.

Old Jonah, one of the workers who had been on the Duncan farm for years, was retired. He had come in from the front of the farm where he always sat near the entrance, coming to get his lunch. The Duncan's had given him a room in one of the barracks. His wife was deceased and his three children were living in other states. On his way to his room, he saw them gathering in the field some short distance away. He made his way down and joined them. He found that they were talking about the speech. He let them finish some of their thoughts. Jonah kind of cleared his throat and said, "Well." They all looked his way. "I hear you all talking 'bout the speech. You know, Mr. Duncan and Mississippi reminds me of the story of Sodom and Gomorrah. We thought we had one who would stand up for justice. Now didn't y'all believe that?" Some answered yes; others kept their peace. But all looked embarrassed. They all believed that Andrew Duncan would deliver them. "I believed in him too, just like y'all. I feel bad inside too. Mississippi is worse than Sodom and Gomorrah. They did find Lot and his family; but we can't find one here. He's been so good to us. No wonder the Bible says all our righteousness are as filthy rags. Some of you remember when he was a little boy about seven or eight. He made better speeches than he did yesterday." Jonah kind of laughed a little. "Lord, that child didn't know we couldn't vote. I think dem white folks up north is just putting on a show. Deep down within, they don't want to see us niggers with anything neither. You know, I think the south can be the straw that broke the camel's back." Someone in the crowd said, "How's that Jonah?" Old Jonah smoked a pipe and chewed tobacco all at the same time. He took the pipe out of his mouth, spit on the ground and he looked around at the crowd. "Well, I let y'all think 'bout the answer to that one. But I tell you this—you see we all down here want to go to heaven, but too many of us don't want to keep the Ten Commandments. In other words, white folk all around this here country want all the life, liberty and pursuit of happiness for themselves. They ain't studying 'bout us. I tell you if you don't believe Mr. Duncan believes in what he's preaching, you's all damn fools. I ain't lived in Mississippi all of my life for nothing. I bet he be telling the same story all around the state. 'It ain't political talk. Dat man means all that stuff from his heart." They all stood amazed at Jonah's words. Seeing they were astonished greatly by his talk, Jonah said, "Y'all better get y'all's lunch so y'all can go back to work."

As Andrew laid there, he wished his mother was with him now, to help ease the tension that lay within him. He wanted to cry—mother mother. But he told himself that he had to be calm. If he acted the way he did this morning, old Sam might hear him and think he was crazy. Old Sam was still sitting outside the door trying to meditate on integration—not yet finding an answer to the question why, in his mind, why his people needed integration? Mother didn't know I won the primary election—he thought to himself.

Mrs. Lucy Duncan showed complacence on the tour. Andrew's heart sang to see his mother her old self again. She mingled with the crowds, shook hands, listened to their problems. She really turned on her southern charm. They spoke in city after city. There were fewer and fewer Negroes in the crowds. The blacks, more or less, listened to the speeches on the radio or TV, hoping it was just political talk. Mrs. Duncan listened seriously to her son's speeches. She didn't approve of all the matters he spoke of in his speeches.

"Dear Friends, we have so many problems to deal with, such as free lunches for underprivileged children, more jobs than welfare, old age assistance, hospitals, federal aid for more homes and industry and better schools. To do all this, we need revenue. Revenue means more taxes and federal aid. Now about our schools, churches and other public places— this stunt they are pulling in Washington is a menace to our way of life. Who are they to reach down and erase what we so firmly believe in? The Constitution is just like the Bible—you get so many perceptions of it. We do have the power to retain the rights of our state and as long as the Negro remains in Mississippi, he shall and will keep the laws of this land. The black man has become envious of his white brother. His evil, which I have seen under the sun, is common among men. The black man thinks he's pure in his own eyes, they are not yet washed from his filthiness. We might not be able to hold on to all the rights of our heritage but there is one right that we will and shall maintain. That is the right to keep our women pure. I just want to add this little note—you know the difference between the north and south? Well, the north is downright two-faced with their blacks, but we are outspoken. When you go to the polls, vote for Andrew Duncan to be your next governor."

Andrew and his committee mingled with the crowd. Mrs. Duncan complained of being tired. She excused herself, and made her way to the hotel a little ways from the crowd. She had to get way to think on her son's speeches. Was this her son? Never before had she heard him speak such evil. He always spoke so kind and gentle to people. She flopped down on the bed. The more she listened to her son's speeches, the shakier she became. This day, she was shaking more than ever. There were more Negroes there than there were in Braidwood. Andrew was so bold with the words. Why one of them might have killed him for such talk. She had to ask him not to be so outspoken. Although she didn't want integration either, she was too American to jeopardize its' good character to the world. All of a sudden, she began to smile to herself thinking—what am I all in a fervor about? This is just political talk, that's all it is. He loved the Negroes so. He had to use the same tactics as his opponents. They were slinging the same mud. They always had the go in Mississippi. He was a republican and he had to be cunning as a fox if he wanted his dream to come true. This thought relieved her so. She rang for the bellboy to bring something tall and cold. Things would be different when he is in office. Even though she felt that someday integration would come to Mississippi. They had to let their proud heads down and let it in. Thinking Mississippi didn't only need integration but more industry and lots more essentials to sustain life, they went from town to town. He made speeches on radio, TV stations, schools, fields, auditoriums, and street corners. They shook hands til they were numb, and till he was hoarse. They were headed for the home base—Clearforest was the last stop before heading home. The committee and Andrew and Mrs. Duncan were fit to be tied. Andrew decided to take Lee up on her invitation. As the Duncan's motored into Clearforest, the sign read 'Population 50,000'. The day was clear and uncomfortably hot. Mrs. Duncan had marveled at some of the changes in the land, but Clearforest showed the greatest changes of them all. She

24

didn't want to believe her eyes. A few towns had grown with a few new houses and new buildings and some industry—but none had grown like Clearforest. Clearforest once was just shrubs and trees. There were small truck farms. The old part of town was just like any other country town you go twenty miles in. Mrs. Duncan just couldn't believe this was Clearforest. Remarking to Andrew, "I love to see this town. My heavens, it has been years since I've been here. I sure don't remember this town looking like this."

The Jackson Construction Company, a few other companies and the U.S. Government waved their magic wand, Clearforest's wooded wasteland was built into a modern municipality. Clearforest was the town where Doff and Lee Rainey lived. Doff made a very comfortable living selling real estate. The Duncan committee stayed at the town's beautiful modern motel. Andrew and his mother drove on to the Rainey's home some miles out. Mrs. Duncan was like a child seeing a circus for the first time. She babbled to Andrew about this and that and of the different places they passed, exclaiming to him there were so many new things to see and places to shop. Andrew gave his mother a short cruise around Clearforest. "So many odd-shaped buildings and bright colors—remember when this place was just nothing, trees and weeds—a one-horse country town. Just look at it. I haven't seen so many houses in all my life. The homes are beautiful, but they don't have elegance and grace of the old southern homes."

Andrew smiled at his mother's remarks. "Yes mother. I do remember when this place was just nothing. This is a changing world and this is the end of the line."

"Oh, we are here already?"

The Rainey's lived on the last street in the last house on Maewood Drive. Across the street, the land tapered off into the countryside. The view was breath-taking. Lee was looking out at the scenery when the Duncan's drove up. Lee yelled to Doff, "They are here!" She ran out to greet them. Lee and Mrs. Duncan gave each other a big hug and kisses on the cheek. Lee threw her arms around Andrew. They pecked each other on the lips. Doff gave Mrs. Duncan a big squeeze that almost took her breath away. Doff then threw one arm around Andrew's neck and almost shook his hand off. It had been years since they had seen each other. Time hadn't changed Lee too much. She did look a little older but her hairdo gave her that up-to-date look. "Mrs. Duncan, I'm so glad to see you back in the saddle," Lee said.

"I tell you, it sure does one good to get out," Mrs. Duncan said. "I have enjoyed campaigning, seeing the country and meeting people. I even met some old friends and people I knew long ago. Some of them have great-grand children." A funny little smile came to her face. I don't even have a daughter-in-law, let alone a grand child. If that son of mine don't get married and have children, the Duncan name will be just a memory. You know it's just the two of us left."

"Oh, I wouldn't worry about that", Doff said. "Some gal will catch that fox soon."

"Who needs to get married when you got two gals around the house?" Andrew said with his face beaming.

"Now Andrew, you know darn well you need a wife. Your mother and Pursa won't last forever." Lee changed the subject. Lee said, "Mrs. Duncan, I just love your haircut."

"Thank you dear. Pursa said my new hair style makes me look like a glamour gal," Mrs. Duncan said blushing.

"Andrew, you look tired. How 'bout a drink? It might give you a lift. How 'bout you, Mrs. Duncan?"

"I guess the both of us can use one. You know how we are about drinking; go easy on the liquor." Mrs. Duncan had held up better than any of the group had anticipated. She showed very little wear and tear. She seemed to have a lot of steam left. Her son on the other hand had somewhat depleted much. He seemed to be holding on with fours.

"You know, Andrew said campaigning is not an easy task. If you ask me, it's worse than picking cotton. I didn't realize it was this much work. I guess when I was a kid, standing on a wooden box, it seemed so easy. Now, don't get me wrong. I'm not backing down. This is my life's ambition. I'll walk, talk, dance, stand on my head and sing til the best man wins."

"That's the determined spirit!" Lee yelled. "Andrew, you do look tired. You and your mother can stay here and relax as long as you like and I assure you—we won't talk politics."

"I might look like an overdrawn mule. There won't be too much relaxing for me. I have to get out there and preach my sermon if I'm going to win. Mother can stay out of the picture if she likes," said

Andrew. The rest of the day, they all sat around the living room, laughed, chatted about the past and present—long past midnight.

As Andrew lay on the old couch, his mind kept focusing on his mother, Lee and Doff.

The third day the Duncan's were at the Rainey's, Mrs. Duncan felt she had rested enough. She wanted to see the town and buy gifts for Sam and Pursa along with one or two others. Most of all, she wanted to look. Mrs. Duncan asked Lee if she would show her the town and they could lunch. Lee made so many excuses why she couldn't spend the day out. Mrs. Duncan felt disappointed but she didn't want to trouble Andrew. He was too busy. Since she wanted to see the town so badly, Lee called her a cab.

Doff and Andrew left about ten that morning. Lee knew that Doff would be out all day, but she figured Andrew wouldn't. He looked too exhausted and they would be leaving soon. She had to make her move. Mrs. Duncan left about eleven. Andrew returned about three. As soon as Andrew returned, Lee talked him into having a few drinks. Lee had long waited for this moment to dig her spear of revenge into Andrew's pride. She recalled the night she told him she would have her revenge.

Lee had run after Andrew all her young life. Andrew was rich and sort of handsome. Many young lambs were written in his little black book of life. Lee always figured she would be the one he would marry. He would often take Lee on dates with other girls and she despised sharing him. At twenty-three her mind and body knew she loved him dearly, and she would have loved to be his wife. That summer was Andrew's first summer home from law school. Andrew had been on vacation from law school for a month. Lee was the only girl he was seen with around town. She refused dates from other fellows and she felt sure she was the only girl he was dating. She had the feeling he would pop the question any time. They went on picnics, swimming, parties, just doing a lot of fun things they loved to do. With summer growing old, she saw less and less of him. She called. He wasn't home. She wrote him notes. She would go to his house and to the farm. He was no place to be found. After the third week, she caught up with him. Lee demanded an explanation why he hadn't been seeing her.

He took her in his arms explaining, "Lee Honey, to be a good lawyer, I have to study long and hard. You do understand, Lee Honey?"

"Andrew, I love you so much," she said as he released her from his arms. She shouted out, "I don't believe you. You are seeing someone else." With tears running down, she ran out the door crying out, "I'll find out!"

Andrew started dating Lee all over again to gain her confidence. She kept the faith until that 'I'll get even night.' It was almost time for Andrew to go back to school. He still hadn't asked that important question. Lee was getting impatient. Two days before Andrew had to go back to school, he took Lee to a dance. They danced for a while, but the dance hall was a bit hot even with the air conditioner on. Lee asked Andrew to take her for a spin in his yellow convertible to cool off a bit. They rode here and there, talked a lot of stuff but nothing sure. Back at the dance, instead of going in, they sat in the car in the 'too hot' night air. Their talk, turned into sweet lingering kisses. Kisses that blanked the mind and fooled the heart and made hot fire in the body. Telling herself if she let her body fill his body's wants, he would ask her the wedding bell question, she did concede his dew within her flower. Believing that he would marry her, she lead him back to the dance. With unclean joy in their bodies, Andrew noticed Lee didn't have much to say the rest of the evening. Taking her home from the dance, she still acted peculiar. When they arrived at Lee's house, Andrew asked in a serious voice, "Lee didn't you enjoy the dance? Are you sick or something?"

Lee didn't answer at first... "I enjoyed the dance." She finally said sarcastically, "I'm not sick, Andrew. What I'd like to know is, when do you intend to ask me to marry you? Are you stringing me along?"

Andrew burst out in the biggest laugh. He thought her remarks were so funny. "Why Lee Honey, I can't marry you or anyone. Going into law and helping manage the planter ranch, I'll just have enough time for a hot time every now and then, not a hot time for a full time wife."

Those words hit every mad bone in her body. It was like fire burning in her heart. Before she knew it, she had slapped him so hard, it made him rub at the sting. Lee let herself out of his car as she departed from his company saying in harsh words, "Andrew I'll get even with you if it is the last thing I do." About a year later, she married Doff who was always second fiddle.

Remembering that unforgettable night, Lee turned on the music. She cuddled up very close to Andrew on the couch in the living room. Without a move of warning, Lee kissed Andrew long and gentle, feeling all the desires and warmth she felt when he first kissed her. Andrew didn't refuse such a kiss. It had been some time since he'd been kissed like that. Terence Honey Thompson, his lady friend he had been dating, went home to take care of her ill mother. Andrew made the next move. He took her in his arms and began kissing her with mad, sexy kisses. Lee freed herself from him, getting up from the couch quickly assuring him that wasn't her intention. She had been a damn fool for his wants once. The angry thoughts of it were still lingering in her mind. She just wanted to see if she still felt love on his lips. Love was still there burning warm as ever. Neither said a word to each other for a moment. Lee stood with her back to Andrew, composing herself for the strike. As she turned and faced him, Lee said, "Andrew do you remember that child you had by Vada McCloud?"

Andrew came up from the couch like a rattler had struck him. "What the hell are you talking about? What child?" Andrew shouted, looking like he just came out of an amnesia attack. "Lee you are making that up. I didn't have a child by Vada."

"Don't you call me a lie, I know damn well you have a child by that nigger. You know how things get around. You could never marry her. She could only be your whore."

"Well, it didn't get to me. You're lying!"

"The word might not have gotten to you, but it sure came from you. You can call me a lie if you want to, but I do know there is a child and I do know that Liz has the child."

"Just shut up Lee! Let me think. Go fix some lunch, I'm hungry." Lee made an exit with that Mona Lisa smile on her face.

When Lee mentioned Vada's name, no child came into his mind. They called her 'V' but her real name is Vada Dee McCloud. Sam and Pursa had five children: there is Sam Jr, JC, Willie and Elizabeth, (they call her Liz). Five years later, up pops Vada. Liz was the only one who looked like Sam—very dark skin, straight cold black hair—tall like Sam but thin. Mrs. Duncan always said if there was such a thing as a black beauty, she was one. She was just that pretty. The boys and Vada favored Pursa but the boys had Sam's height and brown eyes and Pursa's fair skin. Vada looked just like Pursa when she was young—the same reddish brown hair, fair complexion and blue eyes. You would say she was kind of cute.

Chapter 5

The first summer home in three years since his father's death Andrew mourned so over the death of his father. He would lock himself in his room and cry for hours. Sometimes, Sam would find him sitting on the lake's edge weeping. Mrs. Duncan thought it would be best to get him out of the house. She felt the sting of death in her heart too, but she couldn't run. She had to stay home and take care of the family business. Mrs. Duncan sent him to Maine to their only living relative—his father's only sister, Best Wilkinson. For a year, the distinct activities he did: beachcombing, sailing, skiing—weren't what you call doing nothing, but they were not the thing you would be an overwhelming success in either. Andrew got tired of doing these things, not having friends—he had many idle days. Remembering a favorite phrase of his father, an idle mind is the devil's workshop, he enrolled in Harvard to be what his mother wanted him to be—a lawyer. Although he had many letters, calls and pictures from anyone he knew around and about Mississippi and home but these underlying things wouldn't fill his loneliness to be home. He was just homesick.

The pieces began to fall more and more in place, thinking more of Vada and that unforgivable summer and that unseen child—Lee said existed.

They met him at the airport. Andrew got off the plane. He looked over the crowd to see who came to greet him. Over the murmur, he could hear Lee's happy voice say, "Andrew, Andrew. Here we are over here." Seeing them, his face smiled with gladness. Through the joyous smile on his mother's face, he could still see grief lingering from his father's death. Old Sam was there smiling from ear to ear. The car stopped at the short walk in front of the house. The high white pillars and the white face of the house gleamed in the hot sun seemingly adding to gladness of his homecoming. Pursa was standing in the entrance hollering in a happy voice, "Welcome home Mr. Andrew." Andrew threw his arms around Pursa's small frame. They gave each other a hardy squeeze.

"Pursa, it's good to be home. I sure did miss your cooking. As they say—there's no place like home."

"We sure missed you around here. You done grown as tall as one of those Mississippi pines. Y'all come in. It's hot out there."

When they were all inside, there was a loud burst from the gang saying welcome home. Andrew was so thrilled to see so many faces he hadn't seen in a long time. He couldn't speak, being sort of tired from the trip, seeing the old faces and the joy of being home—the tired feeling perished.

Andrew had been home about four weeks. He had gone to one social affair after another with Lee at his side. He was pleased to see how well his mother and Joshua, their foreman, had taken over and kept the vast two thousand truck farm going. When he made his appearance in town, the handshakes were warm and the talks were folkie and friendly. Andrew's speech and dress had changed. That kind of made his friends and the old heads ruffle up their feathers, especially the change in his speech. Sitting in the corner drugstore, Mr. Meade, the old proprietor said to Andrew, "You have gone Yankee on us boy."

Andrew dropped his voice in that real southern drawl, "Now you know I haven't turned Yankee and I never will." They both laughed.

"Boy you sure had us scared there for a while," Mr. Meade said with a big smile on his face. "Boy you sure do look like your paw. How do you like Harvard?" They talked about one thing and then another—the ones who died, the ones who had moved up north or went west. They talked particularly about the blacks who had gone north. But there was someone none had mentioned and he just didn't know who. It kind of bothered him at times, but he never said anything about his thoughts.

Andrew rose with the sun that July first. He wanted to go to the farm and the old place by himself. Coming out of the air conditioned house, he found the morning sun already hot. Thinking to himself—tomorrow may be cooler—going back in the house, he saw his mother coming down the long stairs. Yelling out to her, "How is my favorite girlfriend this morning?"

"I'm fine son. I thought you were old Sam coming in. Why are you going up so early?" She flopped in one of the living room chairs.

Andrew was looking out the window. Turning toward her, he said, "I thought I would take a walk around the old place."

"Walk! Why don't you take the jeep?"

"Boy, we sure have gotten modern around this place. I remember when father used to walk those five miles up to the farm every morning and evening just for pleasure."

"If you want to walk, walk! It will be your feet not mine."

"I see you and Joshua have bought a lot of equipment."

31

"It gets the job done better son. Have you had your breakfast?"

"No, I don't want any. How about you making me a pitcher of my favorite drink?"

"Lemonade, so early. Anyway, I thought you were going for a walk?"

"Well, I have changed my mind. It's too hot outside. Think I'll relax today—maybe read a book, be real lazy like. Besides, I've been going too much. If you don't want to make the lemonade, I'll have Pursa make it but I like yours better. You seem to have a knack for making my favorite drink.

"Alright, I'll make the lemonade." She responded as she gathered herself from the chair. As his mother left the room, he could see she had aged much in the last three years. Her face looked very old. With her mingled gray hair combed straight back in a ball, she looked well past her age.

Andrew collected himself, made his way upstairs, gathered up all the pillows from all the bedrooms, brought them downstairs, and put them on the living room floor. He then went to the spare bedroom, across from the living room, took the pillows there, went back to the living room and made a pallet out of them. Whenever he did this trick, Pursa would get madder than a bear. She would wall her eyes and say, "Mrs. Duncan, we's just ain't raising this boy right." He then went to the study to get a book. While in the study, something on the desk caught his eye—a paper-weight with gather in the inside. Looking at the paper-weight, it dawned on him who it was he hadn't seen. He chuckled a little to himself. It was Vada. How could he forget her? Remembering who, he wondered why he hadn't seen her since he's been home? It took her almost a year to save up seventy-nine cents to buy the paper-weight. He could see her now with two pigtails hanging down to her breast, listening earnestly to his speeches. One day, when all the other children had left him in the middle of one of his fabulous speeches, they became bored. They wanted to play something else. Andrew, seeing she was the one left, said angrily, "Why don't you go too? You don't like my speeches either."

Vada started twisting with her hands in back of her. In a very serious voice she said, "I got a present for you."

"You said that some time ago. What is it? He said as if he didn't care.

Smiling, she held out the little gift wrapped in pink paper with green ribbon discarded from the Duncan house. When she handed him the gift, he was so surprised he didn't know what to say. He opened it. It was a paper-weight with a gather in the inside.

"What am I going to do with this?" Andrew said, seriously turning it looking at the gift this way and that, trying to find its' use.

"That's for you when you be governor—to hold all your important papers down, silly."

Thanking her for the gift - but wishing it was something else - he was happy. Forgetting the book, smiling to himself, he went back to the living room with the paper-weight in his hand. Mrs. Duncan had returned with the lemonade. Andrew held the paper-weight up in front of himself asking, "Mother, where is Vada?"

The question didn't shock her. It only made her shudder. Taking a swallow from the cup of coffee old Sam had brought in, she didn't want to answer him but she knew she couldn't ignore the question completely. She remembered how close they used to be. "Oh," she said, "she's been gone as long as you have—three years. She's staying with JC and his family."

"Oh…What is she doing there?"

"She's going to school, if you must know. Sam and Pursa thought she would learn more there than she was getting here."

"Does she come home during the summer?"

"She hasn't been home for three summers. She had a lot of catching up to do. You know the schools up north for Negroes, they say their curriculum is better than here."

"When I was away, you never mentioned her in your letters. Is she coming home this summer?"

Answering angrily, "She's not your business, son."

As he opened his mouth to say something else, she said quickly, "Pursa said something about her coming home soon."

"I wonder if she still has hope in me becoming governor some day."

"You played governor so much when you were kids. I believed she already thought you were a governor. Remember, she started calling you governor. It was governor this and governor that, until Pursa gave her the same thing that stopped you from making speeches."

Andrew laughed at his mother's sarcastic remarks, tossing the paper-weight playfully. She often wondered who gave it to him. Now, she knew.

33

That summer, V had been home about a month before Andrew made his way down the path that led to Vada's house. As he proceeded down the path, he could hear his mother bellowing to him, "Andrew you come back here. That is going to cause you a lot of trouble one of these days." He acted as though he didn't hear her. In days gone by, V came to the Duncan house with her parents to work, but when she was small, she did more playing with Andrew than working. It was planned, when V came home on vacation, she was not to come up to the big house. As Mrs. Duncan put it, it wouldn't be equitable. Andrew reversed the plan. Vada saw him coming. She ran out to greet him.

"Boy, long time no see," Andrew said. They hugged each other warmly. They then stood staring, smile at each other.

"What's up V?"

"Well, your mother and my folks thought I would be smart for me to stay here and keep house. In other words, I'm a big girl now."

"So I see. You don't look like the little girl I used to know. Pigtails gone, you look cute with your hair curled. I should say you don't look like the little girl I used to know," he mum-m-m, mum-m-med her up and down.

"Not so fast," she said. "You have changed too. You have that mannish look, long tall and handsome."

"I do!" he said blushing. He unconsciously took her by the hand as they took the long path to their favorite spot. They always went to the farthest lake. Vada and Andrew sat on the long grass by the lake and talked.

"It's kind of lonesome around here. I mean around the house. All your brothers and sisters married and off somewhere. The house seems so empty without father."

"I know what you mean. I feel the same loneliness."

"How are JC and the family?"

"They are all doing fine—they have three children now."

"The trees look so different down here." The Spanish moss was swinging in the breeze.

"They sure do. That Chicago reminds me of a people jungle—big tall buildings—love and tragedy playing all at the same time. How do you like Harvard and Boston?"

34

"I like Boston but I like down home better. Harvard, it's okay. I have to study hard to be a good lawyer. Are your folks going to send you back to college this fall?"

"Yes, I'm going to the University of Chicago. This is my last year. I' going to be a teacher."

"That's a good field. Study hard, you will make it."

In the weeks that followed, they reminisced about first one thing and the other. But the talks of this and that wandered into long looks into each others' eyes. For something different to do, they tried to stop seeing each other, but only a day went by. The next day, they were back seeing each other again. Sometimes, they met—they said nothing. They tried so hard to avoid what they both began to feel. They would go fishing or bird watching or just tramping in the woods, trying to shake the feeling.

Before V came home, Lee had Andrew all to herself. He usually made his appearance at Lee's house in his blue open-faced Cadillac more often than one wanted to see a body. Now that V was home, Andrew had rediscovered Vada. Fun, for Lee seemed to slow down. Andrew began to see less and less of Lee and his other friends. Andrew had one interest now, V. His desire for her was so strong on his mind and body, he didn't want to be bothered with anyone else. Lee began to feel lonesome for Andrew. She tried time after time to see him, but the only faces she saw were Sam, Pursa or Mrs. Duncan. She knew too well where he was. To verify her belief, she made her way to that secret place. It was by chance that Lee knew V was home. She was cruising around town when Sam picked V up at the bus station. Vada was getting in the Duncan Cadillac. Although Vada had changed from that girl she knew, Lee still recognized her. They were there alright, laying on the soft green grass under one of the many moss-covered trees. They were lying in each other's arms. He was uttering sweet nothings to her. "Oh, my love, let me kiss thy lips. Love is much sweeter and better than wine. If thy withdraw thyself from me, I will run after thee. You will be glad and rejoice in thee. When thy be afraid of which is high and fears, fear not. I love thee."

"Oh, Andrew, you're just teasing me," she giggled.

"My queen, don't thee feel warm for me. Don't thy like my teasing?"

"Yes, but you put my heart to shame, you fooling me like this."

"Why be ashamed my love. When thy are the fairest among all the women in my heart."

Vada lay there taking in his words of love, smiling as if her heart and soul were rejoicing, as though she had a glorified body.

"Thy buds have blossomed so and thy bed is still green." He rolled over in the grass, locked his arms around her and kissed her just a whisper. "Thy lips are sweet to taste, my love."

Andrew and V kissed each other, one kiss after another, short and hard, seemingly to collect all the wants they had missed.

"I love you V. When I'm not with you, my heart weeps. I seem not to get you out of my mind."

"I love you to, but I'm afraid."

"There is nothing to be afraid of, my love. He kissed her long and tender. Their kisses were hot and soothing and intoxicating like red wine clouding the mind. Vada tried to come to her senses pleading, "Don't Andrew. We mustn't."

"I won't hurt you," he said in a velvet voice.

"That's not it," she said seriously. He stopped the chatter with another kiss. The breathing came hard. The bee entered the flower and gathered all the honey in the comb.

Lee had brought in ham sandwiches for lunch. She started to talk about the child again.

"Shut up Lee, I'm trying to think." He remembered the scolding he got from his mother about messing around with V so much. Mrs. Duncan tried to talk to Andrew about V. In fact, she talked til she was blue in the face. "Andrew, I want this game of hide and seek stopped with you and Vada. Your friends seem to think you have gone back into your shell— like you did when your father died. They really think you are closed up in this old house somewhere going mad."

"Oh, Mother. Let them think what they want, but their conception is a good excuse. What is my favorite girl trying to say—that I can't take care of myself?"

"You know very well what I'm trying to tell you. I'm tired of lying for you. I am tired of telling them I don't know where you are and I am tired of telling your friends you are studying and you don't want to be annoyed. I know you can take care of yourself. Can she?"

"Mother, Vada is a big girl now. Don't you worry your pretty little head off. V can take care of herself."

"Son, it was alright for you two to play together when you kids. You are a man now. You think differently. You look different and you even feel different. Son, I think Lee knows the truth. She is too ashamed to tell them the true story. She feels you belong to her."

"Listen Mother, I am free white and over twenty-one. I am tired of this woman to man talk of yours. To ease you folks' minds around here, I'll change my routine—I'll see Lee and the gang again. I hope that suites you," he said in a very sarcastic way leaving the room.

In the weeks that followed, that summer Lee thought she had Andrew all to herself again. Her heart and mind eased to flight of that of a butterfly. One Thursday in August, Lee had phoned Andrew, planned a picnic for the two of them for the following day to have a last bit of fun with Andrew before he went back to school. They were to drive to Percy Quinn Park. They planned to leave at eight, nine—no Andrew. Ten. Where could he be? She phoned the house, no answer from anyone, not ever Pursa. She wondered where everyone was. Maybe he's on his way. She waited a half hour, no Andrew. She got in her car with the basket full of goodies and went to his house. She knocked on the door, no answer, so she let herself in yelling, "Is anybody home?" No answer so she went out back where she found Pursa picking tomatoes from the patch Sam had put in. "Pursa where is—Andrew."

"Miss Lee, I don't know."

"Oh, that dog!" Lee said. She was so hurt and so mad she could bite steel. The thought hit her in the top of her head of Andrew being with V. It made her all the madder and curious. She got into her car and turned the motor on. She sat there a while, thinking to herself, "No I won't go home, I won't be outdone." She made up her mind to tell him a thing or two, but she really wanted to see if he was with V. The thought of him being with her vexed her so much that she beat her fist on the steering wheel saying out loud, "I'm going to see if he is with her." She spun out of the Duncan drive, went down the highway by the Duncan estate a short piece, turned onto the road that divided the Duncan place from the Clay's. This road went by Vada's house. She drove right into the McCloud's driveway and parked. She got out of the car and made her way to the spot that she knew V and Andrew went to so many times. As she neared the spot, she got off the path and walked with the utmost silence in the weeds and grass. Coming closer to the spot, she could see them through the thickets that grew in-between the moss-covered trees. Getting closer, she could hear them talking. She lay in the weeds like a snake in the grass. Andrew was laying on the ground, V was sitting. All of a sudden, Andrew rolled over on the grass, pulled V down on him—kissing her. Lee cried out within herself, "Oh it's true, it's true." Although it was a hot day, a cool breeze blew off the lake. The call of the wild was all about. Bird were singing. Every now and then, you would hear the honk of a bullfrog. A rabbit jumped over Lee's legs; it almost frightened her to a scream. She put her hand over her mouth and held her breath. Andrew was now lying on top of V. Lee could hear Andrew's voice loud and clear saying to V, "Thy joints of thy thighs are like jewels. Thy breasts are like two cotton balls. Thy nipples are suckling. I love thee even though thou are a black woman. The whole of you are tender grapes. I love you. I need thee close to me. I won't let thee go until I have brought you into my house."

"Stop it, stop it!" Vada screamed. Pushing Andrew off her, she sat up on the grass.

"What's the matter, my love? Have my words hurt you in some way?" He said laying on the ground where Vada had pushed him. Andrew pulled a long weed and put it in his mouth.

"No Andrew, your words didn't hurt me—it's not that." Her voice sounded like it wanted to cry.

"You have been awfully quiet today. You haven't smiled too much either. What's troubling you?" He was puzzled by the look on her face.

Lee was all ears, but her heart was pounding from Vada's actions. Thinking to herself—he didn't speak such loving nonsense to me. His strong passionate words of love and folly made her body feel loose and wanton. It also angered her to hear him express his strong amorous feelings to a nigger girl. It would make Lee angry to hear Andrew speaking his feelings toward any girl—black or white. Lee felt she couldn't take anymore of this abuse. She started to leave. She remembered something was troubling V and she wanted to know the distressing news. She crawled a little closer.

"Andrew, I have something to tell you," her voice sounded sick.

"What's troubling you? You need money for school?"

Vada hesitated a bit, not looking at Andrew but off in another world— "Andrew we have reaped a wild seed!"

"What do you mean?"

"I'm going to have a baby!" she said as if she wanted to burst into tears.

Andrew was up on his feet, quickly like a dog that had wallowed in the grass too long. "A baby!" he exclaimed. "Vada, I didn't mean to hurt you this way. We can run off and get married."

"Married!" she laughed. "You will never be chosen as a candidate for governor—married to a Negro."

"V, my greatest ambition is to be governor. You do have confidence in me being governor, don't you?"

"Yes, I do. With your keen sense human needs and the way you have with people, you have all the makings of a good governor."

"What about you going to college this year?"

"I was thinking about doing way with it."

"Vada, I know we have done an awful thing and I know how you feel about going to college, but there must be some other way. I've heard of girls dying going to those quack doctors and taking different things. I don't want you to die."

"Every time I think about what has happened to me, I knew I should have listened to mama. I got up enough nerve to tell mother. She took it awfully hard."

"What did Sam say?"

"He didn't have much to say. He felt bad to," tears gathered in her eyes and rolled down her face. "Mama said she wanted me to be somebody. She said if you play with fire, you bound to get burned." She said sadly as Andrew wiped tears away with his hand.

"What are you going to do?"

"Mama talked to Liz. I'm going to stay at her place until I have the baby. Nobody will see me out in those woods. I'll go back to college next year."

"What's going to happen to the baby?"

"Oh, Liz is going to keep the child until I am able to take the child someday." With this remark, V's voice sounded as if she wasn't afraid or disappointed anymore. Next year, her expectation will be fulfilled.

"V, I feel sick all inside," his face looked like a sad boy just been caught killing a bird. He didn't feel the relief that Vada felt about Liz and the baby. He took her hand and sort of rubbed them, trying to console her. "I hope everything will turn out alright. If you need anything or money, just call me or write."

"Things will turn out alright. I won't see you anymore. I'm leaving for Liz's place tonight. Andrew I want you to promise me something."

"What is it?"

"Don't tell anyone about the baby, not even your mother."

Lee was glad to hear V's misfortune, but the thought of Vada conceiving Andrew's child, behooved her mind so intensely—she grabbed a hand full of grass up by the roots saying to herself, "Why does a nigger bitch like that have the honor to spawn his child?" The thought of Andrew having her—made her flesh crawl. Feeling she had gained more by listening than by intruding. She cautiously departed as quietly as she had come.

Chapter 6

The thought of a child had come into focus, but all the times he had been at Liz' place, he had never seen a child—not even a toy, not anything that said a child was present.

Andrew said to Lee, "Lee, you remember how we loved Liz' cornbread when we were small.   Remember, we used to call it cakebread?"

"Yes I do!" Lee laughed a little.   "Liz must have made four or five pans of cornbread a week for us kids. It sure was good."

"Well, when Sam and I are up Liz' way or when I am by myself, we have a piece of cornbread and cold glass of buttermilk. Jessie would be there and we sit in the living room or on the front porch. We would talk farming. I tell you, Lee, of all the times I've been there, I have never seen a sign of a child. I remember V said she was that way. Maybe she had a miscarriage. She did mention having an abortion."

"Andrew, I do know there is a child and he's very much alive. He looks just like you when you were young."

Lee knew there was a child alright. Over the years, she made it her business to go up to Liz' to see if the child was still there. The words of Vada clung to her mind—"Liz will keep the child until I am able to take it some day." The road that led to Liz' looked as if it continued. There were patches of woods on either side of the winding road to Liz and Jessie Baker's farm. Many a person found the road was a dead end. The Bakers never paid any attention to the cars that backed out of the road, but Lee used the road to see the child.

"How do you know so much about the child?" Andrew asked with a roar in his voice. "But Lee no one knows but you and me. I don't think you would tell anyone. Furthermore, that's past and gone."

"Andrew, you have everything at stake now—reputation. A scandal like this will hurt your chances deeply. I have heard some of your speeches, mostly the words were sex, sex, sex and the virtues of the white woman. Where is your pride?" she said in a stern way.

"What am I to do with this page in my life?"

Mrs. Duncan was almost downtown when she discovered she had forgotten her purse. Going back to the house, forgetting to knock, letting herself into the side entrance to the kitchen, picking up her purse off the waste-can, where she had left it, stopping to adjust her slip—as she turned to go out the door, she heard the words, "Kill him Andrew, kill him." The shock from the words made her tremble with fear. She reached for the door for support. Standing there too bewildered, too frightened to move—she heard the words again, "Kill him. That's the only way to bury your past." Lee and Andrew were so engrossed in wiping the past clean—it drowned out Mrs. Duncan coming in the house.

"Lee, I can't do anything like that."

"Andrew, you don't know how much he looks like you. If your opponent found out about the child you had by that nigger, you might as well quit now, forget about being governor.

"Lee, that child I had by Vada, if there is one, is just an innocent mistake. It's just one of those things."

"You are talking crazy. If you don't get rid of him, you won't have a chance."

"Lee, I don't know anyone who will do a thing like that."

After Andrew said the words he just said, Lee knew she had Andrew convinced. She had her spear right where she wanted. "You have to do this yourself."

Mrs. Duncan was terrified at the talk she had heard. All she could think of, was to get away. She eased the door shut. She got in the cab. She slumped back in the seat exhausted from fright. "Just drive around cabbie," she said. "I have to think."

The cab driver looked in the mirror. Seeing she looked so white, he asked, "Lady are you sick?"

"Oh no," she said bracing herself thinking, I have to think of something to save my son. She saw now that he meant everything he had said in his speeches. "My son, my son"—she said to herself, "You are a successful farmer, a brilliant lawyer. You're rich. Why is it you want my son? I can't let you kill. Driver, I want to go home."

"Lady, where is home?"

"Braidwood."

"Lady, that's almost a hundred miles from here."

"I know. I'll pay whatever it cost. I am Mrs. Lucy Duncan", she said kind of proper.

The words 'killed him' shocked her more than her son having a child somewhere. As the cab sped along the highway, she began to cry. She wanted to cry aloud, but her pride wouldn't let her. As they drove along, she didn't care to look out at the scenery that she so enjoyed on the tour, thinking too, they didn't tell her about Vada having a baby. Sam or Pursa didn't say a word. They must have felt very crushed. I guess it wouldn't have done any good if we had discussed the child. He must be a big boy now. She always wanted a grandchild, but not in this manner. She thought how she tried so hard to keep V and Andrew apart. I told him time and time again to keep away from that girl—thinking if his father were living—this might not have happened. He would've obeyed his father. She wondered where the boy was? Did he really look like Andrew? Is there really a child? What is she going to do when she gets home? How did Lee know so much? Lee could be lying for some unforeseen reason. If it is true, why didn't they tell her?

The cabbie interrupted her thinking, "Lady, we are entering Braidwood."

"What?" she answered as she pat her eyes with her hankie, then blew her nose.

"We are now in Braidwood. Where do you want to go, Lady?"

"Keep on this highway about twenty miles out. I'll tell you when to stop."

The sun was high in the sky as the cab sped on the highway that led to the Duncan estate. She could see the blacks tending to her crops. Everything looked so pretty and green. Her thoughts went back to Sam and Pursa. It must have hurt them very deeply when they found out that V was bearing an illegitimate child. They must have sacrificed so much to send her to school. She remembered asking them if they needed any money when they told her they were sending Vada to school. She could hear old Sam saying, "Thanks a lots Mrs. Duncan, we'll make out alright."

"Now Sam if you need any money, don't hesitate to ask." She remembered when V graduated from school and college. She was sure of that. Pursa showed Vada in her cap and gown. Sam and Pursa went to see her graduate. When did she have that child? She remembered the gift she gave Vada—a sky blue sweater and a couple hundred dollars. She remembered Sam getting a letter from V telling them she was teaching. She just couldn't figure it out—when did V have the child? There still could be a chance there wasn't a child. As this thought struck her, she became a little relieved. Maybe Lee was making all of this up. The cab was now in front of the Duncan estate.

43

Sam was in the kitchen eating a sandwich saying out loud—Sam said "Who could that be? Maybe Pursa done come home." Coming in the living room, he could see it was Mrs. Duncan. "What you doing home?" As he came closer, Sam could see that she was ill or something was wrong. "Is you sick?" She gave no answer. "Pursa ain't here. She done gone and took herself a vacation all the way to Texas. We were looking for you all in a week or more."

"I know," she finally said. "That's alright about Pursa. Sam, have a seat, I want to talk to you." Sam sat in one of the once elegant chairs. She stood. "Sam I want you to tell me the truth. Did Vada really bare my son's child?" She looked searchingly into Sam's face. Sam stared off into space, hesitating to answer. "Sam, I have to know!" she said in a demanding tone.

Sam looked up toward her with shame on his face. "Yes'm Mrs. Duncan, she did."

The shock of the child reached her. As she swayed she grabbed for a chair. Sam caught her. He carried her frail body, laid her on the old couch. "Do you want some water or something?"

"No," she replied softly coming to herself, "I'll be alright. Tell me when it happened?"

"Well, she got that way in August. That was her last year in college. Do you remember when Pursa claimed Liz was so sick and she wanted to go to Liz' place to take care of her. You had one of the farm hands to do Pursa's work. Pursa wanted to be with Vada when she had the baby. I think that was about April."

"How did Lee find out about the child?"

"I don't rightly know. My baby hid in the house like a scared rabbit. You know how bad she wanted to be a teacher. To keep anyone from seeing her, she stayed in the house most of the time. How that Miss Lee found out, I just don't know."

"Who delivered the child, Dr. Sliver or Dr. Edwards?"

"Pursa did."

"My God!" she murmured dumbfounded that the child was real. She almost forgot what she came home for. "Sam get out the car. We got to get the boy out of town. They are going to kill him", she said in a frightened voice, getting off the couch.

"Who wants to kill the boy?"

"Sam, stop asking questions and do as I say."

44

"You can't go. You look sick."

"We could call Liz, but if we did they would be too excited to know what to do."

"Mrs. Duncan, I can take care of the boy's getting away. You don't have to trouble yourself."

"Sam, I want to go. I want to see the boy."

With those remarks, Sam said no more. Sam drove dangerously fast the seventy miles to Liz' place. The sun still smiling fiery without a cloud in the sky. As the car came up the dust road, they could see Liz and the boy on the weather-beaten porch. As the car neared, Liz could see it was her father and someone else. Liz didn't recognize Mrs. Duncan. Liz hadn't seen Mrs. Duncan in quite some time. Mrs. Duncan had aged considerably. Liz was happy to see her father. Through her happiness, she sensed something was wrong. Sam always let her know when he or Andrew were coming up her way by phoning mother Washington.

As they got out of the car—Liz rushed to them and said, in an uncertain voice, "Daddy, what's the matter?"

"Liz, we got to get the boy away from here," Sam said in a whispering frightened tone of voice so the boy couldn't hear him.

"Why?" Liz asked.

"Liz, they are coming to kill him."

"Who's going to kill him, for what Daddy? I don't understand." Liz babbled loudly.

Sam didn't know why, himself. Sam looked toward Mrs. Duncan to Liz' question.

Mrs. Duncan spoke up, "Liz, I don't want to reveal any names. Please don't ask questions. I do know what I'm talking about. They are going to kill the boy." Mrs. Duncan was looking at the boy. All the time she could see the resemblance so well from the white skin even to the blue eyes. She wanted to say—my grandson. But her pride and shame held the words back. Instead she said, "We are going to send him to Vada."

"To Vada", Liz said with resentment in her voice, "Why she would not know what to do with him."

"She's got to face it Liz," Mrs. Duncan said sarcastically. Does he know that Vada is his mother?"

"Yes," Liz acknowledged. But he's been mine ever since he's been born. I can't let him go", Liz started to cry.

"You must Liz. Can't you understand they are going to kill him" Mrs. Duncan said.

"What kind of mother would she be to him? She sent him money and presents, but she don't love him."

The boy sat on the porch all the time listening to them talk. He too was always glad to see his grandfather. But when they talked of killing, he just sat there thinking it was grown-ups talk and he knew it wasn't his place to interfere. It dawned on him that they were talking about him. With excitement in his voice he said, "Grandpaw I can't leave Aunt Liz and Uncle Jessie. They are all I have ever known as father and mother, except you and grandmaw. If Vada wanted me, she would have sent for me long time ago. I won't go to her. I don't care what they do to me. Let her keep on living high and mighty without shame of me." They looked at each other amazed and ashamed. The boy stood there with his head down. Mrs. Duncan walked over. With her hand she raised his head up and said, "My child, you will have to go. You won't want to die, do you?"

"No Maam."

"When things blow over, you can always come back."

"Yes Maam."

"Liz, get some things for you and the boy. I'll call V when I get back home and tell her you and the boy are coming. We better hurry. There will be a bus soon. We have lost too much time," Mrs. Duncan said.

While Liz was in the house getting some things together, Liz' husband, Jessie, came up. Mrs. Duncan told him the frightening story. He hated to see the boy go, but he agreed it was best for the boy to leave. With tear-filled eyes, Sam and Mrs. Duncan left Liz and David at the station. Making their way home, Mrs. Duncan seemed to be wilting like fresh picked lettuce in the hot sun. Although Mrs. Duncan was very tired, when she reached home she felt she had to call Vada, not only to tell her that her son and Liz were coming but she wanted Vada to come home and talk to Andrew. Maybe she could change his mind about some of the things he said in his speeches. As she remembered, V was the one who kept his spirits up and encouraged his great desire to be governor. The operator got the number.

"Hello Vada, this is Mrs. Duncan."

"Mrs. Duncan!" Vada said nervously wondering what had happened at home. All sorts of things were going through her mind.

46

Mrs. Duncan broke her thought with words, "Vada, Liz is bringing your son to live with you." There was silence.

"Why? Mrs. Duncan."

"They plan to kill him."

"Who wants to kill David? Is dad there?" Vada knew that her mother was away. She had a card from her.

"Your dad is fine. I guess you don't know Andrew is running for governor."

"Yes I do. Mother wrote me about it. When I was growing up, I kept his hope up. When you get older, you forget about your childhood thoughts."

"Yes, I know dear. Somehow Lee found out about the boy. She told Andrew, in his campaigning, his opponent might see the boy, put two and two together and use this evidence in the campaign. If he killed the boy, there wouldn't be any evidence. That's why I'm sending the boy to you. The boy is the spitting image of my son."

"I know. Liz sent me a picture of him. I can't see Andrew killing anyone. I wonder how Lee found out?"

"I don't know," Mrs. Duncan said yelling, banging on the desk. "If he comes to kill the boy, he will find him gone. He won't have to do this awful thing." Mrs. Duncan started crying hysterically. Sam tried to comfort her by patting her on her shoulder.

"Mrs. Duncan, get hold of yourself!" Vada yelled through the phone. He hasn't killed anyone yet. I just can't believe Andrew would kill anyone. I just can't."

"I don't want to believe my son will do such an awful thing. I just don't know," her crying had ceased somewhat. "Vada, I would like a great favor of you."

"Yes, Mrs. Duncan."

"Would you come home and talk to Andrew? You had such great influence over him. He's so against integration. I don't understand him. He seemed to love your people so." She had stopped crying. Old Sam was just standing by.

Vada hesitated to answer her.

"At one time I thought he loved you," Mrs. Duncan added.

Vada didn't add any thoughts to this statement, replying with—"Mrs. Duncan, are you for integration?"

"Well, I wasn't at first. Since Andrew has been running for governor, the many people I have talked with here in Mississippi are still living in days of Uncle Tom's cabin. I got the shivers feeling too many whites are still Simon Lagree. We seem to think we are intelligent intellects but yet we are so ignorant about a lot of things. We want our Negroes to remain ignorant. We can't gain anything but a relief roll."

"That was a powerful statement you just made. Many whites feel the way you do. I can't come home. I may say things that will hurt instead of heal. If it will make you feel better, when I collect myself, I will write him a letter."

"I understand dear, but I still wish you would come home. When you write, please talk to his heart."

"Thanks for saving my son. Let me speak to dad. Dad, why in the devil don't you leave that god-forsaken place?" Vada said in a very angry voice.

"Now Baby, this is home to us. Don't you worry. Now that David is gone, everything will be alright," Sam said.

"But Dad, he might kill you!"

"Now Baby, don't get all upset, he won't hurt me."

"I'm sure Glad Mother is not there. She couldn't stand all of this mess."

"Now don't you worry. I'd better hang up. I think Mrs. Duncan is getting sick. Call when you can."

Chapter 7

When Vada hung up the phone, she flung herself across the bed. She didn't know whether to laugh or cry. So Andrew was going to make atonement for their sin. If he had killed David, I wouldn't have to answer for my sin, she thought vainly to herself. She was astonished at her thoughts. Her vain thinking took her back to that 'whatever you sought, so shall you reap summer." Many a suitor came to Vada's door or her own color, but they came after six o'clock. That's when they knew the McClouds were home. But what they didn't know was that Vada didn't work at the Duncan's anymore and that most of the day, Vada played a passionate love game with Andrew Duncan. The most persistent of her suitors was Joe Charles Thomas. He made it known around town to the other fellows that he didn't want to catch any other dude at her house. Joe Charles was the athletic type. He kept his hair cut close to his head. Tall, but not too heavy, brown skin, not ugly nor handsome. Joe Charles worked on the Duncan planter-ranch. He also lived there. He would come most evenings to see Vada. Joe Charles always talked of leaving Mississippi. He didn't like farm work or the white man's ways in Mississippi. Vada often teased him as they sat under the tree in the chair swing in Vada's yard.

"Joe Charles, you will never leave here. You like pulling those weeds and picking those beans and stuff. You like saying, yes sir and no sir and yes sir boss."

"V, stop saying things like that. You know I hate this place. When I get enough money, I'm going to St. Louis, get me a job and save my money, go to school and study to be a pharmacist."

"A what?" she said laughing at him.

"A pharmacist," putting emphasis on the word pharmacist, looking bleak as she laughed at him. "V when I leave this place, I ain't going to tell you good-bye, so long or nothing 'cause you laughed at me. I sure hate to leave a pretty girl like you to these crazy cats around here."

"Joe Charles, you ain't going to leave this place," Vada said sounding serious.

Getting close to her in the swing, looking around to see if Sam or Pursa was looking from the house, not seeing either one—he got closer to her saying seriously, "V I love you and would like to take you with me. We could get married."

Vada added, "Have a bunch of babies and you'll get one of those penny paying jobs. We will live in the city in the slums or in a shack on the outskirts of town and that will be the way we will live all our lives. I want things much better than that kind of life."

"V you don't have any faith in me at all", he said seriously. When I do leave this grasshopper town, I'll just leave. You don't care nothing about me. I know you loves me some cause you let me kiss you every now and then. A girl like you don't give kisses away just for pleasure. You do love me some, don't you?"

She reached and drew him close to her putting her arms around his neck. She kissed him sort of long on his lips.

"V—don't you do things like that. You get me all stirred up", crossing his legs. "If your folks caught you kissing me, Mr. Sam will run me off this place", Joe Charles said—looking scared.

"Now Joe Charles, my folks know you respect me. I just did that to see what you would do."

Thinking of the innocent love affair she had with Joe Charles, her thoughts fell on Andrew—thinking Andrew wouldn't have stopped at that one kiss. He would have kissed her til she gave in to his sexual desires. She thought she loved them both but in different ways—one for respect and the other for the way he made love to her.

"I love you Joe Charles, but I'm not going to live like a cockroach all my life. I'm going to live high on the hog, have pretty things and have a big black Cadillac like the Duncan's. When I leave in September, I'm not going to tell you good-bye either. This is my last year in school, you know."

"V, are you really going to leave in September?" Joe Charles said sadly.

"I'm really supposed to leave in August. I am making most of my clothes. I don't think I'll finish until September."

"What do you want to be?"

"I'm going to be a teacher. I think I'd love to teach the fifth or sixth grade."

"I won't have enough saved to leave this fall but I will next summer. When you write home one of these days and ask how is old Joe Charles, they will say well that boy has a drugstore all his own and I just might come to Chi Town and say hello to you."

"Well I wish you all the luck in the world. If you have as much ambition as you have talk, you will be a big success."

"V, I'm really fed up with this cotton-picking, weed-pulling, no-voting, his and hers, no-money-paying town."

"Oh, it's bad, but not so bad. Some colored people here have homes, and they own their own farms, and they live happy. The folks up north have their troubles too."

"I know things could be lots better here. I'm just tired of bowing down to these white gods down here. They put poor trash over you. They don't know how to read or write and they can vote, but we have to be over-educated to vote. We never grow up. It's boy this and that. When you get old, it's uncle and aunt. You're never Mr. or Mrs. You even call their little brats Mr. and Miss and you better not look at a white woman—they will lynch you on general principle. The colored woman, to the white man, is like a car. He thinks he can use her any time he's ready," Joe Charles blasting out his feelings. When he made the remarks about the black woman, a queer look came over Vada's face, thinking that statement was somewhat true—but it wasn't like that with she and Andrew. It was just plain love that made Andrew want her. Rejecting his last remarks, she said very calmly to Joe Charles, "Joe Charles it's getting late. We have to get up early in the morning." He gave her a peck on the cheek. Joe Charles said no more about his feeling. "I see you before you leave V." She watched his shadow go down the dusty road.

As Vada laid across her bed in her Chicago apartment clothed in aqua and gold lounging attire, this feeling she had for Andrew, that she thought was love to her then, now was like vomit locked up in her insides. It was coming up as reality. The sickness inside made her think of the words of her mother—"Vada, Baby, Mama don't think it's right for you and Mr. Andrew going 'bout like you are. You might get in trouble. He just ain't your kind. It just ain't right. You don't go hiding places with Joe Charles. Why? 'Cause he respects you. When you got to sneak and hide, you ain't doing right. I's talking to you for your own good and I want you to stop it." Vada never said a word when her mother talked of this matter.

Vada's mind ran back to Joe Charles. Poor Joe Charles. They say he got a good job, but the big city with bright lights, fast living in St. Louis was too much for Joe Charles. He died at an early age of thirty with TB.

She began thinking to herself.—Joe Charles never got to first base. She often wondered if he knew about the child. She wondered how she was going to explain her son to her husband and friends. She was glad her doctor husband was at the office when she got the call her son was coming. If only she made Andrew respect her as Joe Charles did. She wouldn't have to answer to her whore's act. What lie could she tell in place of the truth? Trying to think what she was going to tell her husband, she got off the bed and went through their nine room apartment, looking at all the lovely things they had gained and thinking about the fine friends they had and the trust her husband had in her. They owned the apartment and a lovely place in the country. The furniture in the nine rooms was French-provincial. All the rooms were painted robins' egg blue. Each room was carried out with a different kind and colored accessories. She thought of the lovely china, the silver and the costly jewelry, their cars, the furs and their savings. All these things she always wanted. She had tasted the glory of these precious possessions in the Duncan house, but if she lost her husband because of her bastard son, all these things would be insignificant to her. She had learned what true love was, not respect or sex, but the wonderful feeling that lies deep in the heart. Meditating on the thought if her husband loved her as much as she did him, he wouldn't let the child dissolve their marriage. Vada slumped down in one of the living room chairs, rattling her brain trying to think what will he do, what will he say if she told the truth? Fear began to tremble within. She had come up in the world. She was Mrs. Harry Val St. James. When she married her husband, to him she was a pure virgin. One of the letters V had written to Liz, she told her in a nice way that she didn't want any pictures of her son and not to resurrect her past until she felt it was time. But she never took the time. Thinking today is Saturday, her husband never worked all day on Saturday. Looking at the clock it was almost four o'clock—he was late; she was glad. She hadn't thought of any excuse to tell him. Thinking I can tell him Liz has adopted David and he is coming here to go to school like I did. I could say I have been so busy, I forgot to tell him they were coming. This thought rested her mind a little. Sitting there, another thought struck her. She remembered in one of the letters she got from her postal box from Liz, Liz had taught the boy to call her Aunt Liz, not mother. Saying out loud to herself, maybe David will call her mother. This thought shocked her into prancing the floor like a cat. Maybe I can meet them, rent a hotel room for them and they would stay there until things blow over. No, that won't do. We have a joint bank account. He would wonder where the money was going. She would have to give an explanation for the money. "Just can't lose him. I love him so much", she cried out loud. "Oh God, what can I say?" she stood there weeping in her hands. She was crying so hard she didn't hear her husband come in. He picked her up, carried her to the bedroom and put her down on the bed. She clung to him desperately. With tears running down her face she said, "I have to tell you something."

"Now stop crying, it can't be all that bad. If it is that bad, you can tell me in the morning when you feel better."

"But, but, it can't wait til morning. Harry, my sister will be here tomorrow, she hesitated...shuttering. She is bringing my son."

"Your son. What! Your who?! What are you talking about Vada? You never told me you had a son! Please, tell me you had a good reason for not telling me! Did you think I wouldn't accept him. Darling, what's so bad about having a son?" Harry said looking down at her on the bed.

"You don't understand, I wasn't married!" she exclaimed.

"I think I'm man enough to accept an illegitimate child. I know too many girls have babies, not being married but I can forgive you for this one."

Thinking to herself, I better tell him the whole truth—"Harry I had him by a white boy back home."

Tearing her arms from him, he stood looking at her in laughter. He threw his head back in a loud hideous laughter. His laughter stopped her crying. She looked at him in amazement. He stopped laughing. "You know if they hung every white man for rape and molestation, for every half-breed Negro in this country—they wouldn't have enough trees to go around. Haven't you heard this has been going on for years. Lashing out again—when a colored man plays around with a white woman, when they get caught together, she screams rape to keep her self-righteous and upright in the sight of the world. But the Negro's playing card is hanging..."

"But Harry, it wasn't like that with me," trying to stop his carrying on.

"Now when a white man plays around with a colored woman, if caught together, they are having a good time. If it's rape, they call that having fun. Oh I know you were just his handy lady." She looked at him in a strange sort of way. Harry was on the brown side. "What did he do, come up to you and say, Nigger, if you don't lay with me I'll beat the hell out of you or were you so afraid, you gave it to him with the greatest of pleasure?"

She jumped out of bed shouting at him—"Harry, it wasn't like that at all. I thought I loved him. He thought the same about me. It was just a wild romance."

"Now that's the first time I heard it happening like that. Are you crazy! He didn't love you! He could have married you, you look white enough. I know why he didn't marry you. You didn't have enough money. Most white men will marry a dog if it has money," Harry said in a very smooth manner.

"He did ask me to marry him and he wasn't using me either," she said softly. "He always wanted to be governor. He wouldn't have gotten to first base married to me. Please darling, forgive me and try to understand!"

"Why haven't you told me about this long ago?"

"Our lives have gone along with such ease, I thought I would never have to face the facts." She sat on the bed with her head hung down. "No one knows how bad a mistake this kind of thing is until you realize how wrong it is. But I just couldn't bring myself to tell you", she said looking up at him. Tears started to fall from her eyes again. His eyes met the sadness in her face. The sadness seemed to melt the anger in him. He caught her up in his arms. She cried out, "Please forgive me." He kissed her tenderly.

"Now hush crying baby. I love you," he whispered.

"I feel a lot better now that I have told you the whole truth."

"When you said you had him by a white man…damn…you know how I feel about white folk. I know you understand how a man feels about his woman, especially when he married her thinking she was a virgin," his voice sounded a little tart.

"Please forgive me, please."

"Vada Baby. Forgive me for acting the way I did, but this got to me where it hurts the most, right in the heart."

Chapter 8

TIME – Around 4:00 P.M. same day.

It was around 4:00 P.M. when Lee began to wonder where Mrs. Duncan could be. When she and Doff sat down to dinner, she mentioned it to him.

"Doff, Mrs. Duncan isn't back yet and it's getting late."

"Oh, she's probably gotten caught up at the big shopping center and lost track of time. You know she said she was going to take in a movie to."

"I forgot about the movie."

"Don't worry, she will be in shortly."

"Doff, do you think I ought to wake Andrew to have dinner?"

"If he drank as much as you said he did, he needs to sleep two or three days. You know he's not a drinking man. By the way, you two must have had a ball today."

She didn't reply to his catty remark, just raised her eyes and gave him a dirty look. After dinner, Lee and Doff went into the family room and watched TV and exchanged thoughts about the election.

"Doff, what are Andrew's chances of winning? Do you think he will really win?"

"Oh shucks Honey, the going is sort of tough. But I think he will win. I thought he would talk nigger talk, but he's preaching the true southern gospel. Say, Lee Baby, tell daddy what you have got on the old boy that makes you so sure you can collect whenever you want?"

"Shut up you big mouth. He's just in the next room. Watch TV."

"Is it about what's her name. You know who I mean, the colored gal that he used to be so crazy about?"

"Shut up Doff", Lee yelled softly. "The way you love to talk, you might let the cat out of the bag. All you need to know in a few more months is we will be living like a king. Quit the chit, chat and watch TV. Doff, it is almost six. Mrs. Duncan isn't back. I wonder where she can be. We better wake Andrew. Maybe he knows where she is."

They both went into the living room. Lee got a towel and poured some cold water on it. She brought it back and put the cold towel on his face. Andrew jumped up and flung the towel off his face.

"What are you trying to do to me?"

"We're just trying to wake you up. Your mother isn't back. It's after six", Lee said.

"What do you mean mother isn't back?"

"You remember she left this morning about eleven. She was supposed to do some shopping and go to a movie."

"Oh yes, I remember now. Oh my head. Maybe she met some of them at the shopping center and forgot to call." Andrew collected himself and called the committee. The voice on the other end said she wasn't with them. Andrew hung up the phone saying, "Mother is a smart woman. She isn't lost. Something has happened to her. While they were pondering over the thought of what might have happened to her, the phone rang. Doff answered the phone. "Andrew, the call is for you—long distance."

"Long distance," he exclaimed taking the phone. "It's Sam. What is it Sam?"

"Mr. Duncan, come home as fast as you can. Your mother is awfully sick. I don't think she will last long," Sam said in a frightened voice.

"Alright Sam. I'll be there as soon as I can," hanging up the phone. Andrew asked Doff, "Is there an airport here?"

"Yes, what do you want with a plane?"

"Mother is home. Sam said she is dying."

"Dying", Lee said entering the room with a concoction she had mixed for Andrew's hangover. Lee and Doff looked astonished and surprised. They both looked at Andrew and wanted to ask questions. But this wasn't the time for questions.

"Andrew, you can get a plane out as soon as you are ready. Do you want Lee and I to go with you?" Doff asked trying to be comforting.

"Thanks, I'd rather go alone. Call the committee. Tell them what happened. Tell them to continue with the plans."

The evening light made it easy for the small plane to land in the unplowed field. Andrew had to walk a half mile to his home. He made it in record time. Dr. Sliver was there.

"Andrew, your mother has had a light heart attack. Her condition is not serious. I will have to keep check on her. She is calling for you."

Andrew took the long stairs two at a time. He opened the door to his mother's room. He walked cautiously to the bed. Looking down on her face, she appeared tired and very old.

"Andrew," she said shakingly, "sit on the bed son." He took her hand. It felt cold and drawn. "My son, I came home to save you."

"Save me!" he thought. "From what?" But the questions didn't come.

"My son. When you got your big chance to be what you always wanted to be," she was talking very slow, "it made me awfully happy. But as I look at you, my heart is awfully sad. Your first speech really impressed me. I thought it was just political talk. I guess deep within me, I wanted integration. This evil grudge we still hold from the Civil War, we are just abiding the devil. We keep tension and fear in our blacks for our own iniquity. White folk expect to go to heaven when we die but I don't see how we are going to get there holding a grudge for almost a hundred years." Andrew didn't say a word. He let his mother talk. Her voice was getting weaker and her speech was slower. "I always thought you were a nigger lover. But now—I see all the things you did and said for them were just for your own glory. I know now that you meant every word you said in your speeches. My son, is this the kind of power you want, to keep a man crawling when he reaches up, tries to walk—you push him down, tell him he's not supposed to walk. Do you want someone at your feet to look down on all the time?" Andrew shook his head 'NO' but the words 'NO' never fell from his lips. "If I had known that running for governor would have brought this kind of material out of you, I would never let you run. We must face it. The change has got to come. When integration first started, I didn't want it no more than you did. I am a die-hard too, but I'd rather look like a hero that preached to my country about this freedom and justice for all rather than a coward and traitor in the sight of the world."

"Mother, I don't hate our Negroes. You have no right to say I'm a traitor and a coward to my country. I'm sorry we have different opinions," Andrew said in a sort of angry tone.

Mrs. Duncan closed her eyes. Her breathing was low and she ceased to speak.

"Mother", he said slowly, but frightened. She opened her eyes and raised herself up in bed. With all her breath, she screamed in anger, "You are just a traitor to your country and to the law of the land."

The word (traitor) the second time around seemed to anger him so he forgot how ill she was. He took her by the shoulders and began to shake her with fury. "Mother", he said in a loud angry voice, "All I want is to be governor and have the power to keep those niggers in their place." A frown of pain came over her face. Her eyes closed again. "Mother!" he said. She didn't answer. He began to shake her again and again this time out of fright. The shaking didn't open her eyes. He started yelling,

"Mother, open your eyes." Fear began to envelope his mind. He looked at her still, white body, seeing she wasn't any more. He cried out loud in a piercing way, "Mother, Mother, Mother." The word 'Mother' didn't come from his lips, only the movement of his mouth. The pills had laid his speech to rest, but not his mind. His mind kept thinking about his deadly passion to win the governor's race.

Chapter 9

Although Andrew and his mother were very close, her death did not erase the thought that Lee had so carefully planted in his mind. On the morning after the day they laid his mother to rest, Andrew found more courage than most people to do what Lee said he had to do kill, especially when death was so close to him. Andrew was up early that morning. He hadn't slept all night. He dressed for the hot weather outside. He made his way to the study, went to the desk, pulled out the middle drawer, took out the pistol that had laid in the desk drawer for years. He put the gun in his pocket. Going out of the study, he crossed the long living room. Old Sam appeared in the dining area. He too hadn't slept all night. He had known Mrs. Duncan most all of her life. He was thought of as part of the family. He was so grieved of her passing. With Pursa gone, not coming back for a few more weeks…if Pursa were home, Sam and Pursa could comfort each other. But Sam came to the big house thinking he and Andrew could talk about some of the happy days they had spent with Mrs. Duncan to cover up the sadness in their hearts. But this wasn't the case with Andrew. He had other intentions. As Sam crossed the dining room to enter the living room, he saw Andrew put the gun in his pants pocket. Andrew, with what he had to do so imbedded in his mind, didn't see Sam standing in the dining room entrance. Sam was so shocked and bewildered at this sight. He said nothing to Andrew. Sam unconsciously walked back into the dining room and pulled out one of the chairs. He just sat there with his face in his hands, crying dry tears, wondering what had happened to this man he thought he knew so well. He knew too well what Andrew intended to do. He wanted to yell out, "It ain't no use Mr. Duncan, he's gone." But the words didn't come.

Andrew went like a feather in a high wind the miles up to Liz'. As he drove swiftly along, a thought speared his mind. Of all the times he had been to Liz' place, he had never seen a child, boy or girl. Maybe there wasn't a child after all. There must be. Lee wouldn't tell a big lie like that. They must have hid him every time he came. How did Lee know so much? How did she know the boy looked just like him? He wasn't going to let a bastard ruin his lifetime ambition and his life. Before he got to the house, he parked the car some ways down the road in a thicket of trees. Taking his handkerchief from his pocket, tying it over his nose and mouth, he felt his pocket to see if the gun was still there. He walked swiftly up the dirt road that led to the house. His plan would be simple—kill the boy and hide his body in the woods. Thinking to himself, suppose Jessie and Liz would be home and recognized him, he would kill all of them. Walking off the dirt road into the front yard—Jag and Lady, the hunting dogs of Jessie's, came running out from beneath the weather-beaten old house, yapping their heads off. The barking of the dogs frightened him stiff. He broke out in a sweat and began to shake with fear. Jessie was eating breakfast—coffee, bacon and eggs and two cold biscuits left from the day before. Hearing the dogs yapping so, he got up from the table to see who was visiting so early in the morning. Maybe it was Liz. She didn't say on the telephone she would be back this soon. Andrew had collected himself from the scare. He saw Jessie come out on the porch. Jessie, seeing the man in the yard with a handkerchief over his face, knew that meant trouble. He rushed back to the house fumbling for the key in the door. But there was no key. He remembered that the key was in the top drawer of the old bureau for safekeeping. Knowing if he would move from the door to get the key, the man would come in, scared he held the door closed with all his might. Andrew ran the few yards to the house and pushed the door but Jessie was behind it holding it with frightening strength. "You in there, Andrew yelled, "Open this damn door or I'll shoot right through it." Jessie hesitated. "If you don't open this damn door, I will shoot right through it." Jessie, being afraid, opened the door and let him in. "Now where is the boy?" Andrew asked pointing the gun at Jessie.

"What boy?" Jessie said.

"You know what boy I mean," Andrew said angrily.

"He gone," Jessie replied.

"You are lying." In a fit of anger, Andrew began to beat Jessie with the gun. He hit him again and again. Jessie didn't fight back, he was to afraid. He hit Jessie on the head. Jessie fell to the floor, blood running from his mouth. Jessie began to moan and groan with pain. Andrew gathered him from the floor and shook him vigorously, yelling "Where is the boy? Where is he?"

"Mr. Duncan, Mrs. Duncan came up here a day or so ago. She said that they were going to kill him. We had to get him away. Liz took him to his mother."

"So you know who I am," Andrew said very arrogantly.

"Yes sir," Jessie answered.

Andrew jerked the handkerchief from his face saying to Jessie, "Look at me Jessie. Yes it's me. When you want to tell someone who beat you, I will fix those pigs and that cow and your crops. The sweat of anger on Andrew's face made him look mean. I"ll torture you so you will think you are in hell."

Jessie looked at this man blind-like, trying to tell himself that this wasn't the Mr. Duncan he knew. Straining his eyes, he looked again. It was him alright. Andrew pointed the gun, put his finger on the trigger. Jessie sighed and crumbled to the floor. Seeing Jessie lying on the floor looking as if he were dead, face swollen, blood running from his mouth and head, Andrew panicked, running from this terrible thing he had done. Andrew traveled just like fast lightning, faster than he went. Reaching home he felt secure. As he got out of the car, he started to take off his shirt. Walking in the house he was greeted by Sam. Sam looked at Andrew terrified. Sam had the feeling he had killed Jessie. Blood was all over his clothes. Thinking he didn't have to threaten Sam, he was the great white father. Who would believe Sam. Surely they wouldn't do anything to him for beating a nigger. Supposed they told his opponent of this. His chance would be slim. Although he was still frightened from what he had done, he knew he had to act cool and calm to keep his victim under control. He knew he had to plant fear in old Sam too. Acting impudent, he left old Sam standing in a daze. Andrew went to the bathroom and changed his clothes. Coming out of the bathroom, dressed in a robe, he saw Sam leaving by the way he came. Andrew felt that Sam was trying to escape. Andrew called to him in the gentle voice that Sam knew so well. Sam stopped abruptly but didn't answer with usual, "Yes Sir." Andrew called to him again, this time with sternness. Old Sam responded to the harshness in Andrew's voice. Sam was there on the double. "Yes Sir, Mr. Duncan." Sam tried not to act frightened.

"Sam, take these clothes and burn them and Sam go up there and take care of Jessie." Sam started to leave. "And Sam", Andrew said. Sam stopped but he didn't face Andrew. He stood with his back to him. "Sam take heed to the condition I left Jessie in and Sam tell Pursa the same when she gets back. By the way where did you say she went?"

"She went to visit our boy Willie in Texas. She didn't know you would be home so soon. We didn't expect you until voting time."

"That's alright about her leaving. Don't forget to tell her to keep her mouth shut about what happened around her. I'm leaving this afternoon to catch up with the committee. I want you to drive me to the airport."

"Yes Sir, Mr. Duncan", Sam said slowly, looking sad as he left the room.

It took Andrew only a short while to make himself ready for his political travels. As he was about to depart, the phone rang. It was Lee. She was very angry at Andrew for not letting her know of his mother's death. She had gotten the word by way of the newspaper. She felt that Andrew was getting pinch.

"Andrew Honey. Why didn't you let us know your mother had passed?"

"Lee, it all happened so fast. It hurt me so deeply. Maybe I didn't want to accept the fact that she was dead."

"Doff and I would like to have paid our respects to you."

"I am sorry I didn't call."

"Did you find out why she came home?"

"No, I didn't find out. She died before she could say why."

"Who told you?"

"Jessie."

"You mean, Jessie, Liz' husband?"

"Yes, I had to beat the hell out of him before he told me. Mother somehow overhead you and I talking about killing the boy. She had Liz take him to Vada."

"Andrew, I am glad it happened that way. I feel so much better knowing you didn't have to do such an awful thing. Andrew Honey, you were going to call me and tell me the happenings."

"Lee, I was going to call you. I just hadn't gotten around to it."

"What are you going to do about your mother's things?" Lee was gleaning inside to know Andrew hadn't caught on to her little scheme.

"I'll have Sam pick up mother's things. I'll have someone from the committee pick up mine. I would pick them up myself but I have been out of the race too long. Lee Honey, I wish I could talk with you longer but I have Sam outside waiting to take me to the airport. Talk to you later."

"Chin up, Andrew. I wish you all the luck in the world. Bye." After Lee chatted with Andrew, it made her feel like dancing. She went into the living room, turned on the hi-fi. She floated around the room like a butterfly thinking everything happens for the best. A live body is better evidence than a dead one and I can collect as long as the body lives. I wonder what I was thinking, telling him to kill the boy. Now that I have the cat out of the bag I better start meditating on how I'm going to phrase my conquest.

Chapter 10

Andrew circled over three-fourths of the state of Mississippi. He was on his way back home. He had long left the speeches he had started out with far, far behind him—better roads, corruption out of the government, reduce state taxes. He was on the kick that not only went to the hearts of grown people but the hearts of the children. Andrew was known by practically everyone in this state, being a fine farmer and good lawyer. His kindness and goodness brought out big crowds to hear this man speak. He spoke not of Gulliver's travels but of things that brought out the goodness and the evilness in one's hearts, seeming not to be there. Democrat or Republican or none voters as he spoke, his audience faces' held the look of children hearing for the first time the tale of Pandora and the Magic Box. "Fellow citizens, in a few more weeks we will go to the polls to choose a candidate to run in the primary election for governor. I am one of those candidates. You are looking for a man who will enforce the laws of this state and when new laws are to be passed, they will not pass unless they will benefit the people. Now getting down to the bare facts, we must keep those bugs from crawling in our schools. Next thing you know they will be taking over our women. Would you want to see the white woman with all kinds of colored kids tagging along behind her? Do you want to bear this shame? Think of your heritage. They are like cockroaches. If you let them get out of hand, they will be all over the place. You need a strong man for this job. I will work for the acceptance of the American ideals and the Constitutional rights of our state and for our children, childrens' rights and on down the line. Not distinguished from the social aspirations of our elders, you must choose a man that will recognize and enforce these aspirations. I, Andrew Duncan, am that man. Vote for me when you go to the polls. Thank you for coming." The crowd went up in wild yells and applause. They gathered around, shook his hand, encouraged him to keep fighting to win. Two weeks later, Andrew was back in his home town. He didn't go home. He stayed with Albert Johnson and his wife, one of the committee persons to cast his vote at the schoolhouse which was some distance from his home.

After Andrew cast his vote that morning, in the evening Andrew and some of his followers gathered in the small hall they rented. They waited patiently over coffee, doughnuts and sandwiches for the winner to be announced. It was late in the night when all the results were in. The loud sounds of whoopees and cheers came from the crowd. Andrew had won the primary election. After the crowd quieted down, Andrew made a speech of thanks. "I am very grateful to all those who worked with me so earnestly. There are no words to express my gratitude and thanks to all that voted for me. But I have two more battles to fight and to win. The general election. My greatest battle is when the election is over. That means those who believe in our way of life have to keep fighting until all battles are won." They cheered loudly. He held up his hand to quiet down the crowd. "Please excuse me. I am a little tired. I would like to rest before going home. I thank you all and may God bless all of you."

(Back to Chapter 1)

The sun was up when Andrew arrived home turning into the oval drive that led in front of the house. He peered through the car window as though he were looking for something that was supposed to be there, but wasn't. Coming closer to the house, he still looked for the two familiar faces that always greeted him, but they weren't there. As he got out of the car, he looked at his watch. It said twenty-five til seven. Sam and Pursa were always at the house at six-thirty. He couldn't remember a time when they were late or not at the house except for sickness. Maybe they had forgotten the day he was to come home. But Sam did deliver the car. He, perished the thought and unlocked the door to the old house.

Sam and Pursa didn't forget the day Andrew was to return. Sam still had the telegram that said he would be home the seventh of August. Deliver car to Albert Johnson, 1063 Willowbrood Dr.. Will drive myself home. Look for me early. If I win the primary, the three of us will celebrate. Love Andrew. Pursa had come home before the primary. Sam had told Pursa all that happened while she was away. Along with the telegram, Sam had gotten a letter from Vada. This morning when he was putting on his Sunday pants to celebrate, the feeling of the paper in his pocket reminded him of the letter. He pulled the letter out of his pocket that he had forgotten saying gaily to Pursa, "Got a letter from Vada just before you came." He opened the letter and began to read.

"Dear Mother and Dad,

David and Liz arrived safe. I feel what has happened to you now is all my fault. If I had only listened to you. I knew Andrew wasn't my kind but what I did wasn't right black or white. When you are young, you sometimes do some awfully foolish things. Since David has been here, my life has been cut into two. Harry took it hard at first, when I told him about David, but now he's like an old hen with one chick. They seem to be crazy about each other. Some of my friends have given me the cold shoulder. I haven't told them about David. They sense he is an illegitimate child. It hurts me so deeply for them to shun me. I'll never forget Andrew, David looks so much like him. Sometimes when I look at him, I almost hate him for taking the one thing I worked so hard to become—a teacher. I have resigned from teaching. I guess, in time, I will come to love him as much as Liz does", Sam stopped reading. The words in the letter shocked Sam and Pursa. "Pursa, could this be our Vada writing like this?"

"Pursa began to cry," Told her time and time again to leave him alone. She just wouldn't listen."

"Hush, Pursa Baby, it's all done now."

"I know. But we have to suffer for what she did. Do you think, after things blow over, David can come back home so she won't have to worry with him?"

"Pursa, you just have to stop this crying. You's getting yourself all mussed up for the celebration." Sam felt as bad as Pursa but he didn't let on. "Come on, hush Baby. The Lord will make a way. Maybe things ain't as bad as they seem."

"Lord if Mrs. Duncan were here, things would be different. I'm sure sorry I wasn't here for her funeral."

"Don't' feel bad. You didn't know she was going to die."

"But I just hate I wasn't here. I feel bad all inside", Pursa said still crying. "Sam, do you think Mr. Andrew is losing his mind? That's the only thing I can see that's making him act this way. Lord knows I don't want that to happen."

"I wonder about that too. No, he ain't crazy. He just showing his insides off."

"Sam, those speeches ain't him."

"We mostly live by the outside of a person, not inside. The things he talks about on TV and radio, they come from the heart. I believe he would give up everything he owns to be governor. This is something he always wanted to be from a child. I think he feels no man that's campaigning with him (can keep us niggers in our place) as well as he can. You know a lot of black and white people around town don't believe Mr. Andrew means those words he said in his speeches. It's just political talk. Pursa Baby, as I look back at all that's happened, I am sort of scared to go up to the big house. I's feeling he's not the man we used to know."

Pursa had stopped crying. She started to dust around the house. Trout was looking from Sam to Pursa saying to himself, when are they going to leave? It's breakfast time.

"Sam, we have to go, scared or not. If he comes down here, he will see how scared we is and that might not be good. I can't understand why he wanted to kill the boy. He must be plumb out of his mind. Sam, I ain't going."

"Pursa we's got to go. He done won the first election and we supposed to celebrate," Sam said in a scared voice.

"Sam, I's just ain't going. You better go and see how he's acting," Pursa said with stormy words.

"Trout", Sam called very sadly. Trout jumped up whining and wagging his tail, barking for joy, jumping up on Sam. "Down boy, down you stay here and watch Pursa whiles I go up to the big house."

Andrew had been home about half an hour. He started to get jittery. He couldn't stand the silence that lay in the house. He wondered why Sam and Pursa were not there to greet him. They had never been late as long as he could remember. He took up the phone to call them. they may have forgotten the day I was to come home. He put the phone back on the receiver, thinking about all he had said and did during the primary. They had gotten scared and left. He started to pace up and down the living room floor. Although he wasn't a drinking man he went into the kitchen and made himself a drink. He went back into the living room, pacing up and down, trying to consume its contents. He thought of his mother. He was really going to miss her—wondering if he hadn't shaken her so hard she might still be here. Had he really killed her? He dismissed this thought very quickly. He told himself he wasn't that cruel. I'm not a traitor. She had her thoughts and I believed in what I believe. With this thought, he started to pace from the living room to the study. In his travels from the living room to the study, he tried to think of something to do to ease the lonesomeness. He wished Sam and Pursa or even Trout was there. In the study, something on the desk caught his eye—one pink and the other blue. Sam had put all the mail in a big brass bowl and placed it on the desk. Sam had put the two colored letters on top. Seeing the two colored letters, Andrew was curious to see who they were from. He sensed most of the mail were bills and congratulatory letters but who in the devil were the pink and blue from? He didn't recognize either of the handwritings and there was no return address. He opened the blue one first and began to read.

Dear Andrew,

It's been a long time since we have heard or seen each other. This is Vada writing, remember me? "How well I remember you." He was thinking it looks like our sins have found us out. I have resigned from teaching. I hated to leave my position. It was something I had worked so hard to become. After I had David, I spent three years going to school day

68

and night and all summers trying to become somebody. Now that the bad penny has turned up, I feel that life is not worth living. I hope our sins will be forgiven and we can start life anew. I'm not writing to you to talk about us, but another source. I would not have written you if it wasn't for your mother. "Mother? What—does she have to do with her writing me?" I'm sorry to hear of her death. I always thought she was a great lady. She asked me to come home and talk to you about integration. I started to call you and have a good talk but as dad always said, that would be fighting words. The way you feel and the way I feel about integration and due to all that has happened back home, it would be to no avail. I told her I would write you instead. As you know, I became what I wanted to be, a teacher. Now since integration started, I have tasted the essence of it in many degrees—some just right and some made my mouth want to curse with anger. How irresponsible my people are. How shiftless they are. They are so ignorant. They are not ready yet. What has the Negro done to ask for such a powerful resurrection as equal rights? They don't need anything but a slow boat to Africa. They say nice words too. What is the Constitution for if it isn't for everyone and not just for a certain color of people...poor old Abe Lincoln, John Brown and many others, the men who wrote the great laws of our land. Many black and white men and women believe in lots of kind words that are heart-troubling, but lie around in books and not in too many hearts. There are men and women who bleed and die for this freedom and justice for all. Andrew thought to himself—"His fore parents fought for what they believed in too." They speak of the fast progress we made in the last, almost a hundred years. Even with the so-called fast progress, there is a lot lacking. We have something like taxation without representation. In other words, freedom without liberties and the lack of respect and dignity of the white man. Some think we want integration to socialize and to inter-marry. Socialization and inter-marriage doesn't give us respect or dignity to man or our constitutional rights. We don't only need the federal laws enforced, but the Ten Commandments enforced in our lives. The white man has taught the Negro to respect him, but not himself. I know we have a lot of faults but we are all alike. There are the high and low and middle class but you people put us all in one class. You taught the black man a lot of things but we were born with talents too. I must admit that your people did an excellent job in your style of civilizing and in brainwashing us that the world has ever seen. We lost the tongue we were born with, lost many ways of our African heritage. Some of the slave owners put so much fear in the Negro, they worshipped them like idols. Some of these instillings are still with some of us today because Uncle Tom ain't gone nowhere. This is one of the reasons a lot of blacks spend their money with the whites in the same business the Negroes are in. Slavery bred my people like cattle. Most of my people didn't know what being married was. The white man created one bastard after another. But in this year 1962, don't give the black man the right to keep up this dog-like bastardly in the making. This is one reason our men must become men in this giant program of integration to help curb illegitimate, juvenile delinquency, crime and school dropouts. Regarding our talents, we can all do if we put our hearts and minds into being a good father and mother without the ugly interference of the white man. The Negro woman has always been the backbone of the black race. But it seems as though her back is breaking. I can see it in my classroom everyday. Integration, hopefully, will bring out great talent in my people. After we were so-called 'set free' the Negro man could have held his head high and been a real father and husband to his family. No matter what, the white man would not let him do or be. Through it all, how could he be anything but an I don't care person? Instead, most of our black men turned to bitter things to make him feel he's somebody—things like drinking, gambling, a big car and sometimes stealing. But none of these things fulfill what he is reaching for—that is, to be a real man in the sight of God and man. Have you ever stopped to think what makes you think? Who you think you are? This freedom and liberty and justice are the key words. Andrew really didn't want to finish reading the letter, but something kept him reading on. We ask for this freedom with liberty and justice, the American Negro is to this country like a mother with a bastard child. She wants to love him if he stays out of her way. She wants it to stay in its so-called place. Its growing years, she gave her bastard child the elements from life like a stepmother. She feels she's superior, far better than her bastard child even though she bore it. Over the years she has come to realize it's not our fault we came here in a illegitimate way (slavery). She realizes it is in the family too, just like her other children but it has never fully enjoyed the full pleasures of this freedom and liberty and justice for all. She talks about this sad thing but gives few flowers and throws more rocks. Your people feel so sorry for our brothers across the big waters. You send them food, money—even the blood from yours and the black man's veins to help keep them free. The

70

sorrowfulness you feel for the black's needs, the so-called free northern Negro, can't see Simon La Gree—lives in the north too but more in the south and little Eva is still hollering for help. The only help that comes is black brother get back. The American white has become so arrogant and so important in himself and prosperity has turned his head from which he and his forefathers came—through blood, sweat, terror, disease, poverty, death and wars. Your forefathers labored hard and long in the light of the moon and candlelight. God inspired us all to invent great things to fulfill this American dream. This liberty and justice for all is not something the black man drummed up, but a promise you have been preaching all of your life to all nations. This liberty and justice, the American dream is a big lie to the black man. I hear we have gone communist. Lord help us. I hope my writing like this does not harden your heart to the truth. I hope your soul will find some good thoughts in what I am writing. Remember how we used to talk about you being governor some day. Andrew (thinking to himself) some of the words were silly back then and I was a silly boy. Reading on. We fled from behind the cotton curtain to the states beyond to find this liberty and freedom. We find these liberties somewhat better, but we found opportunity like looking for 'a needle in a haystack'—finding ourselves almost in the same condition but all done underhandedly. There are so many things we should participate in and there are so many things we can do. These things are as much our concern and interest as yours. I know we should do more in helping ourselves and, to me, integration or equal rights will do this—if our men and women take hold to the hand of opportunity. In the past and now the thought of your brother wanting to be superior to us, the feeling of not wanted is so strong in some of us that they have captured that 'don't care attitude'. This feeling has built up a wall of hidden knowledge in ourselves. Our talents and gifts are wasted. The Negro must realize this 'don't care' feeling will only keep him in the bread line. When we try to rid ourselves of this feeling, you will duck our heads back under the water. You are the only one who can tear down this wall and let our minds open to the good of all mankind. This is a need of a people to meet the change as you are preparing your children for the future. I know this change is most enduring for one who thinks he's superior to his brother. The whole thing in a nut shell, that holds integration back, is all of you great white fathers' fear reaping the wild and evil deeds you have sown over the years. There is always a guinea pig in everything we try to acclaim and not without 'who shot John'. Your mother couldn't understand why you were so against integration—you with your angel-like ways. Some are born with this superior feeling and some are taught. Now that integration is budding and not in full bloom, as integration unfolds, black people have to take this great step to secure their future. In a way, we will always be at the white man's mercy but try as we may to be on our own. When integration does burst into full bloom, we should have the trade know-how to go into more businesses of interest other than taverns, restaurants and hard labor, cleaning and other jobs. We also should let our minds probe into science and engineering, inventions and too, we should lend a bigger hand in giving our own black children scholarships to accomplish this paradise we are looking forward to. I feel that our golden years are yet to come. We believe this country is the land of opportunity, for we see it with our own eyes and a piece of it fell on me. I do thank God for being here to reach these golden years. Justice must be done. I hope these words find you and fill your heart. Sincerely yours, Vada St. James

Her letter didn't make him feel any different toward integration. It only hardened his heart. "Who in the hell does she think she is, the Queen of Sheba, to write me such a letter trying to make an explanation for her people. Thinking they are no good son-of-a-sea cocks. They're just no good! Taking up the other letter, he opened it and began to read.

Dearest Andrews, Ha, ha, ha, if you are wondering who is going to drop your secret around—well Honey, it is I—Lee Rainey. If you want this secret kept, just make out a check for $5,000 as soon as you get this letter. Send $2,000 a month. Send it to my home. You know my address. With all my love, Lee.

Speaking out loud to himself, "She can't do this to me. She can't blackmail me like this." He got out his little black address book. He found her phone number. It was Lee who answered the phone.

"Lee, this is Andrew. I received your charming note. You won't get one damn cent from me."

"What makes you think I won't get what I worked so hard for?"

"In the first place, it's not legal. I'll have you jailed for trying to blackmail me."

"Now Sugar, I didn't know what you just said wasn't legal," Lee said in a sort of sarcastic way. "You will pay alright", Lee lashed out. I have mimeographed some hundreds of letters. I have addressed some to your adversary and some to just people. What I said in those letters you wouldn't vote for yourself. You wouldn't want everyone to know you have an illegitimate child, would you? Mr. Goodie Good and you wouldn't want me to send those letters, would you darling?"

"No Lee", Andrew said coldly.

"Darling, think of your pride, your good reputation. I know being governor is your life's ambition. You don't want it thrown to the wind."

Andrew didn't answer her remarks but replied, "Does Doff know about your blackmail scheme?"

"Yes, but he doesn't know what I am holding over your head. He wanted three thousand a month. I told him not to be greedy," she said laughing.

"Alright, Lee, I'll send you the money."

"Wait, Andrew, before you hang up. Think of the money, not as blackmail but as a token to the many years that I wasted my love on you." Neither said good-bye. They just hung up.

All the time Andrew thought Lee was helping him. This want in him to be governor was so strong in him that it blinded his lawyer's immunity. He was like a lamb led to slaughter and he sat there with the pink note in his hand—dumbfounded.

Sam was glad that Pursa didn't come this morning. Sam couldn't believe that this was the man he thought he knew so well he had known ever since he came into the world. He was always a sweet and gentle person in a boyish manner. When his father was too busy, when he was just a kid, he and Sam would go fishing or hunting together. Sam and Pursa and family and all the help were treated as the Bible says—masters give unto your servants that which is just and equal, knowing that ye also have a master in Heaven. But integration had brought out hell-fire in him. Sam couldn't believe that this was the Mr. Andrew Duncan he knew, acting like a madman.

After Doc Sliver left this afternoon, Sam stood at the bedroom door where Andrew was resting for a spell. When Sam thought Andrew was well asleep, he tiptoed into the room where he was to make sure Andrew was sleeping. The sleeping pills had taken affect. Old Sam went back to his little cottage. Pursa was still sitting in the rocker rocking away, singing 'if it wasn't for the Lord, tell me what would I do.'

"Hush, Pursa Baby and listen to me. Mr. Duncan sure ain't the man we used to know. He cursed and called me a black nigger."

"I told you. 'Cause the goose done laid the golden egg, dat ain't no reason he won't still be mean as the devil," Pursa said.

"This is the first time in my life I ever felt being black was inhuman. He ain't never made us feel that we was outcasts", Sam's voice sounded like he wanted to cry. Pursa Baby, I's sure glad you didn't go. Mr. Andrew was always a good man, not easy to get mad he seemed to love our people so, but now I think he hates us. Pursa, we ain't never heard him use bad language before."

"We sure ain't. This integration mess sure got the devil hunching him. I still think he's losing his mind. He's sure acting strange to me."

"Now stop saying he's losing his mind. You know what he told me, that this integration mess is our concern too. I told him I's too old to be thinking about such goings-on. But I's been thinking about dis here thing."

"Sam, don't you start thinking about dis here mess. You be acting like Mr. Andrew."

"But Pursa Baby, there is something about this integration business that keeps dancing on my mind", Sam insisted walking the floor scratching his head, here and there, like a dog scratching in search of a bone he had buried but didn't know where. "You know last Sunday in church and lots of Sundays before last Sunday, Preacher Jackson after his Sunday sermons, they have been discussing integration. But I been let it go in one ear and out the other, but I do remember what he said last Sunday."

Pursa kind of rolled her eyes at Sam and said, "Here you thinking about this integration mess like you going to live 90 more years. Here you's 'bout make up your dying bed."

"But Pursa we ain't dead yet. Preacher Jackson said that our men laid down their lives on the battlefield to help keep this country free. When our boys came back, they came back to the same old hell-fire. He said all we ask is the same equal liberties and better education and the right to vote."

"Hum, hum, you keep on talking that talk you will be crazy too." Pursa said rocking as though she was going to rock out of the chair.

Sam kept on talking, "Lord knows the white man sure got a whole lot to answer for, for he is in authority. For those in authority have to answer for their own souls and for the way they treated their servants. The master more so answers our need by beating our heads and putting us in jail. That's what Preacher Jackson said."

"Preacher Jackson is going crazy too. This mess will drive a dog crazy", Pursa said rejecting Sam's remarks.

"But all the talk I heard around town 'bout this integration business, I have been thinking real hard 'bout this thing. Since Mr. Duncan said it concerns us too. But all these thoughts don't seem the reason to me why we need integration. It's something, way different from all I've heard. But I just can't put my finger on the reason. It will come by and by. I'd better call Doc Sliver and have him give us some advice 'cause when Mr. Andrew wakes up and he is still like he was when he went to sleep, we just can't stay here." Old Sam got on the phone, "Doc Sliver, this is Sam. What must we do 'bout Mr. Duncan when he wakes up?"

"What do you mean, do about him?" Doc said.

"I think he's losing his mind." Sam wanted to tell Doc all that had happened. But fear made him use Pursa's reason why he wanted Doc's advice—not that he thought Andrew had gone crazy.

Doc chuckled a bit, "Now Sam, he's not losing his mind. He is just expressing the way he feels toward integration, you and Pursa probably haven't given integration a thought, one way or another. I can care less, I don't give a damn. My patients are enough trouble for me. Sometimes I wish I could give something from the black bottle. He will be alright after he has rested for a while."

"You think so? If he don't stop acting up, me and Pursa have to leave."

"Leave! Why you and Pursa can't leave him now. He needs you two. You're all he has left."

"He can get somebody else to work for him", Sam said without hesitating.

"I know Sam, but you two are just like a second father and mother to him."

"But Doc, you don't know how bad he's been acting," Sam said in a somewhat frightened voice. What Sam wanted to tell Doc was how Andrew had beat Jessie, called him a black nigger, said other bad words and attempted to kill the boy. But Andrew's warning told him not to tell.

"I can assure you Sam, he will be alright when he has rested. You and Pursa stay with him."

"Alright Doc, we do just as you say", Sam was smiling when he hung up the phone. The assuredness from Doc gave Sam's mind relief.

"What did he say Sam?"

"Doc said, after he has rested, he will be his old self again."

"Lord, I sure hope so 'cause the devil is sure hunching him."

Around 2:00, Sam and Pursa went to the big house. Pursa got busy in the kitchen fixing supper. She had a feeling that everything will be right just like it used to be. She began to sing "I'm going to lay down my burdens" with "Joy in my heart." In came Trout. He always rooted the back door open and let himself in. "Dog, where you been?" Pursa said, "All wet and muddy and hungry. Been chasing a coon, I reckon. You is 'bout the most stay from home dog I done seen. You been gone three days. If a thief came to dis house, you wouldn't be here to bark him away. All you's good for is to feed. Gone get out of my kitchen." Pursa shooed Trout out the door. Trout stood whining for his dinner. "Alright Dog, I'll feed you. Just a minute."

Andrew was himself after a few days rest. Sam and Pursa saw that Andrew took the pills Doc had left. There was color again in his face; the anger seemed to cease; the dark circles began to leave his eyes. He insisted on Sam and Pursa eating in the dining room with him. They talked of many things at dinner that night, mostly how lonesome it was around the big old place. Old Sam and Pursa's children all in different places. Andrew's mother and father gone forever. Andrew wanted to tell Sam it was the letter and the note from Lee that made him carry on like a mad man the first day he came home and the way he felt about integration. Receiving the letter from Vada really angered him, but he wanted to discuss the equalization problem with them in the right manner and, too, he wanted to tell them about the blackmail letter he got from Lee that made him cry like a child. He knew he was getting all mixed up with his thinking. If he could only tell them or talk with someone about his troubles, but something inside—the thing called pride—held these secrets deep within. He thought of Terence, his lady friend. He wished she would hurry home. Maybe she could unbind these troubles within. He spoke of marriage to Terence to Sam and Pursa.

"Ain't she kind of young for you?" Pursa said.

"No she's not. She's past thirty."

"She sure don't look it. When you had her several times by our house, I said to myself, Mr. Duncan done gone and robbed the cradle" they all laughed.

"I would like to start a family and flood the old house with little children again. I'm still young, you know. Then again, I was thinking of giving the old place to the state for a museum."

"We like that part about you getting married the best" Sam said.

"I think I'll ask her for her hand in marriage before I go campaigning for the general election, if that's alright with you Sam!"

"Yes Sir, Mr. Duncan, yes sir."

Chapter 11

On the morning of the fifth day, Andrew arose bright-eyed and bushy-tailed, feeling very energetic. This morning, he decided not to rest. He thought he had rested enough. After breakfast, he had Sam bring the jeep around front. He jumped in the car like a young boy. He then made his way up to the farm. Andrew parked the jeep near the entrance under one of the many weeping willows that lined the highway entrance. This time he didn't bring a box of candy for the children, just himself. As he started into the Planter-Ranch, he hesitated when he saw the Negro Jonah coming out of the entrance to take his usual place along the highway entrance. Old Jonah always sat there on a vegetable box smoking his pipe, chatting with whoever went in or out watching the many cars that went by. Jonah had been with the Duncans as long as Sam and family, but his work on the Planter Ranch was over. He just sat at the entrance passing the time away. Looking at Jonah, a thought touched Andrew. The people on the inside were mostly Negroes and they were the people he was using such bold words to in his campaign speeches. He wondered what they thought about him now. How would they treat him? Thinking they may feel hostile toward him and attack him, he shivered at this thought. As he stood there, he gave himself courage telling himself that he owned this place. He could come and go as he pleased no matter what they thought of him. Old Jonah gave him more courage when he said smiling, "Hi Mr. Duncan." Jonah stuck his hand out for a shake and Andrew shook his hand with warmth, smiling.

"How is everything around here, Jonah?"

"Oh, everything around here is just fine", Jonah said talking out of the side of his mouth, holding a pipe with his teeth. The crop is better than I ever seen them." Old Jonah was a sight with long johns on all summer except for Saturday and Sunday.

"You say that every time I come up here", Andrew said jokingly.

"But they are! We sure miss you Mr. Duncan," Jonah said as he eased himself down on the box.

"You miss me alright. I bet when your people heard my speeches, you wished I would drop dead somewhere", Andrew said with a sarcastic air trying to learn from Jonah how the blacks felt about him now.

Jonah looked at Andrew without a smile on his weather-beaten black face and said, "You know Mr. Duncan, it's like this. When your feelings are on the inside, they are yours but when you bring them out on the outside, they are everybody else's. But, the catch is the way you act when your feelings come on the outside, that's what counts", Jonah said as he took a deep draw on his pipe. He then crossed his arms, looked straight away and said no more.

As Andrew walked into the Planters Ranch, thinking that Jonah said the same words that Sam had said. The living quarters were deserted except for a few children playing in the road. When the children saw him, they ran up to him smiling yelling for candy. "No candy this time young ones." One of them broke from the rest of the children. He ran through the gangway between the barracks toward the packing house yelling happily, "Daddy, Daddy, Mr. Duncan is here." Andrew followed the child, and the other children tagged along behind him asking questions. "Where have you been?"

"Oh, I've been on a trip."

"Where did you go?"

"Oh here and there." The children knew where he had been and had heard most of his speeches. In the words of their parents, don't get fresh with Mr. Duncan. Old Josh, the white foreman, rescued him for the questioning.

"Hi, Mr. Duncan, glad to see you and congratulations", Josh the white foreman said. "Thanks Josh." They walked toward the packing house. "You should see the crop this year", Josh said. "That's what Jonah said", Andrew replied. When they reached the packing platform, the workers had different kinds of vegetables spread out on the platform for Andrew to see. By this time, all the women and men had gathered around with anxious faces to see what Andrew thought of the crop this year.

"My goodness, they do look rich. They look so healthy they don't even look real." The workers smiled. "We have had crops look good years back but the crop this year takes the cake. You all must have worked awfully hard to get vegetables looking this great." Looking about him at the smiling faces of the Negroes, he wanted to ask what they thought of his campaign speeches but instead he jokingly said, "I will give all of you a penny raise." They all laughed but at the same time, in his mind, he would never know how they felt about him or his campaign. They had kept their feelings to themselves on the inside.

He left the packing house, went into the field and chatted with workers out there. He let the dirt run through his fingers. They talked about how good the crops were this year and of family affairs and giving the barracks a new coat of paint. But one subject didn't come up—his campaign speeches nor his winning the primary election. But, everyone seemed to be pleased to see him again.

On the morning of the sixth day—Andrew, Sam and Pursa ate breakfast together. Sam and Pursa ate their breakfast hurriedly. After they had finished eating, they excused themselves. Andrew wondered what was up? But he didn't move to find out or ask questions. Old Sam went upstairs and gathered up all the pillows and brought them down and made a pallet on the living room floor. He then went to the study, chose three books he thought Andrew would like to read and put them on the floor by the pallet. In came Pursa with the lemonade. When Andrew saw Pursa whizzing through the kitchen with the lemonade, he came into the living room to see what was going on. When he saw what they had planned—"Oh no", he cried, "Oh no, I just got out of bed."

"We know but the Doc said you need all the rest you can get and you was gone all day yesterday." Sam gave him the two white pills and a glass of water. "I'm not sick", Andrew protested. "We know, we just want you better", Sam said.

"Okay, I'll rest if you two insist." Instead of reading the books that Sam chose, Andrew turned on the television he had made to match the antique furnishings. Andrew watched and enjoyed television until about 11:00. The ringing of the phone broke up the quiet morning. It rang three times. He didn't bother to answer. Pursa and Sam had been answering the phone. They wanted Andrew to rest without interference. The phone rang again. "Where are they?" he thought. On the fifth ring, he rose and answered the phone. Lee was on the other end of the wire. He hadn't heard from her since he sent her the check. "You got my check, what do you want?"

"I want $25,000 in one lump sum, instead of $2,000 a month", Lee said calmly.

"What do you think I'm crazy?"

"No, that's why I'm asking for $25,000 in one lump. I promise you darling, I won't ask for another penny."

"I won't give you that kind of money. Lee, I'll have you arrested and put in jail. I won't pay."

"Ha, ha, ha," she laughed. "You'll pay." Lee had been thinking when this thing is over, suppose Andrew did not win the election. Maybe his conscience wouldn't hold the shame it held now. He just might have her thrown in jail. "Alright Andrew, go ahead, have me thrown in jail. Andrew you remember I told you I wrote some letters. Now if you don't want to cooperate with me, I'll mail those letters. You will pay one way or the other."

"But Lee you can't do this to me. It's blackmail", Andrew said in a childlike manner.

"I'll give you two days to get the money together", she plunked the phone down in his ear.

"Won't give her one damn cent", he said out loud to himself. He started yelling for Sam, "Sam, Sam, Sam."

Pursa came in to see what all the yelling was about. She could hear the anger in his voice. "Mr. Duncan, don't you go getting all riled up. You got to get your rest."

"Shut up Pursa", he yelled angrily. "You can't tell me what to do. Where is Sam?"

"Outside somewhere", Pursa shook her head as she went out the front door looking for Sam thinking to herself, the storm is back.

When Sam heard Andrew calling in that tone of voice, he felt the same thing Pursa did—the storm is back. Sam came in the house somewhat out of breath asking, "Mr. Duncan, what is it?"

"Get the car out. We are going some place."

Sam brought the black Cadillac around front. "Mr. Duncan, don't you think we should tell Pursa we's leaving. She's fixing lunch."

"No, when she misses us, she will know we are gone", he said harshly.

"Where are we doing?"

"Clearforest, take 134."

They rode all the way in silence. When they got to Lee's place Andrew saw the garage door was open. Lee's car was there but Doff's car was gone. This assured Andrew that Lee was at home. He had Sam drive his car into Lee's garage. He knew if Lee saw his car out front, she wouldn't let him in. He knocked on the kitchen door, right off the garage. Lee answered the door. She was astonished when she saw Andrew with his car in her garage. Why didn't he park out front she thought. Her face turned white.

"What are you doing here Andrew?" Lee said calmly.

"Oh I just stopped by to say hello and talk a bit."

She wanted to say some words, but she stood there dumbfounded and frightened. She really didn't know what to say. Andrew stood in the open door with his foot in it. With a smile on his face, he said—"Aren't you going to let me in?"

Lee could see old Sam sitting in the car. Sam sat there without saying a word until Lee said, "Hi Sam."

"Hi Miss Lee", Sam answered.

"Come in Sam", Lee said, moving to one side, letting Andrew in.

"Sam don't have to come in. He can sit in the car and wait."

"Andrew, it's too hot for Sam to sit in the car."

Lee wasn't thinking of Sam. She was thinking—with Sam in the house—maybe Andrew wouldn't do anything rash.

Andrew moved from the kitchen to the family room, leaving Lee in the kitchen. He turned on the TV. He then called to Sam, saying sarcastically, "sit here and watch TV while me and Miss Lee attend to business."

Lee had composed herself, spitting our angry words "Just what are you up to Andrew?"

"Let's go in the den and talk business", Andrew said taking Lee by her arm and kind of pushing her.

"We can talk here."

"Now you don't want Sam to know everything, do you Honey?"

Instead of going to the den, she led him to her bedroom. She opened the drapes back from the long paneled windows assuring herself if he tried to harm her, someone would see him. Maybe they would get help.

Andrew pulled the drapes closed saying coldly, "You don't want the neighbors seeing me making love to you, do you?" he said with a smutty grin on his face. She said nothing but tried not to look frightened. He walked slowly over to her and took her hand in his. "Lee Baby, I thought all the time you were trying to help me. How could I think such a thought. Being the great lawyer I am, I should have smelled blackmail from the start. You really clouded my mind." She broke away from him. He moved toward her again, she backed away. "You were only helping yourself to my money." He grabbed her by her hand again.

"You made me do this. I thought you would send me a little token of appreciation for my help. I wouldn't call it blackmail, just a love token. I just wanted to get back at you because you didn't marry me. I didn't want the money."

"You are a liar, I didn't need your kind of help." He squeezed his nails into the palms of her hand. She wanted to scream, "You are hurting me," but she tried to show him that he couldn't frighten her.

"I really didn't want the money Andrew. I just wanted revenge. I always loved you and I still do."

"You wanted my money and revenge so you can have your cake and eat it too." He began to slap her. The slaps strung his hand but he kept right on one after another. Her face turned bull red.

"Andrew please stop. Please, you're hurting me", she screamed.

"I want to hurt you just like you hurt me. I'm just hurting your flesh. I'd like to damn your mind." She freed herself from him. She tried to get out of the room. He chased her around the chair and over the bed like a cat chasing a mouse. She screamed as loud as she could. She thought Sam would hear her scream and come to her rescue, but Sam didn't come. "Andrew, please don't hit me any more. I'll burn the letters. I won't say a word about what I know. Please believe me. I'll do anything you say, just stop hurting me." Andrew caught her as she tried to make for the door. He caught her and threw her across the bed. Her head hit the table and turned over a lamp. She laid there—her red swollen face was as white as death. He looked at her. He picked Lee up saying, "Lee, honey, wake up, wake up." She just laid limp in his arms. Surmising she was dead, he let her fall on the bed. He stood staring at her crazylike. All of a sudden he heard voices saying, run Andrew, run, run. You mustn't be blamed for this. He opened the glass doors at the back of the garage, got into the car and drove away, leaving old Sam for the bait.

Andrew had been gone about half an hour before Sam realized the voices in the house had ceased. He was so engrossed in the TV, he didn't realize it was awfully quiet in the house. He got up from the chair in which he was sitting, went down the hall until he came almost to the open door to the den and to the bedroom opposite the den. He stood there a short while, twisting his hat in his hand, getting up courage. Finally he said, "Miss Lee could I have a glass of water please?" He sort of cocked his head to one side and listened for an answer, but no answer came. Sam had a feeling something was wrong. He peeped into the den and then to the bedroom. There was no one there. Seeing another room at the end of the hall, he stood there in wonder. The feeling of something is wrong picked at his mind again. Without another thought, Sam went into the master bedroom. He saw Lee on the bed looking as though all she needed was burying.

Sam put his hat over his face, crying aloud, "Lord what has he done now?" Frightened and nervous, Sam turned quickly out of the room rushing down the hall. Sam wasn't thinking of himself but he soon did. Walking out of the hall into the family room, he came face to face with Doff. Both were surprised to see each other. In a surprised way, Doff asked, "What are you doing here, Sam?" Sam pointed toward the hall. "I didn't do it, Mr. Doff. I didn't do it."

"Do what Sam?"

"Miss Lee, she laying on the bed dead, I didn't do it. I didn't kill her." That's all Sam could say. Doff didn't seem upset but surprised at what happened. Suddenly, Doff thought about Lee blackmailing Andrew. So this is the payoff, Doff was thinking to himself walking down the hall to where Lee was. Doff wondered what Lee had on Andrew. Whatever it was, she must have pulled the string too tight to make him kill her. Looking down on her, he could have given her a beating too for ruining everything he had planned to do with the money. He could have paid off his home, took a trip to Europe. He had such high hopes but it seems like all his dreams were gone. He found life in her body. She was just unconscious. He called the doctor. He then went back to the living room where Sam was—telling Sam she was alive. Sam was relieved to hear the good news, asking Doff, "Do you think she will be alright?"

"I don't know, you better hope so." Doff sat in a chair across the room from Sam, sitting there looking at Sam. Doff grew angry. Getting out of the chair, he went over to where Sam was sitting. "Sam I believe you are lying", he said in a loud angry voice. He jerked Sam out of the chair slapping Sam's face from side to side. "You are lying. You know Andrew sent you to do his dirty work. Where did you hide the car? I'll have you lynched for this."

Sam didn't fight back. He only pleaded with Doff that he didn't do it. Sam was like a child that was getting a beating he didn't deserve. Doff pushed Sam back into the chair. "Sit down there and wait til the doctor comes. When he brings her around, I'll find out if you are lying or not. If you did, me and my friends will have a lynching party. With all this mess your people have stirred up, they won't waste time."

Sam sat frightened, sweat running down his face. He thought of being lynched. He wanted to cry but he only cried a prayer, "Lord, please don't let them lynch me."

In a short while, the doctor was there. "It will hurt a little while", the doctor said fixing up the lump on Lee's head. "Come into my office in a couple of days. I want to see how the bruises are healing. Take aspirin for the pain."

"We will do just that", Doff said showing the doctor to the door. Doff called Sam in the room, "Darling was he black or white?"

"Doff you know damn well Sam wouldn't hurt a flea. Boy, he sure gave me a beating. My face is black and blue." Lee said looking at herself in the mirror.

"Lee Baby, you don't have to be afraid to talk. He will be taken care of", Doff said looking directly at Sam.

"You know who did this to me. Just look at him, he's to scared to move. You know Andrew did this. Why don't you get him if you are man enough?"

These words angered Doff. Sam's eyes popped. His mouth flew open at Lee's remarks. "Okay Sam, get out. Wait in the family room until I find out when a bus is coming to Braidwood", Doff said harshly closing the bedroom door.

"What are you going to do—beat me too? I couldn't help it. The scheme fell through."

"What did you do? Get greedy?"

"Yes, in a way."

"What do you mean, in a way?"

"At first, I asked him for $2,000 a month. After I thought about it, I knew the plan wouldn't work when the election is over, so I asked for $25,000 in one lump sum."

"You did what!"

"I told him I wouldn't ask for any more. He didn't believe me."

"Would you believe a blackmailer if he told you that?"

"No, I guess I wouldn't."

"Honey, why did you mess up? I had all kinds of plans for the money."

"Forget about it. Everything is out the window now."

Andrew was half way home when his conscience made him turn the car around and go back after Sam and to see if Lee was alive. Doff answered the chimes. When Doff saw Andrew, he began to tremble with fear. Seeing Doff was afraid, Andrew walked in with the usual greeting, acting with the calmness of that of a self-made hoodlum. From down the hall come the words—

"Who is it dear?"

Andrew walked back to the master bedroom. Lee saw it was Andrew. She tried to faint but it didn't work. Andrew walked over to the bed and pinched her on her ass as hard as he could. She screamed. Doff and Sam came running.

"What are you doing to my wife?"

"Listen up, the both of you. I didn't make a lot of speeches just for the love of talking, neither did I put all this time in campaigning just for play. I intend to be governor at any cost. I do believe in what I am preaching. I was born not to just live; I was born with a purpose in life. I intend to fulfill this purpose and I'm not letting anything or anybody stand in my way and that means you and Lee." Without warming, Andrew hit Doff with his fist so hard he knocked him across the room. "Get up Doff, I didn't hurt you. That's just to remind you that if you're thinking of taking up where your wife left off, don't try it. It might be boom, boom the next time."

Doff didn't get up fighting, just rubbing his jaw.

"Lee, give me the letters." Lee got out of the bed and went to the den with Andrew behind her. She took out the bottom drawer of the desk and gave Andrew a box from under the drawer. "Lee, if you think of writing some more of these letters, think how bad it can hurt." Lee didn't say a word. She marched herself back to the bedroom with Andrew right behind her. Lee didn't get in the bed. She sat on the edge of the bed, holding her head. Doff stood by helpless. "Lee Honey, it wasn't the money part that hurt so bad. It was my pride. The fact that you tried to act so smart and I'm supposed to be a brilliant lawyer. I should have smelled blackmail when you first came up with your evil scheme. Come on Sam, let's go. Oh, just one last reminder—when you go to the polls, vote for me. Boom boom."

After Andrew and Sam left, Lee and Doff ran to each other. They clung to each other like two lost hunters, scared. This was the first time Lee ever felt she needed her husband. Lee, too, was like a spoiled brat. She didn't love Doff, just used him and his love. Lee began to cry, babbling through her tears, "I'm scared. I'm really scared." Doff tried to comfort her holding her close. "Doff, Andrew hasn't given a thought to his opponent winning. I think he has thought of this election as one of his big cases in court where you match wits with another man. But this is different. The people have you on the stand and it will be him on the stand not them. Suppose he loses and thinks we had something to do with it?"

"Lee you are the one who started this mess. Now you are scared to death. You are just trying to get even with him because he didn't marry you. You better leave him alone before you get us both killed." Lee said no more but complained the lump on her head was hurting.

Andrew and Sam were back home. Andrew was in a happy frame of mind. Sam went looking for Pursa. Andrew went to the study and dialed 446 6450. "Terence, this Andrew, Honey."

"It's good to hear your voice. I miss you so much. I called when I got back but Pursa and Sam wouldn't let me talk to you. They said you had to rest."

"They really have been keeping an eye on me. They think I'm sick. All I needed was rest. How is your mother?"

"Oh Mother is doing fine now. She was pretty sick there for a while. I'm sorry to hear of your mother's passing. I'm sorry that I didn't get to meet her."

"I'm sorry she didn't get to meet you. She wanted to and I know she would have loved you. I sure do miss her."

"I know how you feel. I almost lost my mother. Oh, she said congratulations. Congratulations from me also. I heard you won the primary election."

"I feel I have the general election in the bag."

"Now don't count your chickens before they hatch."

"Why grab the moon, reach for the stars. I know I'm being optimistic, but never underestimate the power of Andrew Duncan. I didn't call to talk politics, I'll be back campaigning Monday; be gone a short while. How about dinner tomorrow night, just you and I?"

"I would love that. What time?"

"Oh, around six."

"I really miss you, Andrew. Love you."

"Love you too, Raindrops. Honey, I don't like cutting our conversation short, but I have some speeches I have to work on. I miss you Angel. See you tomorrow night."

Sam found Pursa in the kitchen. She was as mad as a wet hen. "Where did you and that Mr. Andrew go? You knew I was fixing lunch."

"I told him you was making lunch. He said come on Sam, let's go. The volcano erupted again. He done gone and beat up that Miss Lee. I thought she was dead til the doctor came and brought her to."

"Oh my Lord, what is he going to do next, Lord help him." Pursa sat in one of the kitchen chairs and put her hands together and said a prayer. "Lord, what's wrong with this man? Please Lord help him, Lord to come back to himself. Please help him Lord. Amen."

"Pursa, I think that Miss Lee got something to do with the way Mr. Duncan been acting. I think."

"That's alright about what you think, Sam." Andrew said as he entered the kitchen. Think of something really good to eat for tomorrow night." Pursa and Sam regained there composure and erase their feelings of distraught and fear.

"What do you mean tomorrow night? You haven't ate what I fixed for lunch", Pursa said.

"I'm sorry about lunch. We can eat that for dinner. Now getting back to tomorrow night, I want something real yummy."

"Like pheasant stuffed with pecan dressing, wild rice with mushrooms, hot rolls, green salad and slender strip, coffee and maybe a little wine," Pursa laughed.

"That sounds good Pursa."

"You name the dessert, Mr. Andrew."

"Peach pie with ice cream."

"That sounds real good. A meal fit for a king." Sam said.

"Now that we have the dinner planned, what is the big occasion?" Pursa said smiling.

"Terence is coming over for dinner and I think I will pop the big question."

"I hope you will and I hope she will say yes," Sam said without thinking.

It was Saturday. Sam and Pursa were up early. There was much hustle and bustle in the big old house. Sam gathered the flowers for Pursa to arrange. Pursa and Sam gave the downstairs a cleaning it hadn't had for some time. The crystal glasses, the china dishes and the just polished silver were laid on the just ironed tablecloth. The silver candlesticks awaited for the evening. Pursa paused a minute and thought of days gone by and of the late Mr. and Mrs. Duncan. How many times in the past had she spread this table! It was so pleasing for her to do these things again.

Andrew came down about noon. Pursa give him a bite to eat, then shooed him off. By evening, everything was ready for the big occasion. Andrew came back about three. He had spent the afternoon at the Planter Ranch. When he came into the house, the smell of summer flowers greeted him. Going into the dining room, the table set for two put a sparkle in his eyes and a smile on his lips. The odor of food took him by the nose and led him into the kitchen. He was in a daze. He took a lid from one of the pots. A slap on the hand and Pursa saying, "You leave my pots alone," brought him out of the daze. "Pursa, everything smells so good."

"Everything smelling good down here, don't get you dressed upstairs. I did your white suit."

"My white suit," he exclaimed.

"Just how do you think you will look like proposing in slacks and a sport shirt? You want to look romantic-like." Pursa said with her face beaming."

"I never thought about it like that. White suit it shall be, Pursa." He said joking-like and went upstairs to dress.

Terence, the Yankee gal Andrew was planning on popping the question to, was from Connecticut. She lived in Braidwood several years. She stayed with her aunt, Mrs. Dorothy Thompson, who lived in one of the ranch houses a little piece from the Duncan place. It was by accident that Andrew met her.

Terence's car had a flat tire. There were no houses for a mile on either side. Knowing this, she got out of the car and tried to change the tire herself. Andrew was coming from the Planter-Ranch. Seeing her working feverishly to get the bolts off, being the gentlemen he was, he parked his car in back of hers and walked up to where her car was.

"Maybe I can lend you a hand."

"Oh, you frightened me! I didn't hear you come up. I'll be so grateful for your help."

"I'm Andrew Duncan."

"You live in that big mansion down the road. Oh, I'm Terence Thompson."

"The place is very old, but we love it. I've been aiming to meet some of the newcomers to welcome them to Braidwood, but I have been too busy. I just haven't gotten around to it," he said looking up at her beautiful face.

"It's sure nice here in March. In Connecticut by this time I would have had a good lashing by the winds and cold.

"You're from Connecticut. I stayed in Boston for a while when I was a young fellow. Very pleasant country."

"My uncle is with one of the factories that moved here, Midwest Manufacturing Company. I'm a painter. I thought a change of scenery would do me good and add something different to my painting. I would love to get more acquainted with the people here. How about you and your wife coming to our place and having dinner some evening?"

"Oh, I'm not married", he said wiping the sweat from his brow.

"That makes it unanimous", she said, "I'm not married either." Terence smiled. He had finished changing the tire. Getting up, he took his handkerchief and wiped his hands.

"Sorry to get you all dirty. Thank you so much. I don't know what I would have done if you hadn't come along."

"That's alright. What is getting dirty? I'm glad I could help."

"Let's have that dinner date anyway. How about Friday night, seven?"

"Well sure, thanks a lot for your help. See you Friday."

As she drove off in her white convertible, her red hair blew with the breeze. Andrew stood there thinking, "My, she's pretty." Because of this flat tire, Andrew had been dating Terence ever since.

Terence arrived early. She wore a green flowered summer print dress that brought out the green in her eyes. Her red hair was slightly waved, turned up at the end. Terence came early. She had missed dating Andrew. Although she was some years his junior, he was her type of a man, easy-going and he loved things in life. Sam greeted her at the door in his butler attire. Terence was surprised to see him in his uniform.

"Mr. Duncan ain't come down as yet", San remarked. "Would you like to have a cocktail?"

"No, Sam. I'll wait and have one with Andrew."

From upstairs, Andrew yelled, "you're early!"

"I missed you", she yelled.

"I can't hear you. I'll be down in a second."

"Andrew darling, you look stunning!" She was surprised to see Andrew in a white suit. She wondered what the dress-up was all about.

Andrew, seeing Sam and Pursa in uniform, thought to himself—they are putting on the dog. After a little hugging and kissing, Sam served cocktails. Sam announced that dinner is served. The dinner was superb.

Throughout the meal, they talked about the election, the farm and movies. Sam reminded Andrew that the evening was cool out. "Alright Sam, I can take a hint." The crickets began to chant. Terence and Andrew sat under the Spanish moss trees. He took her hand in his.

"I missed you terribly."

"I missed you too" they said caressing each other.

"The dinner this evening was for a special reason."

"It was!"

"Don't know just how to say this!" He put his hands on each side of her face and kissed her mouth. "I love you. Will you marry me?"

"Oh yes." She said without hesitation and excitement in her voice. They put their arms around each other and kissed in a way that lips in love will always remember. They set the wedding for the last week in September, the week after the general election. Andrew talked of having the first wedding in the governor's mansion in the state, but Terence made plans for a church wedding.

Chapter 12

The race was on. Andrew was back campaigning for the general election. The rest gave Andrew the energy he needed to evangelize the people with his political talk. He and his committee worked day and night, thinking up ways to keep the crowds coming to hear him speak. A lot of his speeches were on radio and television. He wasn't modest with the words. He was firm and earnest. He had high hopes that television and all of his other political tactics would deliver the message and swarm in the votes.

The first of September, the announcement of the wedding headlined the local and daily newspaper in and around Mississippi. 'Bachelor candidate considering having wedding in the Governor's Mansion. It will be the first in the history of Mississippi.'

When Lee saw the announcement in the newspaper, she knew it was the punch she needed to keep her blackmail scheme working. She could have taken a gun and shot herself for not demanding the money, but when she thought of how treacherous Andrew had become, she perished the thought.

Andrew's opponent, Ed Cauly, was fifty years old, white-haired. His white hair gave him a handsome appearance. He had four years of college, one-time sheriff and alderman. He was now Mayor of a European town of nine thousand. He was no amateur. Andrew didn't believe his rival really hoped to win. He had all the whoopee dust and his opponent didn't stand a chance. Andrew treated his opponent with patronizing kindness. Ed Cauley didn't try to gain the peoples' confidence with fancy affairs. His crusaders were all volunteers. He delivered his speeches like that of an old time medicine man. They brought a second-hand truck and trailer and used them as their campaign headquarters and took their stand wherever they saw fit. He also used radio and television. The only thing Andrew and his opponent had in common was they preached the same sermon, only with different words. They both sweet-talked and growled and roared all over the state, they spoke of welfare funds, proposals and changes in taxes, such as state tax eliminations, model plans for the aid of aged, mental and health buildings and the need for state highways, more federal aid for housing and schools and libraries. Their conversation piece was the race issue. The topic—segregation brought out the confederate yells from the crowds that gathered at the meetings. The crowds consisted of mostly whites, in the outside meeting. There was always a few black faces. The blacks that came to listen and the ones that listened on the radio and looked and listened on television were greatly disappointed with Andrew's speeches. Their speeches against segregation held no respect for the law of the land nor for the black faces that listened in the crowd. The word, "D-Nigger" was used fluently. They both promised to keep the public places free of demonstrating from an over-demanding people. Their favorite question on this topic was—what has the Negro done to demand integration? The answer was nothing. They both promised to fight this growing monster with every legal and obscure way they could. They both, seemingly, wanted the Negro (as they say keep the Negro in his place) with the American way of life. The crowds roared and cheered for all the key phrases in their speeches. Both men and their committees had worked hard. They had laughed, joked, sweated, ostracized and criticized, spoke until their voices were just a whisper. They shook hands until they were numb. The joy and the hard work of campaigning had ceased. The day of decision was here and may the best man win. Andrew cast his vote early. That evening Andrew and some of his followers gathered at his home to await the outcome of the election. Sam and Pursa served refreshments. Although Andrew chatted with his guests at different intervals, he thought of some of the things he did from the day he chose to run for governor. He thought of his mother and father. How they would have enjoyed the glamour of politics. He wished they were here now. He thought of the two murders he almost committed to hide his sins. He could hear his mother saying, is this the kind of power you want? To keep a man down, as they say down here, keep the Negro in his place. He saw his mother's eyes closing in death. Lee and her blackmail scheme. Sam and Pursa weren't as happy as they used to be. Remembering all these trials, he still had high hopes of winning the election. He gulped down the cocktail he was holding. He wiped the sweat that came when he thought of all these schemes. He had been a blind fool to let Lee entice him into such gang-like episodes. Now he could see why Pursa and Sam thought he was crazy. The newscaster cut in on his thinking and brought him back from the past. "This is a small fraction of the election returns, nine thousand votes for Andrew Duncan, four thousand for his opponent, Ed Cauley. The crowd in the room lifted their voices with cheers. Terence took him by the hand, remarking in a happy voice, "Darling, it looks like you are in." Andrew smiled and said, "You are counting your chickens before they hatch." Terence was surprised to hear him say those words. Her smile faded. They said no more. By two, he knew he had lost. Ed Cauley was winning the governorship by three thousand votes. The crowd in the room just stood and sat in silence like it was a funeral with all eyes on Andrew. Andrew rose from where he was sitting. He looked at his followers like a boy that had just had the licking of his life. He started to say something. Instead, he walked out of the house into the warm moonlit night. Terence started to go for him, but Sam stopped her at the door. Sam said softly, "Let him be Miss Terence, let him be."

Andrew went to the garden and picked a bunch of flowers in the moonlight. If the person in the house could have seen what he was doing, they would have thought he had suddenly gone mad. He went to the family burial ground. There, at his father and mother's grave, he said to them what he couldn't say to the people in the house, "I have a laugh for you two. I didn't win. Tears formed in his eyes. I wanted to be governor so bad. Being a lawyer was your idea, mother. A farmer was your ambition, father. Being governor is the only ting I wanted to be in life from when I was a child." His face broke into crying. "I will never run again, I have my pride." He stood there talking to them as if they were still in their bodies. "Losing this challenge is so hard to take. I worked so hard and I did so many trying things to win", he said holding the flowers in his hand. "If I had killed those people to hide my sins, it would have all been in vain. I have nothing to hide now. Lee can tell the whole world my secret." As he spoke these words, the agony of sorrow seemed to drain from his face to a contented look. He thought what Sam and Pursa really think about integration since he took the attitude he did toward their people. Maybe the reason I lost is that most of the colored and white people felt this was just one of my passing fancies. They thought of me more as a kind and gentle person, not the type of person he campaigned to be. "Mother, I looked at the black faces when I spit out those bold words I used. There wasn't one drop of malice in their faces, just disillusion. All the black people in this state knew or heard of me. I have helped so many of them with their problems. I guess they didn't want to believe that was the good Mr. Duncan talking. Mother I am still against integration. As Vada said in her letter to me, I can't help what's in my blood. I just have to work it out. I hope she will bear children and bring life back into the old house. I feel so much better since I had this little talk with the two of you. These flowers are the only garnish I could bring for letting me pout out my heart. May you two rest in peace." He then took his handkerchief from his pocket and wiped his tear-stained face. He walked back to the house. When he reached the front door, he braced himself and went in. Terence hurried to his side. Andrew took her hand, patted it to assure her he was alright. "I am sorry the way I acted", he said to his committee. "I couldn't help it." They all smiled with understanding. "Although we lost, it was a good fight. I am truly grateful to all of you for your hard work. If I ever run again, I hope all of you will be on my team. Since my opponent is fighting for the same purpose that we believe in, you can assure yourselves that Ed Cauley will do a good job. Let's all have a happy time. Andrew turned and kissed Terence lightly. He said in a cheerful voice, "Let's have a church wedding."

Chapter 13

A few days after the general election. Andrew didn't come downstairs until a little after the noon hour. He dressed and made his way to the kitchen. Andrew still felt the sting of losing, but he told himself that he must be a man about losing the election. He found Sam and Pursa finishing their lunch and Trout was home for a change.

"Afternoon, Mr. Duncan", Sam and Pursa said.

"Afternoon, Sam. What were you saying about Trout?"

"Oh, this some dog you gave us. He's been home up until now. He told me his gal done run him home and told him to stay home. He's been laying there looking like a sad-faced hound instead of a Dalmatian. He's sure sick that gal sent him home." They laughed at Sam, telling his usual tales about Trout.

"Mr. Andrew, what you like for lunch?" Pursa asked.

"A glass of orange juice and some kind of sandwich. Sam how do you think of such tales about Trout?"

"I don't' know. This dog just tell me things. You know, a dog is like a man. Ain't nothing keeps a man away from home like a woman and nothing but a she-dog keeps a he-dog away from home. This dog is gal-crazy. We see him every now and then—starved to death when he comes back. I guess he didn't eat too much. He is in love."

Andrew laughed at Sam and kind of shook his head as he ate the ham sandwich. "Sam, speaking of thinking, now that the election is over—you said you hadn't given integration any thought. You have heard my side of the story and I know you heard much talk about this problem. I just can't see you two not thinking about this thing. If you were up north where they say everything is peaches and cream for the Negro, I could see you not giving integration some thought. But you are not Mr. and Mrs. Just Niggers. I'm giving you a chance to seek your peace."

"Well I tell you", Sam said, "When you came home from winning the primary election, you said this thing is much our concern too. I been giving this thing much thought ever since that day. I been listening to what the preacher had to say and what other people say but they don't seem to be saying the things that is in my mind. You see, the old Negro always dreams of going home to live with God. Earthly things didn't matter too much. Freedom of the soul, most of us long for, be a Christian in our heart and go home to live with Jesus."

"But wait Sam, don't you think the reason the Negro looked to God is because you were so mistreated?"

"Yes, in a way. I think they looked to God on account of mistreatment. Then again, I say no. We found a God we could trust and found in him a resting place for our souls, but not flesh. I guess mistreatment didn't stop when we found him. Somewhere along the line when they heard 'were you there when the crucified my Lord' I imagine it took a lot of doing to get those idol gods out of the black man, when the white man put us in slavery. I know the Lord had a wrestling time with us black folk making us know who He was but when He did, we came this far by faith. I know my people rebelled and escaped and tried to escape to places where there wasn't any slavers, but we still kept the faith. You know they used to say the old Negro used to laugh to keep from crying. But that wasn't the reason. Our souls were at peace with God. When the soul is at peace, you can bear a whole lot of burdens."

"Amen." Pursa sanctioned. Sam's eyes sparkled at Pursa's amen Sam crossed his legs and kind of smiled and started babbling out his thoughts again. "We black folk used to be pilgrims and strangers traveling through this rich land. We were so rich in the Holy Spirit. My Lord, we trusted the Lord for our all and all. The Lord has been so good to us. He been so good. But we are losing the greatest gift to mankind. That is to do so much with so little. No matter how you people double the price on us, no matter how you people tried to hinder us—we would pray, 'ride on King Jesus, no man can hinder me.' We knew the Lord would make a way somehow. He gave us the way like he fed the multitude with three little fishes and five loaves of bread 'cause we believed. Now don't get me wrong, we ain't all saints of God either. As the song said, 'everybody talk about Heaven ain't going there', but most of us lean on the Lord."

Andrew cocked his head in child-like fashion listening to Sam pour out his thoughts. But Sam's thoughts didn't seem to touch Andrew's heart. He let Sam keep on talking. Andrew believed what he believed.

"The Lord done brought us from a mighty long way. In fact, he brought us all the way. As I look back to the days since that great emancipation up until now, we have had some hard times all over this here land and we done seen some hard seasons on this plantation. You know how this farm got started?" Sam said.

"Remember hearing a little something about the story. In a way, Sam. Remember that used to be father's centerpiece tale at most of the big affairs here but let me hear it one more time, your version."

"Well the story goes that your great, great, great grandfather was a gambling man. He won Spicewood Acres in a game of chance, but when he got here, this place was crawling with my fore-parents. They were sick and starving, trying hard to take care of one another, praying to the Lord not to forsake them as their master had done. The story goes that the owner's wife had died giving birth to their first-born child. The child died soon after. Well, after the death of his wife and child, Mr. Spicewood tried to raise cotton. That failed. Then he tried to raise vegetables like you do here. They dried up under the hot sun. With no rain that summer, things got so bad he just gave up. He up and left the place. He gambled the place off, your ore-parents won. My folk had moved from their cabins that used to be out back. They took over this house. The smell of sickness was foul in the house and my folk was skin and bones, waiting for death to take them. Your folks always ended the story (Oh God! what a sight!) my folk and your folk made this place what it is today. God sent your folk to answer my folk's prayers."

"That's about the way father used to tell the story. Sam, you got off the subject, integration. I know you have said quite a bit on the subject but you haven't gotten through to me. Let's hear some more."

"I done said a whole lot already. But as I look back, we ain't done so bad in this old world even though we ain't built our talents like we should. We seem to be in bondage, in a setting of fear, fear of the white man and ourselves and God—burying our cross so to speak. But we are all our brothers' keeper. We trust in the Lord with all our hearts and lean not unto our own understanding. The fear of the Lord is the beginning of knowledge, but fools despise wisdom and instruction. We buried His word in our hearts and we accomplished much leaning on the Lord." In mumbling words he said, "Something is wrong somewhere." Sam kind of paused in what he thought about integration.

"Now Sam, this is not all that you think about integration. Not a word you said has touched my heart. Go on."

"Hold your horses, hold your horses. I was just thinking how long it took God to deliver us out of bondage. We say we are moving too slow. I wonder who is we waiting on—God or man? God owns the earth and the fullness thereof and they that dwell therein, Psalm 24. God knows we need integration. It's about time we become real brothers. When God let our toils and snares fall from us, every time I think of what's next...it makes tears run down my heart", Sam's voice sounded grieved.

Pursa cried out, "Lord have mercy, have mercy Jesus!"

"You know Mr. Andrew, the Lord took our feet out of the miry clay and set our feet on a solid rock. Now we are losing that rock. I know how bitter it feels to see our white brothers with so much freedom and liberties and we have so less of these things. But we believe in Ephesians 4:2 'with lowliness and meekness, with long suffering, fore-bearing one another in love.' Faith keeps our eyes closed to a lot of trials and tribulations in this world. I say the Lord hates to let those toils and snares fall from us because I'm awfully afraid we are going to forget the giver. After we think we are together, I got a feeling we won't be saying, 'thank you Jesus anymore.' So many of us blacks is at that stage right now." Sam's deep voice sounded like he was mourning out a sermon.

Pursa started chanting softly 'Amazing Grace.' All of a sudden Pursa said, "I got a few words to say about this mess. We always looked at our suffering from a spiritual point of the suffering of Jesus and Paul's suffering for the gospel. But as I look back, we did suffer for the gospel. That was when my folks was in slavery. Out of this suffering came the old Negro spirituals. Now some of the old slave masters did beat and kill the Negroes for serving the Lord. But our suffering for the gospel is gone now. We are free to serve the Lord as we wish. We put most of our talents in being a child of God. This is the only way he had to use our talents. As I look back at it again, all our suffering is in a spiritual point of view. In the fruit of the spirit most of us blacks have shown our white brethren love, joy, peace, long suffering, gentleness, goodness, faith, meekness and temperance in all manner of suffering you people imposed on us. When you people seemed to make our burdens hard to bear," Pursa threw her hands up and yelled, "We would cry out father, I stretch my hands to thee no other help I know. My God, my God. We won't know how to say those words anymore. Lord help us. We have become backsliders now. Proverbs 14:14 says 'the backslider in heart shall be filled with his own ways.' We will believe there is a God, but deny the power thereof. Mr. Andrew I see that through your mind. Don't get me wrong. I believe in integration. It's all well and good. Psalm 133— 'behold, how good and pleasant it is for brethren to dwell together in unity.' This is all I got to say."

"I see you two don't see too much progress for the Negro or for the white people in togetherness."

Sam jumped back in. "I see progress in it alright, love thy neighbor as thyself, do unto others as you want others to do unto you. Do not bear false witness against they neighbor. If thou say thy love God and hate thy brother, you's a lie and the truth ain't in you. Neither shalt thy commit adultery. Whatever you sow, so shall you reap. Thou shalt not steal. This is some of the spiritual progress of integration. But your people is giving my people so much hell about the matter of brotherhood, we are putting God to shame. We blacks, like David after God's own heart. Now I's wondering about that."

"Sam your thoughts are very enlightening but it's going to take a lot of praying, forcing, pushing and shoving and it's going to take a lot of vexing integration down our throats. But every time your people force it down our throats, we will vomit up the confusion back in your faces. We Mississippians will not dismantle our heritage like an old house. We will fight for the principles that our forefathers died for. I don't hate your people. I believe in separation. I'm sorry I don't conceive your people's point."

"Mr. Duncan, it will feel mighty good to put my mark by the man I feels can do the job best. Integration makes us feel all grown up and in the family. We are separated but not equal in a lots of things." Sam said sad like.

"I know one thing", Pursa said banging a pot on the stove, then shaking it at Sam and Andrew, "If I hear anymore discussion about this mess, I's going to dismantle the both of you. We's been one happy family. That's the way it going to be and I do mean that. What we should be talking about is the big wedding."

Mr. Andrew Duncan, the third and Miss Terence Honey Thompson wed the second day of November at one P.M. in the flower garden of the Duncan estate. They sent out many invitations. Yes, there was one for Doff and Lee Rainey and those at the Planter-Ranch. It was a perfect day for a wedding, neither too cool or hot, just right. The southern breeze just whispered over the land, the garden was full with colorful flowers. Beneath the trees stood an improvised altar. An orchestra played as the guests gathered on the lawn in the garden. They came from near and far. Some occupied the chairs, others stood under the many spreading moss oak-draped trees. The strains of the Lohengrain Wedding March began to play. From the house came the bridal party dressed in Madonna blue, caring great sheaf's of peach and white flowers. Then came the bride with her father by her side. Terence' gown was of regal white summer satin, a portrained neckline, long sleeves traced with chantilly lace appliqué embroidered with seed pearls. Terence wore a full length bridal veil. The bouquet clutched in her hand were of sweetheart roses, surrounded by white carnations. She was a picture of beauty.

Pursa sat in one of the living room chairs crying tears of joy. She was indeed happy for Andrew. They were all at the altar. Pastor began the ceremony, "We are gathered today to unite, under God, this man and woman in holy matrimony. This wedding comes out of love of two people willing to cherish their marriage until death do they part. They will care for one another in sickness and in health. I trust that this marriage will be a romance every day of their lives. I hope there will be children to fill this old house. The ring, please. I, with God's blessing, I pronounce you husband and wife. You may now kiss the bride." Lee broke away from the crowd, screaming, why didn't you marry me, I love you so much. Doff ran after her. When is this endless love for Andrew going to stop?"

Terence and Andrew didn't have a reception but they did serve tasty hors d'oeuvres. Some brought gifts. They received many cards wishing them years of blissful happiness. They received a letter from Doff wishing them much happiness and apologizing for Lee's behavior at the wedding. Andrew and Terence went to Bermuda for their honeymoon.

The next day, Lee got to thinking of Andrew getting married. The beating Andrew had given her had worn off and the thoughts of revenge pierced her mind again. The way she looked at it, she hadn't had her revenge at all and she had taken a beating too. Laying across the bed, she thought of Andrew married to that girl. Lee never met or saw Terence until the wedding. She admitted to herself that Terence was very pretty, but why couldn't she be the one he married. Terrence couldn't love him as much as she did. She just wanted a man and money, Lee thought to herself. But Lee knew, within herself, that she loved and hated Andrew all at the same time. As she lay curled upon the bed, she smiled to herself as she made plans for a second try to have her revenge. It was two weeks before Lee made her second stab for revenge on Andrew. Andrew was about to leave for the office. He had promised Terence that he would stop practicing law, but he would take care of the farm business. He was kissing her good-bye when the phone rang. Andrew started for the phone in the study. "You go darling", Terence said, "I'll answer the phone. If it is one of your clients, I'll tell them you can be reached at the office."

"Hello, this is Terence Duncan speaking."

"Mrs. Duncan, ask your husband about that child he had by Sam's daughter." Lee made her voice sound like that of a great mysterious person. Lee hung up the phone quickly implanting the words of vengeance.

The words shocked Terence so she seemed to be stupefied. The clicking sound of the phone being put on the cradle, brought her out of the daze. "Who is this? What do you mean?" She said realizing whoever it was had hung up. Feeling her heart turn over in her breast, she quickly pulled out the big chair at the desk and flopped down, thinking to herself—"What baby? What daughter? What were they talking about?" She sat there dazed. Sam brought in the morning mail. "Here is the mail", Sam said. "Thanks Sam." Looking at Sam, the phone call started her heart beating rapidly. She fell back in the chair looking very oddly at Sam. "Is there anything wrong?" Sam asked.

"No Sam, I just felt a little sick. I'm alright now." Terence said.

"Are you sure?" Sam asked.

"Yes Sam, I'm sure." Sam then left the room. Watching Sam leave, thinking—"Is this the Sam they are talking about? No, she told herself emphatically, it couldn't be. Her Andrew wouldn't go out of his race. She passed it off as some other Sam. With this thought in mind, she made her way upstairs to make herself ready for the day.

In the weeks that followed, Terence acted coldly toward Andrew. Whenever the phone rang, the phone call haunted her. Even Sam and Pursa noticed the unhappiness in her attitude at certain times. Whenever Andrew asked her what's wrong, she would only remark that she had a headache or felt sick of the stomach. Andrew advised her to see a doctor. She said she would. One evening at dinner, Terence had that sick worried look on her face. "Terence, is this sickness bringing the stork to the house?" Andrew asked jokingly.

"No it isn't!" she snapped at Andrew. "Speaking of babies, what about that child you had by Sam's daughter?" Terence asked in a loud angry voice. Sam and Pursa were eating their dinner in the kitchen. Sam almost choked on the food he was eating. Pursa shook her head saying, "Lord, what's next?"

"Why darling, what are you talking about?"

"Someone called about a month ago. All they said was ask your husband about that child he had by Sam's daughter." Sam and Pursa listened for the answer with anxious ears.

"Did they say who they were?" Andrew asked.

"No, they hung up before I could say a word."

"Did you recognize the voice?"

"No, I didn't. You know I don't know many people here."

"Oh, it was probably some crackpot trying to be funny." Andrew wanted to tell her the truth but the words wouldn't come. He felt like a snake.

"Darling," she said with a smile, "I never thought about it like that. That takes a load off my mind. They had me thinking you had a child somewhere. I thought it was our Sam they were talking about." Her smile assured him that she believed him.

"Why darling, I have nothing to hide from you. How could you think a thing like that? Believe me, it's just a joke." Thinking to himself, I can't tell her the truth. It would hurt her too deeply. I can't lose her. I love her too much. I see Lee is at it again. I'll have to really take care of her.

The following morning they lay in bed making love like two parakeets. They both seemed to be very happy, but Andrew had Lee on his mind, wondering when she would strike again, thinking he had to pay her or else suffer the consequences or do something real drastic. Terence interrupted his thoughts with a little peck on his nose asking, "Darling, when are you going to give up your law practice?"

"Oh, in a couple of months or so," he said squeezing her tightly in his arms. Then you will have me mostly all to yourself. After I quit my law practice, I have a big surprise for you."

"What is the big surprise darling? Tell me now," Terence said in girl-like fashion.

"If I tell you now, it won't be a surprise."

She said in a whining sexy voice, "Please tell me!"

He couldn't resist the whine in her voice, "I have planned a trip around the world for us."

"Oh darling, I am so thrilled." She gave him a big hug and a kiss asking, "When will we leave."

"We won't leave until May. We better start shopping for things we need now. Hey, look at the time," Andrew said getting out of bed. I have to be at the office by ten."

When Andrew left the house that day, he didn't waste time calling Lee when he got to the office in town. "Lee this is Andrew. Why can't you leave us alone?"

"I was looking for you to call before now. All I want is for you to say I love you. I don't want bed love, just heart love. Come on Andrew, say you love me. You hurt me with that black gal, now with her. Why do you hurt me with those women?"

He cut the love talk, asking, "How much do you want this time?"

Lee wasn't thinking of money this time, only revenge. She started laughing to herself, so he didn't tell her that Terence didn't know about the child. Vengeance is mine. Since he brought the subject up, she wasn't passing money up. "Honey, a couple thousand a month won't hurt you. That's peanuts."

"You could take me for every penny I've got."

"You have plenty coming in. Think of the shame you brought on yourself."

"Alright Lee. I'll send you the money", he said sadly.

"Andrew Honey, I prefer you to bring it. You can meet me next Thursday at La France around one. We can have lunch and talk."

"Bring it!"

"That's what I said, bring it."

"Alright Lee, anything you say."

"Oh Andrew Honey, gift wrap it. Be sure to tie it with pink ribbons. When you hand it to me, I want it to look as though you are giving me a gift rather than me taking something from you."

"Lee, Clearforest is over a hundred miles from here. Driving there will take up too much of my time. I'll send it."

"You will bring it or else." Lee said in a very cold manner. He didn't say good-bye. He just hung up the phone.

That Thursday afternoon Andrew parked his car in the La France parking lot. Getting out, walking the short distance to the restaurant, he looked about like a thief making his get-away. Lee was sitting in the lounge looking very attractive in a beige box suit with mink collar. Lee greeted Andrew with a cheerful, "Hi Sugar." Andrew said nothing. He followed Lee to the dining room. He looked about to see if there was anyone there he knew. Lee noticed him looking around. She said calmly, "Don't be nervous. Old friends can have lunch together without people thinking." The waiter came, Lee ordered.

"I don't want anything."

"You must eat something."

"I'll have ham on rye."

Lee started the conversation "I'm sorry you lost the election. To be governor is always what you wanted to be."

"That's all behind me now."

"Why don't you try it again?"

"Campaigning is hard work. It doesn't make muscles in your body and brain. I better stick to law and farming."

"Andrew, the reason I asked you to meet me is I really didn't want to come to your house and let your wife hear our conversation. I just wanted to see you. Before I gave you up for Doff, remember the good times we used to have together. Ever since I can remember you meant everything to me. I always dreamed of you marrying me one day. I still love you. Where did your love go for me?"

"Oh! Doff stole your love from me", Andrew said scoring a point.

"No he didn't. I got tired of you stringing me along making a fool out of me. If you had married me, you wouldn't have to deal with me now."

Andrew started to keep the love thing going, but his lawyer's instinct told him not to. Instead he reached inside his coat pocket and handed her the neatly wrapped package. Admiring it for a moment, she put the package in her purse, and remarked, "You did a good job on the wrapping. It looks so pretty."

"Now that you have the money, I'd better start back. It takes almost two hours to drive back."

"Darling you haven't eaten your lunch. Food is good for you. On the other hand, I think you better stay. You really don't have a choice."

"Lee, what can you gain by torturing me this way?"

"Torture! You are thinking about this matter in the wrong way. I feel you owe me something like, making love to me like you used to. I don't call that torture. Andrew looked at Lee as though she was crazy. "You have to find pleasure in giving me what I think is due me. I'm not asking too much, just these little meetings with you, sort of like we used to. I really don't want to take you away from your wife, just a dime's worth of fun."

"Lee, what you are planning just can't happen."

"Oh yes it can. Now next week, I plan for us to see a flower show."

"Next week!" Andrew exclaimed. "I thought you said you wanted the money once a month?"

"That's right about the money." The waiter brought in the food. Lee dove into the food as though she was starved. "Andrew Honey I planned something different for us once a week, a whole day of fun so you can find pleasure in giving me what I think is due me."

"Lee, I can't see once a week all day. I really don't want to see you at all. In two more months, I'm giving up my law practice. I won't have an excuse to get out of the house."

"Once a week, you can plan a day at the farm."

"Josh takes care of the farm. I go there about once a week to see how business is progressing. Lee I don't want any excuse to get away from home. I love my wife and I want to be with her."

"You will meet me next week or I will tell all. I might add a little pinch of salt."

They had finished eating. Andrew looked at his watch, it was past two-thirty. Andrew said quietly, "Lee it's past two-thirty. I will have to go. I'm always home by four."

"You can go now", Lee said as if he were a child. "I'll see you at Cedarwood Greenhouse Garden about eleven. Then you won't have to worry about being home on time. Oh, don't forget to pay the check before you leave."

That Thursday he met her at the Flower and Plant Show. At first, he wasn't interested. He just went along with Lee and the crowd. He listened to the different comments about the flowers and plants, the beauty and the size and the unusual colors and so many different kind. The more he looked, the more interested he became. He bought some seeds for Sam to plant and he bought a couple of plants for the house. He was so interested in the show that he forgot Lee was at his side until she mentioned growing orchids. When they had seen all, Lee asked if he enjoyed the show. "Oh I think it's a great show. How to you like these plants I bought? Oh, I got some seeds too." Lee said nothing.

"I think I'll try growing orchids. Don't you think that will be fun?"

"Yes growing orchids will be great fun for you", Andrew said trying to please her.

"Plans for next week—there is an art exhibit at Chateu and a display at Hale's Department Store in the auditorium on the 7th floor. See you about noon Friday." As she opened her car door to get in, she turned, pressed her lips to his and said gaily, "See you next week love."

It was pouring down raining that Friday. The weather was very chilly for the deep south. He made it his business to be on time. He could have kicked himself for not telling the truth when his wife asked about the phone call. Lee wasn't waiting as usual. Like any person in Andrew's predicament, he became jittery. He started looking into the faces that went in and out of the store, looking at the dressed mannequin in the window with many crazed thoughts going through his mind, wondering where was Lee? She had never been late. What in the devil was she up to now? Just then, someone touched him on his shoulder. He almost jumped out of his skin. "Hi Sugar." He didn't speak, he merely gave her a dirty look following her up to the seventh floor. Inside the exhibit he saw several people he knew. Old Mrs. Carter was the only one he was afraid of. With her mouth, she could set off the third world war. Andrew excused himself quietly from Lee. She started to follow him. She saw he began chatting with some elderly person, so she didn't bother.

"Are you enjoying the show, Mrs. Carter?"

"Why yes Mr. Duncan. As far as I can see the art exhibits are priceless. Oh those decorated Christmas trees are too beautiful for words." Seeing no one with Andrew she asked surprisingly, "Where is your wife?"

"I'm in Clearforest on business. My client is right over there. I'm combining business with a little pleasure. What do you think of that abstract design" he said freezing her mind.

"All abstract designs look rather odd to me", she laughed.

Andrew felt a tug at his sleeve, "Alright, I'm coming. Nice to have seen you Mrs. Carter. Enjoy the show."

Andrew kept Lee moving from one scene to another, trying to beat her at her own game.

"What's the rush Andrew?" Lee questioned.

"I am tired of you pushing me around." He said in sort of an angry tone of voice.

"I'm not pushing you around. I want you to find some pleasure in life with me. The exhibit is striking. I am going to buy a picture and some ornaments", she said trying to keep up with Andrew.

They were almost at the end of the exhibit. Lee paused to chat about a picture in front of her. Andrew walked swiftly out of the door hurriedly to the escalator. Lee caught up with him on the main floor.

"Just what do you think you are doing?"

"Leaving", he sounded off.

"I didn't get a chance to view the exhibit like I wanted to. You won't get away with this."

"Don't upset yourself", he said calmly opening the door for her. It had stopped raining out, but was still chilly. Instead of walking to Lee's car he went directly to his own car. Lee followed him.

"You sure pulled a fast one today." She said.

Pausing at his car asking, "What's up next week?"

"I thought we could see a movie, take a stroll in the park and then have a four o'clock lunch. Let me see, make it Thursday."

"Thursday is Thanksgiving."

"Oh I forgot Thanksgiving was coming. Make it Tuesday."

"Lee let's call next week off. If I meet on Tuesday and Thursday is Thanksgiving, all the time I spend with you, I can't get a lot of things cleared up. Please Lee, be reasonable", he pleased.

She said smiling, "You win this time. But the following week, all the stores around town are giving a big fashion show. They are showing dresses for the holidays. The show will be in the Hotel Magnolia."

"Lee, you can't do this to me!"

"The first show starts at one thirty, the other at seven. Which do you prefer? She asked sarcastically.

"Lee someone is sure to see us there, and all those women."

"You asked for it. The date is Wednesday. Andrew Honey", smiling she said. "If you change your mind about meeting me, I'm quite sure if you didn't think the truth would hurt, you would have told your wife the story of your life before you were married." Seeing how bewildered he looked, she gave him a conquering smile.

Driving home that day, he felt so helpless and so alarmed. He felt what so many of his clients must have felt. He couldn't understand how he let himself not tell his wife the truth. It seemed as though someone has their voo-do working on him, messing up his mind. He thought of killing himself, he couldn't do that. He wanted to live and love his wife. Turning over in his mind about what to do, he was home before he realized. Getting out of the car, going into the house, he flopped down on the living room sofa. Running his fingers through his almost white h air, he felt exhausted sitting there in a quandary. He didn't hear Terence come in.

"Darling, you are home early!" She said kissing him.

"I've got a terrible headache."

"I'll get some aspirin, be right back." He wanted to tell her he didn't need the aspirin. It was just this mess he got himself in. She brought the aspirin and a glass of water. He took the pain killers just to please her. She sat beside him looking at him with sympathy.

"Terence Honey, it won't be until February before I can close the office. I have more work than I thought. He wasn't thinking about the office. He pondered over the trip Lee was taking him on, the big fashion show.

"I think I can manage not having you to myself a little while longer. Mother called. She wants us to have Thanksgiving with them. I told her we would come."

"It will be nice to see your folks again. We really need to get out more."

"Feeling better."

"Yes, you are an angel", he said smiling pulling her close to him. "Just being with you cures all my ills."

The day of the fashion show was a balmy 78 degrees. Andrew did not go to the show. The sight of all those women made chills run down his spine. Instead, he went to one of the department stores, bought his wife three lovely dressed - one peach, one green and the other blue - telling himself if she can be tough, I can too. He put the dresses in the back seat and spun off for home.

Lee was looking her best. She looked as if she was part of the show in her winter white suit. She sat in the lobby and waited for Andrew. Twenty minutes had passed, no Andrew. An hour had gone, no Andrew. She made up her mind he wasn't coming. She was mad as hell. So you win this time but I will get even with you yet. Finally, she went in to see the show. At the end of the show, she went to one of the department stores and bought one of the dresses. Driving home, Lee became more angry with herself for letting Andrew beat her at her own game. Poor planning. She meant these little play-arounds to be fun for her, not Andrew. As she sped along, a sign caught her eye (Moncure, dinner, dancing nightly, finest drinks, every night a famous entertainer, this week Alice Pleasant). The words on the marquee dissolved the anger. Her mouth started to smile again thinking I haven't been to a night club in years. She had her social club. She and Doff went to neighborhood social gatherings. The night club would be just the ticket for she and Andrew to enjoy. The club looked high class, all but the marquee.

First thing Monday morning, Lee phoned Andrew in a very cheerful way. She didn't let on she had been very angry with him for not meeting her at the fashion show. She had to play it cool if she were to have her revenge. "Hi Andrew Sugar."

Andrew went along with her happy mood. "Hi Lee Honey, what's on your pretty little mind this morning?"

"Oh, I've planned a nice little evening for us Wednesday."

"Lee, I'm not coming. I can have you arrested for extortion, deception, harassment. I am tired of this mess", trying to call her bluff.

"Darling, you don't have to come. Stay at home and play house."

"Just what do you mean, stay at home and play house?"

"You either meet me at the club Wednesday or I'll not only tell your wife, I'll tell the newspapers, TV and I just might add a little salt and pepper such as your love affair with me and I might say we share the bed together."

"Alright, you win", he yelled, "When and where?"

"The club is on Fiftieth and Ward. You can't miss it for the big sign. See you at Moncure at six."

"By the way, what are you going to do with Doff, give him some chloroform?"

She didn't answer him, only hung up the phone.

All week long, Andrew thought and thought of what he was going to tell his wife about his Wednesday meeting with Lee. He felt like a heel lying to her. By Tuesday, he hadn't thought of a decent lie to tell her. He made up his mind to tell her the truth. The truth Andrew told his wife was he was going to meet a client, but not the rest of the story.

Andrew looked strikingly handsome in his blue serge suit. The blue suit, white hair and his black mustache gave him a look of distinction. He hadn't been in a night club since his playboy years. Lee was waiting. Lee was looking like a model out of Vogue on his money. Andrew gave the wolf call. Lee had her dark brown hair dyed black, groomed in the latest style she capered around a bit in the pink ice chiffon.

"Andrew, how do I look?" she said smiling.

"I must admit you're very glamorous."

110

"Why thank you dear."

The club wasn't very crowded. There were about ten couples in the very beautiful place. Lee ordered a very dry martini. Andrew ordered a scotch and soda and he wondered why. They both ordered the supper plate. The music was the Guy Lombardo type. Lee started the chit chat. "Andrew I know you love me. You just haven't discovered the fact. I think the reason you didn't marry me is because I up and married Doff. You really didn't want me as a plaything, did you?"

"Lee if you are going to talk that kind of gluey conversation, I just might leave and I might do something dramatic."

Lee looked at Andrew as if he had hit her on the top of her head. "I still love you no matter what", thinking she better cool it, and plus she loved spending his money.

There was silence. "What are you going to do when you give up your practice?" she asked quietly.

"Oh I go up to the farm once or twice a week to keep things intact. I will mostly stay home and play house."

Letting the love talk drop, Lee said, "Let's get a few steps before the food comes."

They concentrated on their dancing trying not to show themselves up on the empty dance floor. They danced gracefully for two people who hadn't danced in years. After the band had played three consecutive numbers, they returned to their table. The waiter brought in the food.

"Yumm-ie, everything looks so good." They didn't talk during the meal. When they finished eating, Lee ordered cocktails. "Keep the drinks coming", Lee said.

"Just one more for me", Andrew said.

Lee gave the waiter a wink. Andrew felt a little woozy after the third drink. Lee felt fine, she hadn't gotten started. The waiter kept bringing the drinks. On the fourth drink, they both had the giggles. Andrew started telling a funny joke.

"I have a funny joke", Andrew said laughing. "I'm not going to meet you anymore."

"Oh that's a good one", she said laughing.

Still laughing, Andrew said, "You remember that beating I gave you for pulling the same thing you are doing now? I can do that again, you know."

111

"Ha, ha, ha," she said. "That is very funny. Let me tell you one. I thought you might get bold and threaten me again," she put her hand in her purse and pulled out a twenty-two. "Bought this along in case you wanted to get rough. You start it and I'll end it", she said sarcastically.

"Lee, put that thing away. I was only joking." This little episode kind of sobered Andrew up. Lee put the gun back in her purse.

"Andrew Honey, let's do make this our last meeting. You get more pleasure out of my schemes than I do."

"Alright Lee, let's do." Andrew was wondering what she was up to now.

"Andrew Honey, I would much rather have a little old check for twenty-five thousand dollars than try to get even with you, and too, you are a smart lawyer. But I don't know how I let you get away with my schemes. I think you love me."

"Lee come off of it. I don't love you and I ain't going to give you another cent," Andrew said in a low angry voice.

She bent over and said softly, "You don't want to be wounded in here, now do you?"

He was all the way sober and frightened.

"I wouldn't shoot to kill. I want you to live so you can explain the wound to your pretty little wife."

He looked at her flabbergasted and frightened, wondering would she really shoot me?

"Now, you don't want a scene, do you Honey?"

He didn't want to let on he was scared and he didn't want to give in to her. "I don't have my checkbook with me."

"I know better. Stop being dishonest with me." She took the gun out again. She held it in her hand under the table. Lee looked around the place. There were quite a few people in the club by now. "You know these people might enjoy a shooting and I might get to Hollywood with my picture in the paper, pretty as I am. With the scandal and all, I could become a star", she said in a devilish way.

"Lee you wouldn't dare!"

"Oh no, I'll give you two dirty thoughts to start writing, one, two."

He took out the checkbook, wrote out the check and handed it to her.

"Thanks Darling, I promise you this is the end. I won't trouble you anymore unless you stop payment on the check. Shall we dance?"

"No, I'm going home. You pay the bill and leave a tip."

"Bye Sugar", Lee sighed.

Lee added the check to her private bank account. She didn't let Doff know about her blackmail scheme this time. She wanted all the money to herself. When Lee got home that night, she calculated getting the money from Andrew didn't satisfy her ego. Taking the twenty-five thousand wasn't the sort of hurt she wanted him to feel. Lee wanted the kind of hurt that he could feel mentally and physically, he wouldn't miss twenty-five thousand dollars. She was letting him off easy. Recalling that night that Andrew told her he was not going to marry anyone, he wanted someone to play with when he was in want, she felt the shock of those words mentally and physically. She couldn't sleep or eat. She lost weight. She was ashamed to face people. Everyone knew he was a playboy. She conceived, one day he would give up being a playboy. Determined to make him feel drama of hurt the way she did, the first week after the club affair, she laid low, putting a fool on Andrew. The next week, she spent time finding out where the boy was, Andrew's bastard son. She first drove to Liz' place. When she got there she thought she was at the wrong place. Liz' house was so dressed up, she hardly knew the place. The place was very still. Thinking no one was at home, this was the break she needed. Putting her hand on the door handle to get out of the car, the door to the house opened. She could see it was Liz. Instead of turning around, she backed the car all the way to the highway. Liz closed the door, thinking it was someone had turned off the wrong road. Lee drove a little way up the highway and parked her car. She sat there wracking her brain, wondering where she was going to get the information she needed to find out the whereabouts of the boy. All of a sudden her face beamed wondering why didn't she think of them at first. Pursa and Sam should have an address book or a photo album somewhere in their home. She started up the car and headed for Braidwood. She remembered Pursa always started the Duncan meals around three-thirty. Looking at her watch, she could make it to Braidwood by five. Sam always joined Pursa in the kitchen, offering his help wherever it was necessary. He mostly serenaded her with conversation.

Arriving in Braidwood, she rode past the Duncan estate with that Mona Lisa smile on her face. She drove on to the road that divided the Duncan place from the Jefferson's. About a half mile down the road, she parked her car. Lee got out of the car and made her way across the back side of the estate—walking through dry weeds, stepping in shallow holes, going through high grass, scratching her legs until she finally came to Sam and Pursa's place. A little tired, stocking torn and legs stinging, she paused to catch her breath, pulling the cockleburs off and brushing off the dead grass. She walked down the short path to the McCloud's house. She turned the knob. All of a sudden a bush of fear came over her. The house was very still. Maybe Sam was inside sleeping or relaxing. Quickly discarding the thought, she went in. Looking around the living room, the picture of Vada in her cap and gown smiled out at her. The picture of Vada brought back memories. She picked up the picture, thinking of days gone by, knowing this wasn't what she came for. She put the picture back. Going into the bedroom, off the living room, sticking around the mirror of an old-fashioned dresser were pictures of the McCloud family and some friends, but the picture of the boy was missing. Thinking they have to have one somewhere, going back to the living room, looking around again—she saw a photo book. Going through the book quickly, there were several pictures of the boy. Now she knew he looked just like Andrew. Next to the phone was an address book. She looked through the book until she came to the name Vada and Harry St. James, 4223 Spanish Drive, Chicago, IL., phone number 535-6783. She took a piece of paper and a pencil from her purse, copied the address. She copied the phone number, just in case. Getting what she came for, she stepped out into the almost dark light.

Almost a week later, Lee plotted in Doff's mind that she was going Christmas shopping. Instead of Christmas shopping, she made her way across town to the other side of the track, so to speak. She parked her car in front of Clearforest's pool hall. She wanted to go in but she felt that would be too unladylike. She sat there watching passing faces, hoping to see one she could trust. Lee had sat for about an hour. She hadn't seen a face she thought was trustworthy. Her patience began to wear. Just as she started the car up to leave, a young red-headed freckle-faced, skinny kid came out of the pool hall. He leaned against the building seeming to be taking in the warm November sun. Lee sized him up thinking to herself, he looks innocent enough. Lee called to the young man, "Young man, will you come here a second?"

He walked over to the car. "What is it lady?"

"What is your name?"

"Van", he said lighting up a cigarette.

"Van would you like to make some money?"

114

"Yes, doing what?"

"Need another fellow. Do you have a friend?"

"Yes, but what do you want done?"

"Do you know where you can find your friend?"

"He's in the pool hall."

"Get him. I'll explain what I want done."

Van came back with a tough looking character. They walked over to the car. Van's friend leaned on Lee's car with a cigarette in hand.

"My name is Bobby Joe. What's yours' maam?"

Lee didn't like Bobby Joe's looks or the way he talked. By the looks of things, she didn't have a choice. "My name doesn't matter."

"But it does if you want us to do a job for you", Bobby Joe said very foxy-like.

"My name is Miss Lee", letting them think that Lee was her last name.

"Well Miss Lee, what you want done?" Bobby Joe said.

"Get in back, I'll drive you around a bit while I explain what I want done."

"What is the job?" Bobby Joe said.

Van said nothing. He just listened.

"I want you to kidnap a boy", Lee said straight out.

"Kidnap", they both said, rising up from their seats.

"Down boys," she said, "It's only a nigger boy I want kidnapped."

"A nigger boy. Now I've heard everything", Bobby Joe said flabbergasted. "Just what do you want to kidnap a nigger for, but just to kill him. It couldn't be for money."

"I don't want this one killed. I want this one alive and it ain't for money."

"You haven't told us what you wanted him for", Bobby remarked.

"The boy's father is dying. The boy's father keeps asking for him. We called and wrote his mother. She refused to let him come to see his father. I don't think she should refuse a dying father's request, do you?"

"I guess not", Van said in a confused sad way.

She could see their faces in the rearview mirror. Lee could see Van's face. He believed her but the look on Bobby Joe's face showed some doubt.

"Now that we have heard the story, how much is in it for us?" Bobby Joe asked.

"Two fifty apiece", Lee said.

"Make it five, we will take the job", Bobby Joe said.

"Okay, five hundred", Lee said.

"Where is he?" Van asked.

"He's in Chicago. I'll pay all the expenses. I have hired a private pilot to fly us there. We will leave on Tuesday, but we will have to stay over night. You two have to make up your own story to your folks about staying over night", Lee said.

"I have a pad of my own", Bobby Joe said. "Van need a cock and bull story, he's still at home."

"As I was saying, we have to stay over night. All kids go to school between seven and eight. We will seize him on the way to school, bring him back here and then take him to his father."

"Simple enough, but what is the nigger to you?" Bobby Joe asked.

"His folks have been with my family for years."

"I see." Bobby Joe said. Van just listened.

"I'll pick you two up around six Tuesday at the pool hall." She let the boys out and went on her way.

Christmas was coming on. Andrew and Terence were in the living room trimming the Christmas tree. They looked like happy angels with halos over their heads. They had finished trimming the tree. They sat gazing at the beautifully lit tree. Although Andrew was looking at the tree, his mind was on Lee. She hadn't called or written. What was she up to? Andrew's mind couldn't conceive what Lee had conjured up to really get her revenge.

Monday evening at dinner, Lee had her lie ready to tell Doff. "Dear, Dad called today. Mother is sick. He has to go out of town on business and wants me to come over tomorrow to sit with her, if it's alright with you."

"You know it's alright with me. Boy, this dinner is good. You haven't fixed this kind of dinner in a long time—roast pork, French green beans, sweet potatoes and pineapple upside down cake."

"I won't be back until Wednesday."

"Stay over some days, if you have to."

"I'll be back Wednesday. A loose man might get himself in trouble."

"Lee Baby, what makes you say a thing like that?"

Lee got up from the table. She went to his side and sat on his lap. She put her arms around his neck, kissed him sensuously remarking, "Sugar a woman has to keep her eye on her man."

116

The next day, Lee put in her small suitcase just enough things for over night. Her final touch was a twenty-two in her purse and her heavy coat. The boys were waiting. They got in the car and off to the airport they went.

"Don't you boys have heavy jackets?" Lee asked.

"The weather is nice here. We didn't think about a heavy jacket," Van said. "I ain't got one anyway."

"I ain't got none either", Bobby Joe said.

"It's cold in Chicago this time of year. I guess you two can make out with those light-weight jackets. We won't be out in the weather that much", Lee said.

"They didn't talk much going to the airport. The boys took in the beautifully decorated stores and houses along the way. When they arrived at the airport, it was dust dark. Lee parked her car. Van took Lee's luggage and coat. Bobby Joe took the overnight bag they had between them. They walked out to the plane where the pilot was waiting. They boarded the plane and they were off.

"What time do you think we will get there?"

"It depends on the weather. Have you boys ever been on an airplane?"

"No, and I got butterflies in my stomach", Van said.

"I think it's very exciting", Bobby Joe said. Bobby Joe had butterflies too, but he didn't let on.

They were almost to their destination. Lee started crying. The boys looked at each other surprised.

"Are you frightened, Miss Lee?" The pilot asked feeling uneasy.

"Oh no. I got to thinking about the boy. It's a shame you have to beg a child to come home to visit his dying father. I don't know what to think of some kids nowadays", Lee said in a convincing voice.

"I thought you were frightened to tears", the pilot said feeling relieved. "The boy will probably come home after you talk to him."

"I hope so", Lee said drying her eyes.

"Look, we're coming into the airport. Hold onto your seats", the pilot exclaimed.

The plane landed. The pilot walked with them through the terminal. "Is there a motel near?" Lee asked.

"Yes, the airport motel is not far from here. Take a cab. There is always one waiting. See you in the morning." The pilot was on his way.

Lee and the boys rode to the motel in silence. Lee asked the driver to wait. Lee registered herself and the boys. She gave them some money to get some dinner and the keys to their room. "I'll be back in a couple of hours. Wait for me in the lunchroom."

"Where are you going?" Bobby Joe wanted to know.

"I'm going to talk with the boy. We might not have to persuade him to come home", Lee answered.

"See you at the lunchroom", Bobby Joe was with unbelief.

Lee got in the cab. "I want to go to 4223 Spanish Drive. Take the clearest route to this place. I have to drive back here tomorrow."

"Okay lady." The cabbie was delighted with taking the clearest route. It meant more money.

Lee looked at her watch to establish the time. Along the route, she jotted down the names of the streets the cab took. It was the long way about a fifty minute drive. The sight of Christmas was everywhere. The cab stopped. "You are here lady."

"Oh I don't want to get out. I just didn't want to spend all day tomorrow trying to find this place. The place was one of those well-kept, three story greystone houses converted into apartments. Christmas sparkled from the windows. She looked at the big apartment house, wondering which apartment was Vada's.

"Where to lady?" the driver asked, interrupting her thinking.

"To the nearest you drive it rental."

She drove the car very carefully along the route she had jotted down. Back at the hotel, she ordered dinner and chatted with the boys a bit.

"Did you get to talk to the boy?" Van said excitedly.

"There wasn't anyone home. We have to do what I planned. He probably wouldn't come if I did talk to him. Oh yes I rented a car."

"What kind is it?" Van asked.

"Think it is a Mercury", she said putting the last bite of food in her mouth. "I rented the car for the simple reason if I called a cab, I might be late getting here. We have to be on time. Do you fellows feel nervous about doing this?"

"Kinda", Van said.

"I can't see why you are nervous about kidnapping a nigger, Van."

"I've never did anything like this before. I can't help it if I feel shaky, Bobby Joe."

"You should be like me and Miss Lee, calm."

118

"Bobby Joe is right Van. Since this is a small matter, try not to be nervous, you might mess up things/"

"We better turn in. We have to leave at five."

"Five!" Bobby Joe exclaimed.

"Yes five. It takes about fifty minutes or more to get there. Don't know what time this kid leaves for school."

"Have you ever thought he might be out of school?" Bobby Joe said kind of putting a flaw in Lee's thoughts.

"If I figure correctly, he is about seventeen. This should be his last year in school and if I know his mother, he will go until he finishes. Be sure to get all your things together. We are leaving for the airport as soon as we get the boy. Let's turn in. I am sleepy", Lee said.

With the boys' help, they arrived at 4223 Spanish Drive around 6:15 A.M. They parked the car a little ways from the house. Van remarked it was such a nice neighborhood. Chicago really excited him. He didn't know a town could be so big. 6:30 A.M., no boy. Lee kept looking at her watch. "This is sure nerve-wracking", she admitted. Every now and then, someone would pass along the sidewalk. Cars zoomed by. 6:40 A.M., no boy. "I wish I smoked", Lee said. "I didn't know this kind of waiting could be so frustrating."

"I'm cold Miss Lee. Turn on the heat", Van said.

"Maybe he ain't going to school today", Bobby Joe hinted.

There seemed to be more people on the street, more cars going to and fro. Lee began to think the boy might not be there. She should have called the number to see if the boy was really there. 7:10 A.M., "Look, that's him. The boy coming down the walk now," Lee said excitedly. David wore a brown leather jacket with some of fur on the collar. The collar was pulled up. He wore no hat, but gloves. They all were very shaky and tense now. Lee thought she was seeing Andrew all over again at seventeen.

"Thought you said he was black", Bobby Joe questioned.

"He just looks white", Lee said.

The boy walked toward the car. "Wait til he passes. Here Bobby Joe, take this."

"What is the gun for?" Bobby Joe wanted to know.

"To frighten him", Lee said with a 'to do it' tone in her voice.

"You are going through a lot of trouble just to get a boy to see his dying father", Bobby Joe said putting the gun in his pocket. The boy passed the car. The boys got out of the car, walked swiftly up to the boy. Lee was along-side now with the car, scared.

"Get in the car", Bobby Joe said as he put his hand in his pocket. He pushed the gun in the boy's back. David began to tremble with fear. As cold as it was, David's face trickled with sweat. He was too frightened to say a word thinking to himself, they are going to kill me, oh my God. Van opened the car door, David didn't move. Seeing the boy was too frightened to move, Bobby Joe took him by the collar and shoved him in the car, getting in himself. Van got in quickly in the other side of the car. Lee took off down the street like a bolt of lightening. She was going so fast she almost turned over.

"Slow down", Bobby Joe yelled. "You are going to kill us."

"Don't kill me, please don't kill me!" David cried. "Where are you taking me?"

"Stop whining, ain't nobody going to kill you." Van said in his slow-talking manner.

"You are, I know you are", David repeated.

"Shut him up, Bobby Joe", Lee ordered.

Bobby Joe slapped David hard across the face. "Now shut up."

Behind that hard slap, David was too scared to say another word. They all sat in nervous silence all the way to the airport. At the airport they all got out quickly including David, thinking if he did move, he might be killed. Leaving the car at the parking lot, they found the pilot waiting in the lunchroom.

"Set, let's go", the pilot said.

They followed the pilot to the field. Lee and the boys' nerves had settled down. They somewhat, had accomplished their mission. As they boarded the plane, David said, "Mr. I don't want to go back. They will kill me."

"They are not going to kill you. They're taking you to see your dying father. You owe him that much respect. Climb aboard", the pilot said.

David's fright changed to wonder at the words the pilot said. The plane taxied off the airstrip into the wide open spaces. David got to thinking about what the pilot had said. His Uncle Jessie had been such a good father to him. He never thought much who his real father was. Maybe they were telling the truth. David felt a little relaxed at this thought. No one said a word as the plane winged its way back to Clearforest. Riding from the airport, Lee got the idea it was too early to take the boy to Andrew's house. It was still day—Andrew and his wife would see them. She didn't want to be seen.

"Bobby Joe, will you keep the boy at your place until around six?"

"I thought you were taking him to his father's house now", Van said surprised.

"I've changed my mine", Lee said.

"There will be a slight charge—about twenty dollars", Bobby Joe said. David's face turned pale when Lee said she changed her mind. He wondered what she was planning to do with him. Was she really going to kill him? He wanted to say something to save himself, but he didn't want to anger them, thinking it was best to sit quietly and listen.

"I'll pick the three of you up at six", Lee said again.

"By the way, when do we get paid?" Bobby Joe asked casual-like.

"As soon as we deliver the boy", Lee said. "Which way to your place?"

"Go past the pool hall five blocks, turn left on Sagmore. My house is the fourth one on the left. A half hour later, Lee drove up in front of Bobby Joe's place. It was a shabby two-story building. Van and Bobby Joe got out of the car, David followed without being told. Half way down the street, Lee backed the car back to Bobby Joe's place. As the boys were entering the house, she yelled at Bobby Joe, "Will you come here a minute?" When he got to the car, she stuck out her hand—"The gun, she said.

"Oh yes I forgot." He gave her the gun. She put the gun in her purse and drove off. Bobby Joe stood watching her car move down the street wondering what was she up to. He watched until she turned the corner.

Lee didn't go home. She drove downtown. She first drew out the necessary money she needed. She then shopped around for Christmas presents. Looking at her watch, she still had time to spare. With the rest of the time, she had lunch and took in a movie. Lee kept her date on time. She sat in the car and blew the horn. The boys filed out of the house like three little kittens—Van in front, David in between with Bobby Joe behind. The street light revealed their faces. Maybe she wouldn't have to pay them at all. Instead of getting in, Bobby Joe leaned on the car. Van and David got in.

"I want my money now", Bobby Joe said.

"I'll give you the money when you deliver the boy", Lee answered.

"I said I want my money now", Bobby Joe said in a very demanding way. Bobby Joe had one foot in the car, holding David by his arm. "Out of the car, boy." David just sat there. "I said out of the car boy", Bobby Joe said snatching David out of the car.

"Alright, half now and the other half when you deliver the boy" Lee said. She opened her purse and counted out two-seventy for Bobby Joe. She handed him the money. "Now give Van his part."

"Let Van speak for himself."

"I'll take my half too, Miss Lee", Van said.

"I see I'm not trustworthy", she said as she gave Van his half.

"It's not that we don't trust you. We just want a little assurance. Okay boy, get back in the car now." They drove off.

"Did you have any trouble with him?" Lee asked feeling a little angry with the boys.

"No he was as gentle as a lamb", Van said.

"That's his father in him. Did he say anything?"

"The only thing we got out of him is that his name is David. Where are we going now?" Bobby Joe asked.

"To Braidwood, that's where David's father lives", Lee said happily.

At the Duncan house, the gaily lit Christmas tree showed someone was home. Lee parked her car near the dark entrance. They walked on the dark side of the house. When they got almost to the house, Lee stopped them.

"What now?" Bobby Joe wanted to know.

"When you get to the house, open the door."

"Suppose the door is locked?" Bobby Joe asked.

"The Duncan's never lock their doors. I know. I have been there too many times." The name Duncan rang a bell with Van and David, but neither said anything.

"As I was saying, open the door and push him in, far enough that he will fall on the living room floor, right in front of them."

"I thought you said you were taking him to see his dying father", Van said.

"Never mind what you thought I said. Do as I say now. I'm paying you two. Here, put these handkerchiefs over your faces. They won't recognize you two with these on." They put the handkerchiefs on. Lee ran up to the window where a big evergreen stood. She could see Andrew and his wife sitting, chatting on the couch in the living room.

Bobby Joe turned the knob on the door so easy that you couldn't see it move or hear the clicking sound of the lock. He then threw open the door. Van and Bobby Joe rushed down the hall to the living room. They pushed David so hard he stumbled half way across the living room floor before he fell flat on his face. When David got up from the floor, he looked directly into the face of his image, his father.

Chapter 14

Andrew jumped up, his eyes blared out in shock, his mouth went open, his face went white. Andrew and David stood, staring at each other.

"Andrew, tell me it's not true. You lied, you lied", Terence screamed. "You were lying all the time", she began to cry as though her eyes were raining tears.

Andrew's face had sunk into a crazy stare, his shoulder slumped in. He looked like a man waiting for death to take him.

David looked from Terence to Andrew, trying to understand.

"Andrew, tell me it isn't true", Terence said tugging at his sleeve, trying to get his attention. Seeing she couldn't get Andrew's attention, she ran upstairs in a crying rage.

Lee walked away from the window with that smile on her face that seemed to say, revenge accomplished.

"Are you my father?" David asked.

"Yes I am" Andrew said with a funny look on his face. "I can't deny you, you're so much like me", he said as he sat down on the sofa for support. "Sit down boy." David sat in a chair across the room. "Boy", he said looking at David, "All I can say is that I am sorry I brought you into this world as a bastard."

David hung his head in shame looking at Andrew. David said, "I have heard of you, Sir and I have seen pictures of you. But I have never put our looks together and I never dreamed a man like you could be my father."

"It happens to the best of us." The shock drained off a little as he talked to the boy. "People would never accept me if I had married your mother."

"I understand sir."

"If it will help you to bear the shame, I will give you my name in writing, within the law."

"Thank you Sir, my foster father has adopted me."

"What is your name?"

"David Hemp St. James."

"That's a nice name. I have so much to offer you. If you need or want anything, write or call me. Have you finished school? What is your ambition?"

"I will finish school this year. I would like to be an electrical engineer. Don't you think you better go and see about her?"

"No David, your coming here has ended my marriage. There is nothing I can say that will bring her back."

"I'm sorry sir. I didn't come on my own. I was kidnapped and brought here."

"I know who brought you here. She wanted to destroy me and she has", Andrew said in a very sad voice.

Chapter 15

It was around six when Vada remarked to her husband that David had not come home. He played basketball late sometimes, but never this late.

"Maybe he's at Mark's. Why don't you call him?"

She went to the kitchen phone and called Mark. "Mark, this is David's mother. Is David at your house?"

"No, he isn't. He wasn't at school either. I usually wait at the window looking for him. When I'm late, h e comes up and waits for me. This morning, when he got almost to my house, I saw him get in a car with two fellows."

"Thanks Mark for the information." Going back to the dinner table, she looked bewildered.

"I think David has run away."

"Run away! What are you talking about?"

"Mark said David didn't go to school. I thought we were doing such a nice job, making up for lost time. He seemed so happy with us."

"Now don't think like that. Maybe he thought if he asked to visit Liz, we might get the impression he wouldn't come back, so he went on his own. I'll call Liz." Harry got Liz on the phone. "Liz this is Harry. We think David has run away. We feel he is coming to your place. When he gets there, tell him whenever he makes up his mind to come back, we love him and he can come back any time."

"When did he leave?" Liz said excitedly.

"He left this morning. We don't know why he left."

"Harry, I am sorry to hear David ran away. When he gets here, I will get in touch with you. Let me talk to Vada."

"Liz, she is too filled up to talk."

"I understand. Will get in touch when I hear anything."

Harry and Vada sat at the table trying to eat their dinner.

"Harry, I don't think David ran away. He was too happy here. At least he seemed to be", Vada began to cry. "I have grown to love him so much. I know he loves Liz more than he does me. I know I was wrong for not raising him. I am sorry I didn't."

"Dear, don't carry on so. He'll come back."

"When I was young I was ashamed of him. I love him and I want him back", Vada said through her tears.

Harry got up from the table and went to her side and tried to comfort her. "Hush now, he'll come back when he has had a little visit with Jessie and Liz", Harry said trying to comfort her.

She hushed a bit. "Harry, do you think he would come all the way here and kill him?" She got up from the table and started pacing the floor.

"Dear, you are feeling perturbed for nothing. He'll be back, come on, stop crying, try to eat something."

Mark said he got in a car with two boys. I don't understand that. All of a sudden a thought struck her. She went to the phone and called Mark again. "May I speak to Mark?"

"Just a minute please", the voice on the other end said.

"Mark, this is David's mother again. Were the fellows that David got in the car with—were they black or white?"

"They looked white, as far as I could see. He seemed to be put in the car, instead of getting in by himself."

"Thanks Mark. Harry I think they are trying to kill David again. Mark said he got in the car with white fellows. He said they seemed to be pushing him in the car instead him of getting in by himself."

"Maybe they are trying to kill him", Harry said.

"Can't you see they are trying to kill him again", Vada yelled as she ran into the bedroom. "I'll kill him if he has killed David. I'll kill him," she screamed.

Harry ran to her in the bedroom. She was on the phone. "Who are you calling?" Harry asked.

"That rat of a dog, Andrew Duncan", she said waiting for her call to go through.

"Here is your party."

"Andrew, have you got my son? You tried to kill him once. If you have had him killed, I swear I'll kill you", Vada said in a very serious angry voice.

"Vada, your son…" she didn't let him finish the statement. She kept on screaming words at him in the phone.

"You know you sent those men here to kill him. Andrew, how can you have an innocent child like David killed to hide your sin."

"Vada, what are you saying is not true", he finally got in.

"All you are thinking about is saving your self-respect and that big name of yours."

"Vada, listen to me. He's here", Andrew yelled.

"I don't believe you. You are lying", she cried frantically through the phone.

Harry took the phone from her. "Did you really kill David, Harry asked?"

"No, no. I didn't have him killed. He hasn't been harmed in any way. He's right here. I'll let you talk to her."

"Hi Dad, I'm alright", David said with assurance.

"I am so glad you are safe son. Your mother is so upset about you. I'll let you talk to your mother.

Vada took the phone.

"Mother, I'm alright. It was a little rough, but I'm okay", David said happily.

"What happened? How did you get there?" Vada said seeking answers.

"It wasn't him. It was some other folks. They said they were taking me to see my dying father. I didn't understand what it was all about, but I'm alright."

"You go to your grandfather's and stay. I'll come and get you in the morning."

"Mother, I'll tell you all about it tomorrow", David said.

"I had better call your grandfather. I will have them come and get you. I'm not rushing you off but I think it's best", Andrew said.

"I understand sir", David said.

Sam and Pursa were all out of breath when they reached the big house. How come he's here, Mr. Duncan?" Sam asked.

"Lee had him brought here", Andrew said sadly.

"I'll sorry about all this mess", Sam said.

"It's not your fault Sam. This is good-bye David." They shook hands.

"I don't know what to say, but I am glad to have met you" David remarked.

Andrew walked them to the back door and he watched them walk down the path to Sam's house until the darkness gathered them in.

The loud sound of the radio sent Terence running down the stairs. Reaching the end of the stairs, she saw Andrew opening the desk drawer, taking out the gun. She turned off the radio in the study. "Andrew, put the gun back", she said softly, horrified.

He didn't seem to hear her. He put the gun to his head.

"Andrew, listen to me; put the gun down. You don't want to kill."

He looked at her and said, "I have nothing to live for."

"Yes, you have me."

He still held the gun to his head. "I know you are through with me when you saw the boy", he said with a silly stare.

"I was only acting like a silly woman. I was only thinking of myself. When I saw the boy, I did feel hurt. Please forgive me", she said wrapping her arms around his body.

He took the gun down from his head, but he still held it in his hand. Feeling her body close to his, he felt less tense.

"You can talk to me darling", she said calmly holding her fears and wanting the truth within her. "I love you, I don't want you to kill yourself. I want you around so I can love you. Things aren't that bad. Put the gun back. Let's go in the living room and talk this thing out."

He looked as though he didn't want to obey.

"Terence, Darling", Andrew said looking at the gun in his hand, "You know I seem to solve everyone's problems but my own. When trouble comes my way, my brain seems to lock. I can't think straight. Killing myself seems the best way out."

"You really haven't had any real trouble in your life. That's why you can't handle your own. You had very little trouble with your help. Sometimes the crops didn't turn out the best. But this problem is dealing with your sin. That is a big difference and that calls for confession. Now put the gun back."

"You are right", he said, putting the gun back. "I guess I have been a fool for the devil. I'm supposed to be a smart man, brilliant lawyer."

Terence didn't say a word. She took him by his hand and led him to the living room. They sat on the sofa. She put her arms around him, laying his head on her breast, holding him close to her.

"I did have a child by Sam's daughter. I was young, bold and foolish. Lee was always in love with me. She resented the fact that I didn't marry her. She made a promise to me that on day she would have her revenge. Lee has had her revenge in more ways than one."

"When you got the gun out, you were doing just what she wanted you to do", Terence said softly.

"I realize that now. I haven't told you what started this mess. I have to tell you the whole story."

"Darling I don't want to know the whole story. As they say down here, let it be."

"I think it's best you know the whole story. Should have told you the story of my life the night we got engaged. It all started when I was nominated to run for governor. With me being against integration probably brought out all the things that happened. He told her how Lee talked him into want to kill the boy, how he beat up Jessie—Sam's son-in-law and how he acted toward Sam and Pursa the day he got back from winning the primary election. I almost hated all black people because I was so much against integration. When I got that letter from Vada, it really made me hate colored people, people I had felt sorry for and helped all my life. I had no malice for them, hate just seemed to grow. I cried like a baby when I got that blackmail letter from Lee. I imagine Sam thought I was crazy, crying on him like I did. I was really hurt, thinking of how I let Lee lead me on the way she did." Andrew's voice sounded as though he wanted to cry, but he held the crying in. "I'm supposed to be so smart."

There was silence in the room. Terence had a queer look on her face. Her mind could not believe all that he had said, but her heart told her that she loved him and she felt sympathy and understanding for him.

Andrew broke the silence, "Terence do you want to stay with me knowing all of this?"

"You want to know something, I probably would have acted the same way if all you said happened to me. I love you", she said smiling.

"I love you to. I want to keep you. I have been such a fool. You don't know how foolish you can be when you try to hide your sins, but the good Lord said the truth shall set you free." Andrew felt so relieved telling her the whole true story.

Chapter 16

Vada got off the plane in Jackson, Mississippi at 7:00 A.M. She took a white cab to the bus station in downtown Jackson. She had to wait an hour before the bus left for Braidwood. After she entered the station, she stood for a while deciding where she was going to sit. At one end of the station, the sign red 'colored.' The other end read 'white.' With all the advertisement around where the signs read 'colored and white'—these signs stood out like a naked man or woman, a sin and shame. Knowing she could pass for white, she thought of sitting in the white section but her conscious led her to the colored side. There were quite a few people in the station. They either were leaving for Christmas vacation or for good. Sitting idly waiting, a wave of terror came over Vada. It dawned on her she didn't check with her mother or father to see if Andrew was telling the truth. He might have frightened David into saying everything was alright. It was Andrew who was going to kill David. He just might kill her too. By the look of things, Andrew might not be the same easy-going, good-natured young man she left back home all these many years ago. She was so hell-fired mad, she just had to come home and tell Andrew a thing or two. In her frightening thoughts, she didn't have to come home. She had told Andrew a thing or two over the phone and David could have come home by himself. Wishing her husband had come with her for protection, thinking a man like Andrew in Mississippi is somebody. Whatever color you were, it didn't matter a damn. Vada had lived in Chicago for such a long time, she had forgotten the set ways of the south, not that Chicago was such a goody, good town. Her mind went back to the black people in the station. They were not going on a visit. They were going up north to stay where the dream of life was somewhat different, better than down home. She thought of the migrants from the old country. They were permitted to roam and go places they pleased to find their dream, but her people (looking for that same dream) went up north, as they say, trying to find that dream. Remembering as a young girl back home, around the household and on the Duncan farm, the talk of night riders, seeing crosses burning, lynching a Negro for rape or for so-called rape. The sound of the hounds drummed in her ears. They were on the hunt for one of her people for something he might have done or he might not. You could hear of a Negro woman submitting herself to a white man just to satisfy his middle man, submitting out of fear saying yes to the big boss man when you knew he was wrong. Vada was shaking within, frightened from the memory her home state. She began to perspire. She took off her fur coat putting it over her arm. Her trim figure showed off the light-weight netted emerald green two-piece suit. She took her powder puff from her purse, dotted her face gathering up the sweat. Thinking she was frightened to death for own self. Why she had a good life in Mississippi! She tried to shake off the memories of the past, but they lay haunting all of her thoughts of some of their ways, of thinking of just ignorance. It wasn't ignorance. They knew right from wrong. They had a grudge. They were taking it out on her people, still sorry they didn't win the Civil War. Off the sidewalk, nigger; get back, nigger; stay in your place, nigger. Her thoughts went back to Andrew in his wanting to kill. No, no this isn't the Andrew she knew. Mississippi was all she was thinking, but it wasn't like that in the town where she was born. Oh they had their ups and downs, but never a knock down drag out affair. In the letters and calls from her mother over the years, her mother always wrote that Andrew was the same sweet gentle person, always doing good wherever he could in and out of his law practice, with very little pay or no pay at all. If Andrew had changed, she wasn't going to let Mississippi and her ways, neither Andrew frighten her and she would get in her words first and she wasn't going to call him Mr. Duncan. In short, she was respected as Mrs. Harry Vince St. James. She, too, had fallen among the stars. 'High now brown cow.' Letting her thoughts roll high, her fears rolled away like a storm out to sea. She thought of Liz and the happy reunion she had with her. Liz was the same old Liz. She still wore her hair in the same old style, her long hair (now mingled gray) braided to one side. She tried to get her sister to get her hair cut and styled in the latest coiffure. Liz said she had no time for hairdo's—too much work on the farm. Vada always laughed to herself whenever she thought of Liz' husband Jessie. Jessie looked like a yellow-belly catfish in jumper coveralls. He looked so funny to her. A little smile came to her mouth thinking of different ones back home. Even the white folk were warm and friendly. Breaking the warm feeling that had taken over her fears, she heard the station-messenger call—Whitfield, Learned, Eution, Carpenter, Crystal Springs, Braidwood and McComb. Vada boarded the bus. She went directly to the back of the bus. Vada flopped down by the window, putting her coat over the seat. The bus leaving the station made a tour of the capitol, a sort of sight-seeing a-do.

The bus went down the street showing off the excellent cultural buildings. Riding through Jackson, she could see the town was still beautiful, the old places stood out as arrogant as ever. Quite a bit of the new—moving out the old. It had been a long time since she was home. She thought of the many times she visited kinfolk and friends. Some had moved away, some gone on before. Vada never took time out to visit her folks, although she had pictures of her mother and father. But she wondered what they really looked like now. Vada's brothers, Sam Jr. and Willie always came to see her. Her brothers came home once a year. Although James (JC) lived in Chicago (whom Vada stayed with until she got on her feet) she visited him over the phone, then went by his house. She told herself she wasn't high-toned. He had his circle of friends and she had hers. The sight of chickens, hogs, lazy dogs, pigs and horses, cows, plowed and unplowed fields, made Vada forget about taking a nap. The sight of the countryside in Mississippi took her back to her childhood days. She had seen these things before. Going home made them seem so different. Thinking it had been so long since she was home, she didn't see much change in this part of Mississippi. There's too many weather-beaten houses along the way. A new house appears every now and then. The highway was paved. She could see, over yonder, a cloud of dust, a man in a wagon with a team of horses. Seeing the cloud of dust meant that the back roads were still dirt roads. Mississippi was slow in progressing or was she just letting her ignorant grudge hold her back from making a great empire out of a beautiful state, withholding progress from her natural resources to the good earth. Mississippi says, I accept others if they accept my way of life, my way of making love with others. The bus came to a halt outside the two-by-four station. The sign read 'Briarwood.' Vada was back home. No black Cadillac, no Dad. Maybe he will be along shortly. She started to go in the little store station. Through the window she could see an old white man behind the counter and another drinking, what else—coffee. As small as the store was, it had benches for the colored and one for white. Changing her mind about going in the station, she pranced up and down in front of the station. Cars were passing—none was the black Cadillac. Vada gave a thought to calling her father. A cab rolled up and stopped a little distance from where she was standing. Out came a tall, dark fellow about Vada's age. He walked up to her.

"Vada", he said.

"Yes I don't believe I know you", she gave him a blank stare, and then with a shout Vada yelled, "Bubble Eyes, is that you?"

"None other", Bubble Eyes said, gleaming with joy.

They threw their arms around each other in a joyful hug.

"Now Vada girl, don't you come calling me Bubble Eyes. My name is Cleveland Julius Jackson. Sure been a long time girl, long time," he said rolling his big bubble eyes side to side, sizing up Vada.

"It sure has been a long time, I guess too long. Well, Mr. Jackson, how is everything with you?"

"Fine, as that cat you are wearing. I live in Jackson now. I have been visiting my folks on the farm. Mr. Sam asked me to pick you up, 'cause he was a little shaky from the happenings. V, how is everything in your corner?" Cleveland said picking up Vada's luggage, giving her the once-again with his big cotton white eyes.

"Oh I'm going to be alright", Vada said.

"I see you're looking mighty fancy. What is that you are wearing? A cat or a rabbit," he teased her feeling the mink collar on her coat.

"You always was a teaser", she said smiling. "Where is your brother?" Vada asked.

Cleveland, very gentlemanly-like, helped Vada into the back seat of the cab. He then put the luggage up front with him and they were off."

"That brother of mine lives in Chicago, too. Talking about crazy, he is real crazy."

"Where does he live? I would like to stop by and visit with him some."

"You don't want to see him. He done drink so much of that stuff, he's uglier than me, you know. He used to be kind of handsome. He looks like a hippopotamus ninety years old. He gets drunks everyday. I don't know how he keeps a job. He owes everybody. He ain't got nothing and he ain't married either", Cleveland said with some anger in his voice.

"That's too bad. Maybe he will change some day. Next time you're in Chicago, stop by. Dad will give you my address."

You know Vada, Tab got a better job than me. He makes more money than me but I got more than he has. I got a five-room house and I owns my own cab. Some of us seem to think it takes a world of this and that to get along. All I can hear nowadays is education education."

"You was born in the day when you didn't need so much education. You must get an education in these times and days to come. There will be no getting by", Vada stressed.

"I know that. I wish I had gone to college, but you know there are three kinds of fools. Now there is the fool, the damn fool and the educated fool. The educated fool is the worst one. They think they know everything. With all that sense they suppose to have, you would think they know that they don't have everything. If you don't have common sense with education, that makes you a real fool and that's what my brother is."

"Ah, just pray for him. How's your folks?" Vada said trying to get Cleveland off his brother's case.

"They are fine. Mother is fat and sassy. Dad's still preaching at the farm and my Uncle John preaches at your sister's town. I am getting married next year, I think in June." Cleveland laughed at his "I think'.

'Well congratulations. I wish you God's blessings."

"Thank you V. Do you want to go to your folk's house or to the big house?"

"You better take me to the Duncan's. Mother and father are there by this time of morning", Vada said as they rounded the road that went by the house she used to call home.

"I heard that Mr. Andrew is trying to make a round carrot. They say it is supposed to have more a fruit-flavor than a vegetable taste. They have a lab somewhere making this crazy carrot", Cleveland said laughing.

"Now I have heard everything. Maybe he will get people to eat more carrots with a different shape and taste. I wish him success. Vada said kind of laughing at the idea too.

"Well, here we are", Cleveland said as his cab rolled up in the Duncan driveway. Cleveland got out of the cab, then let Vada out. Then he took out the luggage.

"Thanks Cleveland. How much is my fare?"

"Oh, the ride is on me. It was just nice seeing you again. It has been so long. Try to have a nice time while you're here."

"It is a joy to see you after all these years. Thanks for the ride. If I don't see you anymore, I wish you success in marriage."

They gave each other a big hug and off Cleveland went.

Vada picked up her bag. She stood looking around the old place. It was the same as she remembered. She could see her father hadn't lost his touch. The yard was neat and trim as ever.

Terence Duncan answered the knock on the door. Vada looked for her father to open the door. Vada introduced herself. I'm Mrs. Vada St. James, Sam's daughter."

"Oh come in. I'm Terence Duncan."

"Where is mother and dad?" My, she is pretty Vada was thinking.

"Due to all that has happened, I gave them the day off."

"That's kind of you. Before I go down to the house, I would like to speak with Andrew. All the way down here, I kept asking myself, over and over again what happened to him to make him act the say he did! As I remember Andrew was so kind."

"I asked myself the same question until he gave me the answers. Darling you have a caller", Terence yelled upstairs to Andrew.

"Be down in a few."

"I think you folks should hear the story too. They were here with him day after day. He owes them an explanation too", Terence went to the phone and called the McClouds, "Sam, you and Pursa, come up to the house and bring David. Your daughter is here."

"Thanks for calling. We'll be right along", Sam said excitedly.

It took Sam and Pursa and David half the time it took to walk to the big house. They came in the back door as usual. When they entered the dining room, Vada ran to greet them.

"Mother, Dad, I'm so glad to see you", she cried.

They hugged and kissed one another. Tears of joy came streaming down their faces. Vada then took David in her arms and cuddled him with a mother's love. I'm so glad you are safe, son", Vada sighed.

"Oh, I'm alright", David said.

"Stand back Baby. Let Mama see how you look. Bless Jesus, you done put on some weight. The hair is a little redder. Other than that, you still my baby", Pursa took Vada in her arms again and gave her a real hug saying, "It sure been a long, long time", Sam and the rest stood by smiling from ear to ear.

"I am sorry trouble had to bring me home. Least I could have done was come to see you two every now and then."

"That's alright Baby", Sam said, "We understand. You did write and call some time."

136

Andrew was half way down the stairs before they saw him. He stood there on the stairs staring at Vada. He descended the steps with a big smile on his face. He walked over to her, "Vada", he exclaimed, "I'm so glad to see you," he said shaking her hand vigorously. "It's been a long time, hasn't it?" Andrew said.

"Yes it has", she said as they eyed each other.

"Vada I am sorry you had to come home in this unpleasant way", Andrew said with sadness in his voice.

"I'm sorry too. What I don't understand is a man of your intelligence, why didn't you cope with this situation in a different manner?"

The rest of them listened to the two of them talk.

"If you had thought, you could have done what your mother did, sent David to me", Vada said with some malice in her voice.

"Vada, you don't know Lee. She is a shrewd woman. She blackmailed, she threatened me. I guess I wanted to be governor at any cost. If I did send the boy to you, she still had a trump card, the boy. Can't you see—everything was built around the boy. David I am sorry to say, if you didn't exist she wouldn't have a scheme. I gave her a beating that frightened her somewhat. She stopped intimidating me for a while. When I got married, she threatened to tell my wife about David. The blackmail started all over again. Like a fool, I gave her money. Getting that letter from you only helped the hellfire along."

"Lord have mercy", Pursa said.

"I never thought about the child until she brought him up. I really didn't know if there was a child. She convinced me. I thought if she told my wife, that would end our marriage."

"How did she find out about David?" Vada asked.

"I don't know. I asked her but she wouldn't tell me. If I only left you alone", as mother said, "Your sins shall find you out."

"Suppose you had an illegitimate child by a person of your own race, wouldn't the facts apply the same?"

If I had an illegitimate child by someone of my own race, it wouldn't matter as much as this child. I am against integration. If my opponent found out about the boy, he would have crucified me. I would lose everything I stood for—my pride, respect. Now all these things I've done, the agony, the pain, the tears, the time and the effort—were all in vain. I lost the election", his voice sounded very grave, a man defeated by his own self-destruction.

137

All eyes were looking at David, but Vada stood with her arms around David as if to protect him.

"I am so sorry you lost. It may be for the best. I remember when I was a little girl. I used to call you governor. I know how much you wanted to be governor. It was your life's ambition."

"I wanted the governorship so bad, it clouded the right way of trying to think up ways to get people to vote for me, hoping Lee wouldn't ruin my chances to be governor. The more I thought about integration, the angrier I got. I was a bundle of hate and confusion. It's all over now. I'll never run again. But if the boy didn't exist Lee wouldn't have anything to threaten me with. She built all her ideas around the boy.

David hung his head down. He walked toward the dining room. He wanted to get away from all this disgraceful talk that hurt him so deeply. He didn't ask to be born. Andrew, seeing the boy walking away, went after him. "David wait." David kept walking. "Wait." David stopped. He turned around and faced Andrew. He was biting his lips to keep back the tears. "I'm sorry you had to hear such raw talk, but it is the truth. I don't hate you, I know it's not your fault that you are here. Please forgive both of us for bringing you into this world illegitimately." Tears tumbled down David's face. Andrew gave him his handkerchief from his pocket. Since things are over and done with, you can come back home and live in peace. Just remember, any time you need help, call or write, I'll see you are taken care of."

"Thanks Andrew", Vada said. "I can give him all the help he needs. In other words, he can only be my son. I hope, in time, integration has reached the point where he can be whatever he wants to be", Vada said with her head perched high, with a bit of anger in her voice and the look of shame on her face.

"I'm sorry Vada that I don't feel the way you do about integration. I just can't see your peoples' point."

"I wish you could think of integration as a step toward progress for my people. It's a shame my people can't have the great opportunities this country has to offer. We are Americans too."

Sam, Pursa, Terence and David had their thoughts on integration but said nothing. They listened to the two of them have it out, so to speak.

"I don't see integration your way."

"Can't you see this as a great challenge for this country to prove to the world it can practice what it preaches and keep its' house in order?"

"Please, please Vada, let's not talk about integration. I've buried my feelings on the subject. Please let me be", Andrew said.

"But Andrew, I thought you would be all for this togetherness."

Andrew didn't answer her.

Vada said no more. She looked at Andrew, the one person she thought would be for equal rights. She thought to herself, how could he lay with me, talk sweet words to me and have the kindness of a good man but deny her people the salt of the earth.

"Now, getting back to all that's happened, I feel I owe all of you an apology. The Lord said the truth shall set you free and confession is good for the soul. All the years I've been a lawyer, wrong doesn't make right. I don't know what happened to my thinking. The months I campaigned for governor, I built up a hate in myself that I didn't know was in me. The first day I came home from winning the primary election, I guess Sam thought I was crazy. I came to hate Negroes. I really blew my top." He looked around at the faces sitting in the room. He saw faces of sympathy. "The only thing I can say is I am truly sorry about everything."

"We understand", Sam said smiling.

"It's a load off my mind", Andrew said with a sigh of relief.

Everyone in room showed understanding, but there was pity too that a man with so much generosity and intelligence and, supposedly a God-fearing man, wouldn't get through his head -behold how good and how pleasant it is for brethren to dwell together in unity-. There was silence in the room.

Chapter 17

A loud knocking on the front door broke the silence. Sam answered the door.

"Morning Sheriff Bates."

"Morning Sam, is Mr. Duncan in?"

"Yes sir, come on in."

"Morning Sheriff", Andrew said surprised to see the Sheriff. "Now Sheriff, what gives me the pleasure of seeing you. You know I'm not offering my assistance anymore, I'm retiring."

Sheriff Bates had called on Andrew many times in the past for his assistance to help some poor soul. "Yes, I know. It's not your help I need this time. I have a warrant for your arrest."

"A warrant for my arrest!" Andrew exclaimed.

"Lord have mercy", Pursa said.

"Sheriff, what's this all about?" Andrew wanted to know.

"It seems someone gave Mrs. Lee Rainey a terrible beating last night and she claims you did it."

"Why Sheriff, I wasn't out of the house at all last night."

"Can you prove that?"

"Yes, my wife can verify that."

"My husband was home all evening."

"I need more proof than that."

"What time did it happen? Andrew asked.

"Oh, between eight and nine."

"David, tell the Sheriff who brought you here."

"What's he got to do with it? Sheriff asked.

"A lady by the name of Miss Lee and two fellows just a little bit older than me—one called Van and the other, Bobby Joe. They brought me here a little before that hour. I know he couldn't have beat her", David said trying to defend Andrew.

"I better tell you why she brought him here. This is my son. She brought him here to hurt me."

Sheriff Bates was so shocked he didn't know what to say. He looked from David to Andrew, seeing the resemblance so deeply he couldn't believe his eyes. Sheriff Bates had known Andrew all his life, but this was the first time he heard of him having a son.

"Who is the mother?" Sheriff Bates knew that Andrew hadn't been married before.

Vada dropped her head. The whole room seemed to float in silence with shame. "I'm the mother", Vada said holding her head high.

Sheriff Bates looked at Vada. "I don't believe I know you,"

"You don't remember me. I am Sam's youngest daughter", Vada said.

He searched her face trying to recall. "No, I believe I do. Andrew what's all this got to do with you being arrested?" Sheriff Bates asked.

"I'm coming to that", Andrew said. Andrew told the Sheriff the whole story from the beginning to end. "You see Sheriff, she is still trying to have her revenge."

Sheriff Bates stood there shaking his head in disbelief of all Andrew had said. "It looks like you can file some charges too. But by your story, you had more reason to beat her than anyone."

"I know it looks that way. I know who did it. I'm not going to take the blame for this mess. All I ask is for you to take me to Clearforest. I know I can find proof there," Andrew said with assurance."

"Alright Andrew. We will go to Clearforest if that will clear you."

"I want to go with you darling. I don't want you to go alone," Terence said with love.

Andrew walked over to Vada. "Take care of the boy and have a Merry Christmas", Andrew said with kindness on his face.

"Thanks, you have Merry Christmas too."

Shaking David's hand, Andrew said, "You have a Merry Christmas."

"Thanks Sir. Due to all the trouble you are having, I hope you and your wife have a wonderful Christmas", David said with sincerity.

They left. Pursa started spouting tears saying, "Lord, Sam, what's going to happen in this house next? Will they put him in jail?"

"Hush, Mother, don't cry. Everything will turn out alright", Vada said putting her arms around her mother's shoulders trying to console her.

"Pursa Baby, you have to stop this crying. I don't believe you been asking the Lord to help us to bear these burdens. You been crying about everything."

"All these years we lived here, we ain't had no mess and upsets like we done had these last months. Sam I have asked the Lord to help us", Pursa said drying her eyes.

"We's been blessed as far as trouble go. We all have to bear a cross. I guess this is ours."

"Dad, I told you and Mother, any time you wanted to leave this place, you two are welcome to live at our place in the country", Vada said.

"Now Daughter, don't go talking like that. We can come and visit you but we's going to make up our bed right here", Sam said dejecting Vada's statement.

Vada closed the subject, knowing no matter what she said, they would never leave. "Mother, you think they would mind if I look around the house?"

"Go ahead Baby, they won't mind", Pursa answered.

"Vada", David said.

"David, the bearer is Mother", Vada said with a chill in her voice feeling hurt inside when David called her Vada.

"Mother, may I look with you? I've heard so much about this place. Grandfather and grandmother talked so much about it too." In all of his years, David gave many thoughts to why his grandparents hadn't brought him to see the place where they had worked and talked about so many years. Now he knew.

"You may come along." Vada remembered only once Mrs. Duncan ever having the inside of the house painted and papered. They first gazed in the dining room. It had light cream walls with forest green drapes. The chairs were forest green with white stripes showing wear. The backs of the chairs had carved ornaments in the center of the crest-rails. The dining room table was draped with a hand-made lace tablecloth. Over the fireplace hung the late Mrs. Duncan's father and mother. On the opposite wall was the late Mr. Duncan's father and mother. The pictures were hand painted. The huge china closet held some of the family china, crystal and cut glass. On the silver chest were two large solid silver candle holders. The spare bedroom downstairs was a bright yellow, dirty yellow now. As Vada remembered, the twin beds in the room had feather-ticking. She flopped down on the bed to see if they were so. They still had the feather-ticking. The drapes were a dreary brown. The two chairs in the room and the spread on the bed had big yellow and brown on them. In days before Vada's time, the kitchen was separate. As time made a change, the kitchen she remembered, was attached to the rest of the house. The huge fireplace, where they used to cook, was still standing. The bit pots and the kettles, skillets, even the old charcoal irons were still sitting there for show. On the left side of the kitchen was an all-electric kitchen,

142

everything to get the work done faster from the cabinet to the pots and pans and other essentials for these days and times.

"Boy, the dishes I used to wash here. The parties they used to have, they were just fabulous. I can see mother keeps things neat and clean as ever", Vada said.

"Boy, some house", David said excitedly as they roamed through the house. All his growing up days he often wondered why his grandfather hadn't brought him to the Duncan house. He had talked so much about it. The events that just passed, gave him the real reason why.

They went upstairs. The late Mr. and Mrs. Duncan's room was in the colors of blue, ivory, and gold with white and pastel rose with a touch of red. The theme was of Asian descent. All the beds were draped with white canopy. There were fireplaces in every room with hook throw-rugs on the floor. What used to be Andrew's room was now Terence and Andrew's room which was very manly. All of the furniture about the house was French provincial. There were two guest rooms, one was with all pink and white. Vada always loved this room. Looking at the room, she thought of the late Mrs. Duncan. The reason this room was so feminine was deep down within her, she wished for a girl child, which she never had. They looked in what used to be the entertainment room. The only thing in that room which reminded her of all the gaiety the room used to hold was the grand piano. Vada took her hand, wiped the dust away and played 'Silent Night.'

"Vada", David said, "I mean Mother, I didn't know you could play."

She kind of smiled and said, "I play very well. Andrew taught me all I know. In my day, a boy playing the piano was sissy. He made the teacher promise not to tell anyone he was taking lessons and he told his friends I was taking lessons. He plays beautifully." They went back downstairs.

"Mother, the house reminds me of the rooms at the art museum you took me to", David said.

"Oh yes they do. You know David, even though she's gone, she lives here still", Vada said—her mind recalling old memories.

"Who, Mother?"

"Old Mrs. Duncan. She was a wonderful woman."

Except for the kitchen and the bedroom downstairs, there was a red carpet covering the living room, hall, study and the dining room floors. What Vada loved about the living room was the mural painting of old St. Louis in the horse and buggy days. She remembered that Mrs. Duncan

143

gave a big party to show off the mural. There was a big to-do about the painting. Most of her friends felt she should have a painting of the old deep south, but she wanted the mural to be the talk of the town. It was for weeks.

"Mother, the place still looks the same", Vada said looking around the living room.

"Yes Baby, it still looks the same except for the TV and the Hi-fi and the air-conditioning. Things are beginning to wear", Pursa said looking as old as some of the things in the house.

"Mother, Aunt Liz wants us to see how they have fixed up the house before we go home."

"Now son, you know we couldn't go home without going to Liz'. You still miss her, don't you son?"

"Mother, we didn't look in that room over there!" David said pointing to the study, avoiding her question.

"Oh that's the study", Vada said as they walked into the study.

"Look at all those books", David remarked.

Vada started to smile when she saw the paperweight still on the desk. She picked it up. "Son I gave this to Andrew when I was a little girl."

"What is it for?"

"He asked the same question as you did, when I gave it to him. I can hear myself now saying it is a paperweight to hold your important papers down with, silly, when you get to be governor", Vada said kind of laughing as she put the paperweight back on the desk.

They went back into the living room. "Father, I want to look around the grounds a bit before we go to see Liz. David, you want to come with me?"

"Yes, Mother, I'd love to see where you use to live."

"Y'all go right ahead. We'll wait right here til y'all comes back. I sure hope everything turns out alright. We all have our faults Mr. Duncan is a good man", Pursa said as if she wanted to cry.

"Don't worry Grandmother. I heard he was a great lawyer. He can get himself out of his mess", David said trying to assure his Grandmother.

"David, you still want to come with me?" Vada said again.

"Sure Mother, I would love to come", David answered.

Vada and David looked around the grounds until her heart was content but when she went to the spot where David was conceived, she made haste to the little house where she born and raised. As far as she could see, everything was the same except for the TV set. She and David went out back. There was the little garden her father and mother cared for in spite of the farm vegetables. Vada pulled some of the leaves from the turnips and ran them under her nose. She then picked one of the big red tomatoes and took a big juicy bite remarking to David, "There's no garden like Dad's garden." After looking at her father's flower garden, they made their way back to the big house.

Chapter 18

Sam got out his choice of cars, the gleaming black Cadillac, and off to Liz' they went.

The mid-morning weather was a mild 59 degrees. Arriving at Clearforest, Andrew had the Sheriff drive straight to Van Barbara's house. Terence stayed in the car. Van was just getting out of bed. He slipped on his pants and answered the knock at the door. Andrew and the Sheriff entered. Van was surprised and frightened to see Andrew.

"Alright Boy, give it to me straight. I know you did it and I'm not taking the blame", Andrew blurted out.

"Did what, Mr. Duncan?"

"You know very well what I'm talking about."

"How did you know it was me? We had handkerchiefs on our faces."

"Last night, when you and the other fellow pushed the boy in the house, I recognized your red hair. You and my wife are the only two people I know who have such deep red hair. When the boy mentioned your name, I knew it was you. What did Lee do—double-cross you two? It's the reason you fellows beat her."

"I didn't lay a hand on her. It was all Bobby Joe's doing. We figured the story Miss Lee told us was a lie. She said she was taking the boy to see his dying father. We thought there was more to it than she said. She didn't know I knew you. We thought she was doing this for money. Bobby Joe wanted more money. The Sheriff didn't know what to make of the boy's story. But Andrew listened to the story with much belief. "Bobby Joe had her let us off at his place. Me and Bobby Joe got in his jalopy and followed. When she got to a patch of woods, he forced her off the road. When she got out of the car, she had a gun in his hand. She and Bobby Joe struggled over the gun. He knocked the gun out of her hand."

"What did you do—pick the gun up and start beating her", Andrew said trying to throw his story off.

"No, I didn't touch her. The only thing I did was to pick up the gun. I put the gun under Bobby Joe's car seat. I guess it's still there. Bobby Joe told her he wanted more money. She said she wouldn't give him another dime more. Bobby Joe got mad and he started beating her. She fought like a tiger. She picked up a stick and hit him real hard and that made him more mad. You could see everything. The moon was shining bright as day. He took the stick away from her and he struck her several times, real hard. She moaned and fell on the ground. I am telling the truth. I didn't lay a hand on her", Van said with much assurance in his voice.

"Boy, why did you get in this mess? You know this is going to hurt your mother deeply. It will probably break her heart. What's wrong with you? As soon as you get out of one jam, you get in another."

"I don't know. I'm just stupid, I guess", Van said.

"Finish dressing. Let's get Bobby Joe", Andrew said.

The Sheriff, Van, Andrew and Terence drove to Bobby Joe's with Van's direction. This part of the town was the same as Van's. The houses were weather-beaten. The only care the people had was that they had a roof over their heads. Van, Andrew and the Sheriff got out of the car. They went upstairs to Bobby Joe's room. Van opened the door. They went in. The room was unkempt and the smell of beer and beer cans was all about the room.

"Wake up Bobby Joe", Van said shaking him. They know what happened.

"They don't know nothing", Bobby Joe said sleepy-like.

"Get up boy", Andrew said, jerking Bobby Joe from the bed.

"What's this all about? What do you call yourself doing? I ain't done nothing", Bobby Joe yelled.

"Andrew shook Bobby Joe and gave him a hard slap in the face.

"You don't be hitting me Mr. I said I didn't know nothing", Bobby Joe said standing face to face with Andrew. Andrew and the others could see the scratches on his face and hands and bruise spots on his body.

"Where did you get all those bruises?" Andrew asked.

"Boy, just where did you get those bruises?" Sheriff Bates said getting his bit in.

"I had a fight with my gal last night", Bobby Joe answered looking real mean at the bunch in the room.

Andrew grabbed Bobby Joe by his arm and twisted it behind his back.

"Dog, stop, you are hurting me!" Bobby Joe wailed.

"I'll stop when you tell the truth boy", Andrew said.

"Sheriff, make him stop!" Bobby Joe yelled.

"It's up to you boy. Why don't you tell the truth?" Sheriff Bates said.

"Alright, alright. Let my arm go, I'll tell the truth", Bobby Joe said.

Andrew released his arm.

"We did it. She made me do it. She thought she was getting away with something. I showed her how to run a show."

The Sheriff and Andrew went to Lee's place.

"I think you'll have the last laugh Andrew. Lee is in the bedroom. They sure gave her a beating. I wanted her to stay in hospital but she wanted to come home. They said she would be alright, but I doubt that. Her mother is coming tomorrow to take care of her", Doff said grievously.

Andrew and Terence followed Doff down the hall to the bedroom where Lee was. Lee's face was swollen and her body was black and blue. She looked terrible.

Lee looked at Andrew through her swollen eyes. "I see you have the last laugh. They beat me. Look at me. Why don't you laugh?" she screamed. Lee started crying hysterically. All of a sudden, she began to cough vigorously, blood tricked out of her mouth. Terence pulled some tissue from the box on the night table and put it to her mouth. Doff ran to the bathroom and brought back a bath towel and put it to her mouth.

"Andrew, will you call an ambulance? I'm taking her back to the hospital. I know she should have stayed. She was crying to come home. I let her have her way as usual", Doff said sorrowfully.

They all were nervous and somewhat frightened at the sight of blood. The coughing stopped but the blood was still trickling down. It took the ambulance only seconds to get there. Doff, Andrew and the Sheriff rode in the Sheriff's car. Terence rode in the ambulance with Lee. Terence felt Doff was too perturbed. At the hospital, they admitted her at once.

When Doff arrived at the hospital, he demanded to see his wife. Andrew persuaded Doff to wait in the waiting room. Doff couldn't sit still. He went back to the Emergency Room. The attendant there would not let him in. Doff protested kicking on the Emergency Room door. "Nurse, I want to see what they are doing to my wife."

"Mr. Rainey, get hold of yourself. You can't see your wife at this moment", one of the nurses spoke with firm words.

"That's my wife, she means everything to me. I want those doctors to do all they can to save her", Doff loud-mouthed.

"Why Mr. Rainey, you wife isn't going to die. She is going to be just fine", the nurse assured Doff.

Doff looked surprised at the nurse' remarks. This statement kind of settled his mind. Andrew talked Doff into sitting on the couch in the waiting room. After Doff calmed down, he said to Andrew, "If my wife dies, I'll get them if it's the last thing I do. Andrew, tell me, what did Lee have hanging over your head?"

"You knew she was blackmailing me. The evil she had hanging over my head was I had a son by Sam's daughter, Vada. I sure like to know how she found out!"

"So that's what it was", Doff said in surprise.

"Lee went to Chicago and brought the boy here. The boys she had helping her, wanted more money. She refused to give it to them. They ended up beating her. She's been wanting to hurt me ever since that night I told her I wasn't going to marry her. Bringing the boy here, is her revenge to me and my wife and she got a nice sum of money from me too", Andrew said spilling the beans.

"I know she always loved you, but I love her—that's all that matters. You knew I loved her when we were just kids. I loved those big cow-like eyes and that shiny dark brown hair. Those things just set her apart from the rest of the girls. God knows I love her. She's my doll", Doff kind of smiled talking about his love for his wife. It kind of consoled them all— Doff speaking so sentimentally. "I can't hate her though her sins may be as red as scarlet, to me they are as white as snow. I'm really sorry about all of this. We have been friends ever since I can remember, but we never know what life holds for us. Doff got up again and went back to the desk. "Nurse, can't I see my wife?"

"Mr. Rainey, be patient. As soon as I hear from the doctor, I'll let you know of your wife's condition."

Andrew led Doff away from the desk, sitting him down on the couch. He tried to comfort him with words, "Lee will be alright. She just got a little excited."

"But I don't like that bleeding. If she dies, I will get those boys personally", Doff said with a vicious bark.

Sheriff Bates spoke up, "The law will take care of them Mr. Rainey."

They all sat around waiting to hear from the doctor. No one said anything. Almost an hour later, the doctor came and talked to Doff.

"Mr. Rainey, the bleeding has stopped but I think we should keep her under observation. I'm sure she will be fine in a few days", the doctor said.

"Doc, can I see her?" Doff asked.

"I think it's best for you to go home. Come back tomorrow when she is better. She is asleep. I gave her a sedative. She needs to be quiet", the doctor stated to Doff.

"But Doc, that's my wife. I want to see her now, don't you understand?" Doff growled at the doctor.

"Alright Mr. Rainey. You can have a few minutes with you wife."

Doff took Lee by her hand and kissed it, but he looked at her as though she was dead. Tears filled his eyes. A nurse walked him to the waiting room. From there, he was driven home.

Chapter 19

When Vada, Sam and Pursa arrived at Liz' place, Vada called her husband stating David was going to spend Christmas with his aunt and uncle and friends back home. With Christmas being a week off, she was going to stay around about three days. She didn't know how wonderful it was being home again in almost twenty years. Vada's heart cried over the fact that she was leaving David to have Christmas in this place that used to be home. It would have been David's first Christmas with her and her husband. Vada found much happiness having a child around, the child she hadn't wanted all those years. She thought how much she hated him all his young growing up years. He had always been Liz and Jessie's child. Now she loved him to, very much. The first day Vada spent a glorious time. She and David went fishing in the little creek some way from the Baker's house. David got a kick out of his mother trying to bait her hook. She dropped the worm out of her hand three or four times. When the worm started to squirm, "Hold your nose. I'll get him on", she would say.

"Mother, I'll bait your hook", David said laughing.

"Wait a minute son, I'll get it on. I'm not afraid of worms. I haven't had one in my hands in years. They feel more like a snake than a worm." They caught a mess of perch. Vada was overjoyed with the catch. She was really having fun. She had on David's pants and jacket and Liz' old blouse. She looked out of style and funny, but she loved it. She and David tramped through the woods. Vada let her hair blow out of shape with the mild warm southern breeze. She lifted her face up toward the sun to forget the cold wind of the Chicago winters. The warmth of the sun made her feel good all over. Vada and David did a little bird-watching like she and Andrew used to do. They looked for a tree to trim. They did see a bluebird, a robin and a red-winged black bird. They found a pretty shapely tree to trim. Back at the house they all had a hand in dressing up the tree. Even Jessie added his touch in decorating the tree. This was something Jessie had never done. Vada being around brought out the urge in all. They all were so happy to see her and it was the season to be jolly. Vada thought she would spend a day visiting the neighbors, but Liz gave a big Christmas party instead. Giving the party was the very thing for Liz to show off to the neighbors. Time for the party was six to nine. How all those people got in those five rooms, only the Lord knows. The guest'

faces reminded you of the United Nations with some countries missing—
with Africa speaking for itself. The guests who came early were the only
ones that really got to see the beautiful remodeling job on the house. The
ones that came late had to go home for chairs. Some of the children had to
sit on their elder's lap. Liz served chitterlings and spaghetti, green salad
and cornbread. They started early that morning preparing the good. Liz,
Vada and some more ladies helped clean the chitterlings. They thought
they would never get finished cleaning them. Vada kept saying, "I wish
we had thought of something much easier than this!"

"We!" Liz exclaimed. "This was your idea. You said you hadn't had a
good dish of chitterlings unless you were invited out. I hope you enjoy
them."

"I do too", Vada said in a tired and disgusted manner.

Jessie built a big block pit in the back yard. He took charge in cooking
the chitterlings. They wouldn't have gotten all those chitterlings cooked
on Liz' new electric stove. Chitterlings floated its aroma about like bar-be-
que, but they have the enchanting odor of limburger cheese and about the
same delicate taste. Preparing the rest of the eats threw Liz, Vada and the
ladies in such a tired loop, they had David call and drive around to ask the
neighbors would they be so kind as to bring a small pan of cornbread.
They all came with cornbread in hand. Before the eats, they talked about
farming, who died and who had babies, who left town and that giant
subject—integration.

Old Mr. Moore, teacher and principal of Airindale's little five-room
country school, kicked off the subject of integration.

Preacher Jackson said, "I knew it, I knew it. We would wind up on that
subject, as sure as I am sitting here."

"You got any objection if we talk on the subject?" speared Mr. Moore.

"Oh no", answered Preacher Jackson. "We just can't talk nowadays
without bringing up this subject. It's either burning in the mind or it is
spoken out with the tongue."

"Well", said Mr. Moore, "We here in Mississippi haven't got too far
getting our equal rights, but we are all able-bodied men and we fear no
evil. We are ready for the trial. Our aim is to do this thing in a peaceful
way and we will turn the other cheek if we have to. We all must keep a
peaceful mind, no matter what. An angry man is subject to do and say a lot
of biting words and violence into the madness. He will be sorry for when
the fire passes." The whole house went quiet as light even the little

children. Some things seem to say listen, listen, this concerns you too. They listened like rabbits having their ears cocked for danger.

"You know, most people in every generation want their children to have it better than they had it. Better education, homes, jobs and the like. There is nothing wrong with farming and common labor—somebody has to do it. But we have been under this manner too long. It looks like we are going to have it hard here trying to get it better for this generation, let alone the next. We don't have a grain of a mustard seed for integration here", said Aunt Hannah kind of sorrowful-like.

"Aunt Hannah, the Lord said the mustard seed will grow into a big tree; just give it a chance, it will grow", old man Henderson added.

"But this thing been growing for years. Let us tell it, it ain't even stuck its' head out of the ground", Mr. Moore said getting in the conversation again. "White folks think we are kids, everything grows up but us. The good Lord said, be fruitful and multiply, and replenish the earth and subdue it. By these scriptures, God wasn't leaving us out of the things of this world by no means. Man himself has shut his fellow man out. This really gets me. If I can lay with you, surely I can sit down beside you."

"Mr. Moore, have you thought about the laying part like this? Say there once lived a king. This king went out and had a peasant. King meaning white man; peasant meaning Negro woman. One day, the peasant got tired of living apart from the king with all her children she had by him. She got tired of her and her children being his slaves and she got tired of the trifling little things he was giving her and his children. She wanted everything that made this life worth living for. She felt she was as good as he. But to him, it was alright for him to lay with her. But it isn't right for her to enter his kingdom. She strolled by his palace one day. Seeing her with those different colored kids, all of a sudden he realized he had done wrong. He remembered a phrase, you have to reap what you sow. He didn't want this to happen to his kingdom. No matter how wrong he was, he would do everything in his power to prevent this horror happening to his people, rich or poor", Liz said with no offense to her sister. "After all, we are Americans too."

Vada sat very quietly listening to them talk and what Liz had said hit home-base with her. But she knew Liz didn't say words to hurt her, but just to make a point.

153

Larome Wright, a veteran of World War II and the Korean War, got out of the army because of his discontent with a segregated army. Larome put in his dollars' worth, "You know the Negro has fought in all this country's wars to keep this country free and other countries free." His face looked very grave. He stood as if we was in church giving his testimony, twisting his handkerchief in his hand. "I have seen men with their heads shot off, men's eyes shot out, tongues cut out, bodies mangled, so many dead men that the blood ran down like water being poured from a pitcher. The stink is indescribable. Your stomach turns over, you vomit until you think you're going to die yourself." Both ends of mouth sloped down and his eyes looked as though he was living the battles all over again. Everyone in the house got the feeling that death had crept into the house. "These men had cried, sweated, been shot in any part of the body you can imagine. They carried their cross, so to speak, and so did us black folk. They all was fighting for what we were trying to get peacefully, a new birth of freedom", he bellowed. "Every time I think about it, I get mad. Our men out there getting all shot up and killed for the white man to do what he wants to us. It's always nigger you stay in your place. We are the ones keep the fire for freedom burning. It just ain't right. That's all I got to say", Larome Wright's heart bubbled over and this was the first time his friends heard him talk this much, even his wife. He was always the quiet sort.

There was silence. They were all taken off their feet to hear Larome talk like this. If a man of this sort' mind can be triggered to speak out, it's time for the Negro to change his mode of living.

Vada broke the silence, "I have listened to some of your thoughts. I must say I am deeply touched by your feelings on equal rights but there is one thing I can say about the south, you know where you stand down here. The north wears a thin veil over her face. At first you don't see through her. After you've been with her for a while, you can see she is an ugly American too. You hear them say we want you people to have your equal rights and we think you people are entitled to have your rights, but there is always a big—but. But we don't want integration forced down our throats. It takes time for progress. Maybe it does as they say, haste makes waste, but we have waited a long time for equal opportunity. I feel we need integration for the Negro to challenge ourselves and integration to meet the world. But there are some things we do that helps keep this thing at a slow pace. We must cast some beams out of our own eyes!"

154

"What do you mean Vada?" Larome said, speaking out again.

"Well, you see, most Negroes in the north think they have it made, but they haven't. If they would stop and tell themselves that we are all about in the same boat—the northern Negro has one paddle; the southern Negro doesn't have any. If the north Negro would offer more of the right hand instead of the left, they—ain't—got it better either. I must confess we have gained a lot of material things with some integration. Believe me, we really had to scuffle to make ends meet and there is still Uncle Tom. He hasn't gone anywhere. He's still all over. You know, the white man did the greatest brainwashing job in the world. Many of slaveries, ya, sum's and fears are still with a lot of us. That's a hindrance. There is the I don't care bunch, the loud-mouths on the job, in the homes, on the street, on the buses. There are the get-eveners—I'm going to get even with the white man up north for what the white man did to me down south. That's not right. We can't do evil for evil, expecting to get our rights."

All ears were open to what Vada was saying. Some didn't agree with her, but no one interrupted her thoughts.

"There were places that used to be open to us; they are closed now on account of the way some of us acted, acting like monkeys as if it were our passion. We don't have to do a monkey-shine to be seen. When we get a job, we try our best in doing what the big boss says on the job, not because the white man down here is a slave-driver, but because we feel it's our duty to do as he says. Sometimes he will get smart too, but most of us come to reason here. But when some of us get up north and we get a little more liberties, instead of coming to reason, we curse, sometimes coming to blows. Not that we can't be wrong and pretty nasty. There are blessings in doing things in a nice way. But, every time we mess up on the job, they are laying for us like snakes laying for frogs. That gives the white man an excuse to fire us and put a white man in our place. You see, the white man is coming from the country and down south and overseas, just like the colored man—he is going north, east and west, like we are. Lots of them are unskilled and uneducated too. They are taking the jobs that they used to call the black man's job. Only the lowest and the poorest would take such jobs. We really have to fight for our rights in all things. And another thing, anything the black man makes money out of, please believe me, your white brother will be in it too. And if you don't watch him, he will steal it right out from under your nose. There are some that say we should take up arms, really fight for our rights. We'd probably get the weapons

155

from the devil. Fighting with weapons, we would be in a real struggle for freedom. We have to stop, look and listen and cast beams out of our own eyes."

"Miss Vada, what makes you think that white folks shit don't stink. They do every sinful thing we do. I can say most of them try to hide and cover up their sins the same as we do. Miss Vada, you talk like white folks are gods and angels. They ain't no better than I am." There was a murmur at this young girl's remarks.

"Why! Earnestine, you shouldn't talk like that." The girl's mother said, sounding very embarrassed.

"Mama, I heard you say that many times."

"I don't care what you heard me say. That don't give you the mind to say what I do. You ain't grown yet", Earnestine's mother growled.

Getting into what Vada was talking about, a young lady said, "white folks get away with more because they are in authority. When you get right down to it, we all need a good housecleaning. What makes me mad is when one of us messes up, they put all of us in one class—no good."

"Getting back to what Liz had to say", old Mother Washington said with the look on her face of a sweet little old fat lady with rose brown skin showing wrinkles, "I think we need integration in all things because of both races. The black and white is messing around more and more. Some are marrying and living with each other. They's bound to have babies. Integration will take away the look of embarrassment for the mixed kids. But I think when the white woman and the black man get too hot and heavy together, that will be the killing of the goose that laid the golden egg. I can have your black woman anytime I want. But don't you mess with my white woman."

"Mother Washington, you sure know what to say", someone in the room said. "And too, it will take care of the Negro that wants to be white, without sneaking and hiding in fear of his fellowman telling someone he or she is black and it will take care of the job and housing and public places. A lot on both sides think integration means to sex-a-grate. As the old saying goes, the white man has left enough of his leavings that a black man shouldn't want a white woman. They say the black woman has been so misused that she ought not want to look at a white man." Old Mother Washington claps her right fingers into her left, rolled her thumbs outside in. She added these words, "This saying don't mean that the white man won't reap the wild seeds. We all have to reap what we sow."

"You are so right Mother Washington", Brother Jackson said. "You know what they said too—we got brains we ain't used yet", Brother Jackson chuckled.

A very tall man about sixty made his way to the living room where the cock and the hens, who seemed to know so much, were seated. He crossed his heavy long legs, leaned on the door facing, speaking in a typical southern Negro voice. The sound of his voice broke the laughter and the talking. "I don't understand the way you all feel about this mess. As for me, them white folks can keep every damn thing y'all niggers is talking about fighting for. I like the way it is now. I likes to be with my own peoples."

"Pea White, you talk like a fool."

"Wait, Moore. No one butted in whiles you was talking and I ain't no fool. Now you shut your mouth whiles I have my say", Pea White was yellow and ugly and mean with it. "I got nothing against white folks and I ain't in love with them either. I work with them and for them all my life. That Mr. Duncan's foreman, Mr. Josh, is the one that made me know I had enough guts to do something on pride and respect. That's the reason I got that patch and the worker I have now. Them poor white folk, over yonder hill, used to come and visit with us. Me and my woman would drop in on them every now and then. Since this mess started, they don't come around anymore. The cold peace is gone. White folks look on us niggers here like we's vultures, ready to leap on us if we make that right or wrong. I'm so jumpy nowadays I feel like a frog. I go along with Mr. Duncan in a way. I sure thought he would be for integration. Only God knows the heart. All I ask of them whites is to give our black children the same education and same jobs and a decent hospital. They can keep all the rest of that mess, as far as I's concerned. I's raised and educated nine without all this mess", Pea White had his say and he kept his beliefs.

Vada took in more of Pea White's small talk than she could stand. Saying in a voice that controlled her anger, but with firm words, not talking low, "I'm so glad not too many Negroes take the stand that you are taking, Pea White. If our fore-parents could hear your kind of talk, they would quiver in their graves. I think they would be pleased the way we are conducting ourselves. They wouldn't dare take the chance we are taking now because of fear. Our fore-parents didn't struggle, fight, sweat and die in vain. We may not gain the victory today, but there is a tomorrow." When she spoke that last sentence, life and the pursuit of happiness seemed to pop into the house like a crocus blooming out of a wintery snow. The faces in the house beamed with smiles. There was a sparkle in their eyes. There was a murmur of words "Girl you sure know what to say."

"You sure is telling the truth."

"Tell him a thing or two."

Pea White opened his mouth to say something, but Hattie Mae beat him to the words. "Mr. Pea White, aren't you tired of paying double for everything you buy, last to be hired, the first to be fired, fed up with unemployment, decayed housing, rat-living and the sound of 'black get back', being discriminated against wherever you turn. We are not trying to move them out like they did the Indians. We just want justice. One of these days we will note in Mississippi. We have been discriminated against too long in a rich country."

Pea White stood with that look on his face that said, I's mad and I's ain't mad. He didn't know what to say. He stood rolling his blood-shot eyes at the folks in the house. All of a sudden he put on his hat and yelled to his wife to come on, "We don't have to take this mess." They left without saying good-bye.

"This is the first time I ever saw him not having the last word", laughed Mr. Moore and others.

"Wait Mr. Moore, let's not pat one another on the back for telling the ignorant the truth", Vada remarked.

"We sure have to do a lot of praying and marching. Sit-ins and sit-outs to get our rights down here, I guess just about everywhere else too. There are a lot of states like it is here. You can't stoop and eat or use the restroom. You buy gas but you can't go to a motel or hotel anytime you think you need a rest. I just can't see how white folk think. This is a need of a people not a want. Well, I guess we will be all on one accord one of these days", Mr. Thomas said shaking his head.

"Brother Thomas", Preacher Jackson said, "There are a lot of good white folks in Mississippi. But they keep talking about their heritage. The only thing their heritage left them, was evil thoughts in their mind. We all thought that Mr. Sam's boss, Mr. Duncan, would be the man who would stand up for us black folk. He has done some mighty nice things for us black folk, mighty nice. You know some people are just good-hearted and I think he was just that way and, too, I think there are a lot of kind white people in this country. But they don't want to believe that most Negroes are living in an undemocratic world without equal rights in many things. This is one reason this integration problem is not being solved in a family manner, and another reason the problem is not being solved in a family manner, is when the high courts handed down the great order that black and white must go to school together, if that President Eisenhower had the respect for the law of the land and any respect for the Negro, he would give a fireside chat that would surpass Mr. Lincoln's Gettysburg Address. Since President Eisenhower didn't speak out for the laws of the under God, many whites have shown what that president showed, no respect for the laws of the land, that's all I have to say."

"I'll say Amen to that", said Mr. Moore. All said Amen.

There was a strong Amen in the house. The house went silent. Vada rose to kick off the discussion again, but Deacon Wells beat her to the draw. "Vada, I don't mean to cut you short, but I just like to get a word in. We's been taking stock of ourselves. I's been listening to y'all talk. Y'all done talked about this, that and other. We are forgetting who's birthday is coming up soon, our Lord and Saviour Jesus Christ. I"s wondering how many of us is on speaking terms with the good Lord? If we's saved, and we believe that God hears and answers prayer, we ain't got nothing in this world to worry about. Y'all down here on this earth trying to get what man got on paper. What we all need, black folk and white folk, is to get what God got in the good book. Where is y'all's faith?" said Mr. James Mack.

"Now wait a minute, Mack," barked Preacher Jackson, "Are you trying to tell us we haven't got the faith in God? You are making a mighty big statement there. I know you don't know what you are talking about. I know I have the faith."

"The way y'all act and talk says so. Y'all's faith sounds so weak. In Mark 11:22-23, Jesus answers, 'He said unto them, have faith in God. For verily I say unto you, that whosoever shall say unto this mount, be thou removed, and be thou cast into the sea; and shall not doubt in his heart, but shall believe that those things which he saith shall come to pass; he shall have whatsoever he saith.' What things you so ever desire, when you pray, believe that you receive them. Y'all's faith sure sounds weak to me", said Mr. Mack.

"But Brother Mack, I know our faith ain't weak. It's them white brother's belief is weak. They's just quenching the spirit. That's all.

They know right from wrong. Some folks get's too grown" Preacher Jackson said.

All ears were cocked to hear the duel of words. The Deacon, Brother Mack and Preacher Jackson were all sitting in the living room. They were sitting a little way from each other. Those in the other rooms crowded in the two doorways that led to the living room trying to hear words of wisdom between the judge and the judger.

"That may be true, Deacon Wells, but what happened, we let everyone hear us. That's alright if others help. I know the old folks got restless at times. But something within said, be still and know that I am God. They would kick the devil out and go back to the great power of prayer and wait on the Lord. Their prayer was answered without sound brass and tinkling cymbal."

"Deacon, you're forgetting these times. God helps those that help themselves. This is a need. If we don't throw our weight around and force them white folks into some kind of action, they will take another hundred years filling the Constitution for us. That Civil War was a whole lot tinkling cymbals and sounding brass" Preacher Jackson said laughing.

"Deacon Wells, "I'm with you", said Jean Amay, a young woman of thirty and mother of six. She stood in the doorway that led to the living room. Squirming around in her arms, a little one of nine months. "If you are a true Christian, white or black or any race, you pray and wait on the Lord. As one singer put it, he might not come when you want him, but he is right on time", Jean Amay spoke with a very tender voice. "Most of you know the Lord has been better to us than we have been to ourselves. We all know the Lord is a way maker. He's our burden-bearer. I feel like Deacon, he'll fight our battle if we just keep still. In the years before this mess started, we progressed faster than any race under the sun with all the evil underhand and misuse. We thank God for that. Jesus is the hope of the world", Jean Amay said turning out of the room with tears running down her face.

Sister Wells got up from where she was sitting in the living room, looking more like an Irish washer woman than a Negro. "Life is bitter and life is sweet. Sometimes we have to take the bitter to get the sweet, Amen. The Negro used to have joy that was unspeakable. We were burdened with life's cares seemingly unjustified but we laugh, cause we had Jesus and that was enough, Amen. Children we ain't sending up our thanks to God like we used to. You know children, we would be just walking along, out of the blue sky, we would say, thank you Jesus because he has been so good to us black folk, Amen. Nowadays we got all kinds of funny beliefs. Every time I go to a church conference, I hear more and more of this off-the-wall tale on the Bible, Amen. Children, we ain't sending our children to Sunday School and morning and evening service like we used to do. And another thing, children ain't peeping in the window to see the Holy Ghost. Children, we have to hold onto God's unchanging hand. We gots lots of muddy waters to cross before we get that piece of the pie, Amen."

After the strong Amen in the house, as we say, another country was heard from, a New Yorker by the way of Mississippi—old Mother Washington's son, Edward Charles Washington. In Mississippi, he was just called Edward Charles by whites and Negroes, even though he was over fifty years old. But in New York, he was known as the prominent Mr. Edward Charles Washington. He looked like his mother but he had more of the Jewish look. He stood up in the crowded living room. He spoke very distinctly without the southern accent. "Hope you people understand that when this integration business gets straightened out, we have a whole lot of catching up. In that education line, we have to wake up our brains and learn how to make money. You see with these servants or servant jobs most of us do now, we got paid every month on the first and the fifteen. We got our little money and that is that. To make our dreams come true, we really have to work extremely hard. I know what I'm talking about. Some of you know I have a small paper in New York. I go to bed working. I wake up working. What I am getting at is we really have to put our talents to work. One thing we have to learn is to obey each other as boss. When the white boss is over us, we obey. This one hard thing we must learn to be successful. You know what I am talking about. That's all I've got to say."

"I'd like to get a word in", another voice said in the room. That voice was none other than the Mr. John Holmes Smith, another New Yorker by the way of Mississippi. Ed and John always came home around Christmas. They would stop off in Tennessee to visit some folk John knew, then on to Mississippi to visit Ed's mother. "You know the way these whites talk like we haven't done anything to make this world a better place. All we are trying to do is to open the door to put our minds at rest so we can do more in making this world a better place and be the true American family. Don't forget we have to learn our history. We have done many great things in music, inventions, medicine, science, so forth and so on. We have to get more and more into the political world. Come on Ed, let's go outside and see if Jessie's got those chitterlings done. Nowadays, when we come home, it's not much fun anymore—that real down-home fun. It's just melting in that conversation called integration. I am getting tired of discussing the subject. Come on Ed, let's hit the cool."

Standing in front of Vada was a little boy about six or seven wide-eyes, dark brown skin, saying in a very concerned way, with a frown on his face, seeming to get straight what he wanted to say. He finally said, "Miss Vada, just what do us colored really want?"

"What do we colored people want?" Looking down at his solemn face, "Young man we are not asking for the world. The Negro wants the same in all things as our white brother—in education, housing, jobs, public accommodations and the same human respect with love and dignity the white man expects from all men. Slavery infested a sore that no other country has between two people. But without this sore, this nation wouldn't be the country it is today. We and our fore-parents helped bare this country's pain with our sweat, blood and tears. We are not looking for our inheritance, as power or greed, but just being part of the great American family in all things. All the Negro's life, he has only tasted the true American way that most white folk lived and enjoyed in sadness and in love and in injustice—do you understand what I said?"

"I think I understand, Miss Vada."

An old feeble voice came from the kitchen, "Miss Vada, this dignity and respect, I think I's been respected as a man in Mississippi. I stay in my place, as far as white folk is and as far as my own peoples is. I think this dignity is within a man as far as I can figure out. Respect comes from you and another man. It's all in the way you carry yourself. I hope out of this comes a bunch of people that will know God. But I see down the road, we never belonged to the club. We's all will be together, yet apart."

"Yes another thing will keep us out of the club," barked Edward Charles, "Is—if we don't have money, we have to look like it. We go buy a scrumptious house or not so fine house, nice car in a nice neighborhood. About this house, we sit on the front porch and eat, lay on it, comb our hair, play in the front yard till all the grass is gone, then we take the drapes and tie them in a big knot. The front of anyone's home should be for beauty and self-pride. In fact, the front and the back should be your pride and joy. What I'm getting at is, they say one monkey don't stop the show but as far as the white man is concerned, that's all it takes, is one monkey to make all black people look to them less than heathens. But we are not all alike."

Vada and the rest of the house didn't add words to Edward Charles' little bit.

A voice in the house cleared his throat very loudly. All the guests in the house seemed to drop what they were thinking and focused their attention on him. Him being Booker T. Jefferson. Booker T. had been back home in Mississippi about five years. He lived in St. Louis about twenty years. He was a big-timer, done everything, seen a lot of living and gone a lot of places, made fairly good as far as a black man and spent the money as fast as he made it. The words he was about to say to the folks in the house, if someone had told him years ago the words he was about to say, he would have called them a liar and cursed with words of the devil. "I'd like to get my two cents in. Y'all might think I'm crazy to say what I think about us. To me, slavery was a blessing in Mississippi and I don't think as many colored folk would be in this country today according to the number of true Africans in this country. I know slavery was a bitter pill. We wasn't forced to take this bitter pill for nothing. The black man was brought here for the same reason. The white man was brought here to build a great empire and to exercise his gifts and to believe in one God. Not to keep the old ways of Africa, but to do great things, to serve a true and living God and help make this country what it is today. The promise they make in the Constitution, they got so high and mighty, they decided to keep us servants of servants. But we must keep the faith,. As they say, the mind is a terrible thing to waste, we will overcome someday."

"I say Amen to that", Johnny Bea said. Johnny Bea had six kids. Two in high school, the other four in lower grades. They were at the party. "They are so afraid they won't get to be kinds and queens. This integration business has frightened some to hate. There is the money part. Money puts most of them in equal classes. I don't care how much money we get, that don't give us equal rights either..." Johnny Bea said sitting down, looking kind of sad.

A feeble voice, that of old Mrs. Gladney, going on 90, heard and saw a lot of happenings in and around Mississippi. She had never been out of the state. She had her little say, "When this thing gets straightened out, they will still make us black folk pay and don't y'all forget, we are afraid to venture and scared to adventure, always scared that the white man will steal or cheat us out of our talents and creation. I guess all our lives we been haunted by fear. Fear of spooks and ghosts. We can't hang onto old fogey-ism. We are in the wrong time of life to hand onto such crazy notions. If God be for us, who can be against us. Nobody but the devil. I hope to vote one time before I die. Vada, the floor is yours—seems to be the speaker of the evening."

"Oh well, I don't know everything but I am somewhat like Dad. When I get started talking, I don't know when to stop. I teach in an integrated school. It kind of worried me—how did the black children feel about going to school with the white kids. Their feelings didn't occur to me at first. I only thought of getting our equal rights. I asked some of the children how they felt about integration. Some said they felt at home, other wish they were back in their black school. Some say it will take some time to get used to. In a way, I thought they were being blessed, then I asked my son how he felt."

David dropped his head in a somewhat shameful manner, wishing his mother hadn't brought him into the subject.

"David said he feared something bad was going to happen. It seems you could see hate on some of their faces, but some too, did not care at all. They too were feeling up and down. I told him, he who overcometh fear, conquers all. We must keep our trust in God."

"Hew, hew, mercy me, we must keep the faith. If the good Lord don't hear us, the devil sure will. The one thing that's going to kill the goose that will lay the golden egg is when them black boys and them white gals start messing around with each other, everything will be alright until that mess starts. They can mess with your women, don't mess with mine. And another thing, money is the root of all evil", a voice said somewhere in the room.

No one in the room commented on what was just said. But one said, "Man, you's sure telling the truth. I knows one thing, we's Americans too."

Vada took up the subject again. "We are asking a greater part of the heart than lots of us think. They didn't have it easy neither. They had to endure trials and tribulations but in a different way from our struggle. They think they built this country all by themselves. We had a big hand in it too. I know they have broken our hearts in so many ways. Trying to obtain our equal rights with love and law, they have become so self-righteous, they can not face the real facts, we are being mistreated very unjustly. We must become a part of that heart that says freedom, liberty and justice for all. If not, it will be just a myth on paper." Just then, Jessie yelled in the back door, breaking her thought, "When is y'all going to eat? If I heat these chitterlings one more time, they won't be fitting to eat. Y'all done talked enough talk on that conversation. Come on, let's have some fun."

Liz surprised Vada with a pre-Christmas celebration. Vada had not celebrated Christmas in such manner since she had left home. Up north, they didn't wish their friends afar Merry Christmas with fireworks. The fireworks were also used to scare away evil spirits. The bright glow lit up the dark night. They sang merry songs of Christmas. To Vada and the rest, it was the happiest they had in a long time.

The day came for Vada to go home. There was much crying between Liz and Vada. They cried so much they almost had Jessie and David in tears. Jessie had to put his foot down and tell them they had to stop all that bawling. They could always visit one another. Jessie went outside to see if his tic tic was going so he could take Vada to say good-bye to her father and mother and to spend a little time with them. But Jessie's old car just wouldn't start. Vada called Andrew. Andrew gave permission to use one of the cars. Poor old Sam drive the ninety miles to Liz' place like a teenager. No one gave a thought to Sam being 80 and he might be tired of driving, but Sam didn't complain. Vada was sort of sad to take David back home to have Christmas for he had many Christmases with Liz and Jessie. But she knew it was best. On the way to get Vada, Sam stopped by and told old Josh to spread the word that he was bringing his daughter by for all to see.

On their way back, Vada talked to her father about some of the things that were said at the party. "Dad, Andrew was hardly mentioned or some of the things that were said in his speeches. I just knew he would stand up for equal rights. If it hadn't been for integration and if he had won the governorship, it might not have been a giant step forward, but if the governor stands up for the law of the land, most law-abiding citizens will follow."

"Daughter, we all thought he would stand up for integration. When Mr. Andrew came home from winning that primary election, I knew he meant everything he said. I said to myself, fool, this is Mississippi. I didn't care how good he is, it don't make no-never-mind. But it would make all of us black folk in Mississippi feel mighty good to know he thought so much of us."

"Oh well, we'll overcome some day." A large crowd had gathered outside the commissary. Vada's coming to the farm was like a hero's homecoming. Vada felt she didn't deserve such a goodly welcome and good-bye. The day was sort of chilly but they all wanted to see Mr. Sam's daughter they thought so high-toned that she never wanted to live their kind of life anymore. All of Sam's children had come home many times over the years, but this was the first time Vada had ever come home. She wouldn't be home now if it wasn't for the happenings. They all knew the story. But they still wanted to see Mr. Sam's daughter, the daughter Sam talked about so much. All that knew her were pleased to see her. Those who didn't know her were happy to know she had made something out of herself. The farmhands, who knew her, had great big smiles on their faces and there was much kissing on the cheek. The farmhands who didn't know her, there was much hand shaking. Vada had her mink coat thrown over her shoulder. One of the little girls in the crowd rubbed her hand over the coat. The mother said to the child to keep her hands off of the coat. Vada said freely, "Oh it's alright. I remember when I used to fee Mrs. Duncan's furs every chance I got." Vada could see most of those she had grown up with had left to find Heaven on earth or just moved to other parts of the state. There weren't too many faces she really knew such as Josh, some more of the old folk and a few of the kids she grew up with. Sam and Pursa didn't do much visiting during the week. Sunday was their day. They had great times visiting the farm and going to church and visiting neighbors. Sometimes at Sunday service and at Wednesday night prayer meeting, Sam and Pursa would tell about the nice presents Vada sent them. Sam always wore the diamond watch and Pursa her diamond ring. Sometimes Sam would say, "She wanted to buy us a car. What do we need a car for? We got three cars in the garage now." Sam spoke of the Duncan cars as if they were his. Sam felt so proud showing off his daughter. She looked so refined and successful. Sam was happy as a bee in a field of pink clover having her meeting first one and then another. Looking around at the faces she knew, Joe Charles came to mind. He had gone on before. Careless living in the big city and TB met him on the road of destruction. Joe Charles hated farm life and Mississippi. Leaving the hate, he never reached the point of success. She let Joe Charles drop from her mind.

Vada pulled her mink coat close around her, keeping out the cool breeze that shipped through the thin blue dress she wore. "It was nice seeing and meeting all of you. Sorry to leave so soon. I'd like to spend some time with dad and mother before I leave."

Pearly Mae grabbed and hugged her real tight. "We understand. It has been a long time, girl. Be sure to come back", Pearly Mae said with a smile on her face.

"I'll be back. Look for me this summer. I truly have enjoyed being home. You all have to visit me in Chicago."

"We will do just that V. Sure wish you had more time. Sho enjoyed seeing you once more and again", Mr. Coffee said with a long smile.

"V", old Jonah said, "I don't think I'll get way up to Chicago; that's a kind of far piece for an old man like me."

"Mr. Jonah, I would love to have you visit me and my family and see what the rest of the world looks like. Dad is thinking about visiting me when the Duncan's take their vacation. They will be glad to have you come with them."

"Sure Jonah, if we go we will be glad to have you come along to see how those northern folk live", Sam said with a big 'Ki Ki'.

"Thank you for the invite", old Jonah spit a mess of tobacco juice on the ground and knocked his battered black hat to one side of his head. "V, I got to think about going that far."

"If you wish to come, you are welcome at any time", Vada said, getting in the car.

The ones that didn't know her personally had gone back to their cares after wishing her Merry Christmas. But the ones that knew her stood smiling, waving good-bye and a hardy Merry Christmas, with come again.

"See y'all around", Sam said driving off with a big smile on his face. Vada waved until the Cadillac turned out of sight.

Sam took his daughter by the school where she had spent many happy hours at learning and play. On the Duncan farm, one thing one had to do, black or white, was get a learning. The little wooden church stood out like a rock. It hadn't changed a bit. With a little snow, it would make a good print for a Christmas card. Vada viewed the church. She thought about the Wednesday night prayer meeting. She remembered going to church several times during the week and three times on Sunday. Nowadays, she only gets to Sunday morning services, sometimes to an evening program. Thinking how far she had gotten away from the church, she went every

167

Sunday. These modern times, you just don't have the time, besides people have more to do nowadays than singing and praying and praising the Lord. She threw the church out of her mind. Looking kind of melancholy, she said, "Dad I hated Mississippi as much as Joe Charles, but I never let on. That is one reason I never came back. Looking back to the farm, I hated the farm and the house-work. Those things were like filth to me. Looking at the common things now, they hold some of life's fondest dreams. In the country-life, God is everywhere—in the wide open spaces, you can see, in the trees, birds and the bees and in the good earth. God seems to be all around the country-life. In city living, there are only a few things there where you feel God's presence, in the wind, rain, sun, ice and the snow. In the city man is everywhere. We can't live with the common things. They look bitter—then again they look so sweet and precious to me now. We need integration to wake up those brains we haven't used yet, more on the professional side of life." There was sadness in her voice. "Looks like Mississippi and many other states want to hold on to their way of life no matter what the law says."

"All I got to say is us colored folk kind of look at this injustice done to us in a spirit light, our cross to bare. We have to watch as well as pray. Daughter, I hope this thing don't steal our souls and I hope I get to vote one time before I die. My concern is really for the lost, sin-sick souls. Get up Cadillac; let's show this pretty girl her hometown."

Cruising down the highway, Vada could see time had made a change. "Dad, whatever happened to the Mitchell's and the Potter's?"

"Oh, the Potter's and the Mitchell's sold out to the few factories in town. This is the reason for this division over there. There is another mess of houses across town."

"Do they have any colored workers in the factory?"

"They have a few. You see, Mr. Duncan is a smart man. You know he always paid good. He paid the workers more than the factories. When the factories moved here, he started giving them half salary in the winter months."

"Whatever happened to the Carey's and the Smith's?"

"We hear from them all the time. Both families and all of their children are all in California and they are doing fine. You remember they both had nine kids. We hear from most of the workers that lived on the farm and many of our friends that moved away. We get Christmas cards from all over the states", Sam said joyfully.

"You know, I bet I wouldn't recognize too many of the kids I grew up with. It seems so long ago. Dad, is this uptown Braidwood?"

"Sho is baby girl. All these things came after the factories were here for a while."

"If this town looked like this when I was growing up, I wouldn't wait for Saturday to come to town. I would put my feet in the road everyday. Just look, supermarket, five and dime, laundromat, so many places to shop for clothing, office buildings, jewelry shops—my goodness, so many different places." Vada was so excited in her hometown, she stuck her head out the window as though she couldn't see enough with her sight on the inside of the car. "I just can't believe my eyes."

"Daughter you sound just like Mrs. Duncan when I first brought her up here. She was like a child seeing fairyland for the first time. You should have seen her before she died. She always wore her hair in a ball. She got that white in the latest style. She looked ten years younger", Sam said smiling from ear to ear. "Pursa said she looked like a glamour gal. She really got herself together to go campaigning."

"I can imagine how pretty she looked."

"For a long time, all Mrs. Duncan would do was go up to the farm. She helped keep the books in order, fooled around about a couple hours then back to the house. She stayed in that old house like a bird in a cage. When Mr. Andrew was nominated to run for governor, she was like a young horse in spring. When she came home that day, she looked like a wilted head of lettuce. She was tired and disgusted. I carried her up to her bedroom. I called Doc Sliver. As she lay there, she looked up at me, her tired blue eyes full with tears. "Sam", she said, "Is this my son? What kind of monstrous power does he want? Does he think he's some kind of God that wants people to keep bowing down to him?" She talked very slow. "Sam, when I heard some of his speeches, I thought it was all political talk, but when he was going to kill for what he wanted to be and as we say, keep your niggers in your place..."

Doc came and he sensed it was her heart. He wanted to put her in the hospital but she didn't want to hear of that. I kind of felt sorry for Doc. He was kind of sweet on her. He was the only one that came to the house. He knew she was leaving us. He stood looking at her with tears in his eyes. He tried to stop her from talking, but she kept right on.

Vada listened with a sad look on her face.

169

"Sam, I hated this thing integration too. But I made up my mind this integration was this nation's business. If niggers want to grow up, it's about time. I think if they didn't try to get equal rights, they would be crazy. If whites were Negroes, they would have had equal rights long ago. As white folks, if we don't stand up for democracy for people of other colors, what are we standing for?"

"I am very disappointed in Andrew too. You never know how a person really feels within their heart until you touch the thorns underneath the rose. Then you know how bad the rose can hurt."

"All I got to say is this mess sure did stir his heart in a bad way. Still in all, he's a good man. Cadillac, ease on down the road. We's almost home."

Sam and Vada found Terence and Andrew decorating the front of the house. Sam got out of the car, walking in a fast pace with Vada trailing behind him. "Mr. Andrew, what y'all doing with all dis here mess?" Sam said in a demanding voice.

"Sam, we're fixing up the place for Christmas. Don't you think it looks pretty?" Andrew said kind of smiling.

Sam kind of stood back a bit, as if to get a good look at the decorations. He knocked his hat to the side and scratched his head. Andrew knew whenever Sam knocked his hat to one side, his answer would come by and by.

"I think the decorations make the place look just beautiful. I like the way the greens are arranged over the door, with the gold balls and angels with that red velvet swag. And those trees with the gold angels with the big white ball with all that silver dust. The tiny colored lights will show up the whole place."

"Thanks Vada, I'm glad you like it", Terence said smiling, "We sure worked on it hard enough."

"I like it too. We haven't had this place spruced up like this in years", Pursa said looking at the door and then the trees.

They all stood around looking at the decorations. All of a sudden Sam's mouth flew open, "Mr. Andrew, did you go back yonder and cut down my trees?"

"No Sam, I didn't cut down your trees", Andrew said laughing at Sam. Terence and Vada sort of smiled too at the way Sam spoke of his trees. "We bought them uptown. Now Sam, don't you think this place looks Christmas-like for the first time in years?"

Sam went up on the porch, examining the trees, looking from one to the other. "Trees sure do look alike. Y'all got one in the house, ain't that enough?" Sam started smiling, shaking his head, "If they ain't my trees, I think the place looks pretty, mighty pretty. Is there anything I can do?"

"I think not Sam. Thanks a lot for asking. Terence and I will clean up the mess. You and Vada have a lot to talk about before she leaves. We ate breakfast in the kitchen. You can sweep off the table for Pursa."

They all got a laugh out of Sam. As far back as Andrew could remember, Sam always swept off the kitchen table. Andrew had to shake his head about the tales Sam told about his dog Trout. Terence, Andrew's wife, found life in the south a lot different from the little town in Connecticut from whence she came. In the little town, there were very few Negroes. Race was no issue. After moving down south with her aunt, Terence didn't go out much. Whenever she went on a painting spree, she was always by herself. Going about in this way of life, Terence didn't feel the real southern way of life. After dating Andrew for about three years and then marrying Andrew, Terence got the real face of the southern way of living. She saw in Andrew the love he had for Sam and Pursa and all his workers and they had the same kind of love for him. But underneath this love, she got the feeling that the Negro was just a child or a nobody in the sight of most of the whites. You are my illegitimate child, I bore you, bred you and I raised you up by my hand. You will always be in my hand. Sometimes she saw a cold hard hate, then again there was that laughable kind of love she saw and felt between the black and white. She saw the Negro as a servant child—no matter how old you get, you just ain't grown up enough to do as you please or go wherever you please. The black child says I'm many years old. I'm big enough to go for myself and do as I please, go where I please, buy what I want, live where I want. Terence sometimes saw love in the eyes and hate in the heart. Terence found understanding in Pursa and comfort in her singing. She was amused by Sam, just as Andrew was. Terence loved the different way of life, with its' bold, naked way.

Sam and Pursa and Vada had gathered in the kitchen. Pursa was doing the dishes. Sam took the broom, swept off the table and then the floor. Vada put her coat on one of the kitchen chairs. She then took the towel off her mother's shoulder and started drying the dishes. "Mother, I'm really enjoying myself. I kind of hate to go home. Down here is far change from Chicago. Here you are on the go, but more at a slow pace. I wish you and dad had come to the party."

"Baby, your dad and me is old and we just ain't up to going much and we's still upset over the happenings. Glad you is having a nice time. What do you think about downtown?"

"I was shocked at the change, so many places to shop, but you no eatie here." They all laughed. "Mother, I wish you and dad would leave this place", Vada said sadly. "You two are old now. The least I can do for you is take care of you in your last days. I know what you are going to say—this is home. But you can find home someplace else."

"We knows that baby", Pursa said harshly.

"Dad, you and mother can stay at our place in the country. You can have chickens, a garden, pigs if you want. You can have anything you want. Besides, Andrew is married now. You two have worked hard all of your lives. It's time to take a rest. If you pass away, they have to get someone else."

"Daughter, we's knows all that. This is still home to us. This little work we does around here keeps us from getting stiff. If we left this old place, homesickness would kill us", Sam said in a somewhat forward voice.

"If you two are staying here in hope of outliving Andrew for an inheritance, you can't outlive him", Vada said in a cold sort of way, trying to vex them into leaving.

"Daughter, we's ain't waiting around for money. Can't you get it in your head, this is home to us. It ain't Heaven, but home. Another thing—sin is everywhere. And another thing, we's been sixty-five a long time ago. We get a check every month and we have money of our own, and another thing, Mrs. Duncan left us ten big ones a piece."

"You old rascal, you didn't tell me that!" Vada said smiling putting up the last dish.

"You didn't ask", Sam said sarcastically. "Mr. Andrew done gave us the check already. We done put it in the bank."

"Well, I be a dog with shoes on. God bless the people that give."

Looking straight at Vada, Pursa said, "Mr. and Mrs. Duncan and Andrew was fair with us. The will read if we died, the money would be equally divided between all you children." Pursa said in a voice that said I hope that straightens you out.

"Well all I have to say is that I am surprised and shocked, but it was awfully nice of them. Wait til Liz and boys hear about this. I know I haven't been home in years and I know I haven't seen you two once in years. I often wondered why you only came that one time to visit me— that one time?" Vada said pacing the floor now. "I would just like to make an Amen for me not coming home. Come and stay, at least three months."

"Ha, ha if you get us to stay three months, you would lock us in your place. We would have to break out and walk all the way back to Mississippi", Sam fell out laughing at his remarks.

"Ah, Daddy, how can you think of such things?"

"Baby, Mama knows you mean well", Pursa said sitting in one of the kitchen chairs. "You haven't been selfish in a way. You sent us nice things you called every now and then. I think you done found out for yourself there ain't no Heaven on earth for us blacks. Me and your father built our lives around God. God has been good to us down here and we thank God for it. Baby, Mama wouldn't trade all the shacks in Mississippi for all the slums and mansions up north where they say things are somewhat better. You see daughter, we got Jesus and that's enough. About us visiting you that one time, we seen you was married and living high on the hog. You was doing alright for yourself. We didn't see no reason to visit some more." Pursa really didn't say the real reason they didn't visit anymore. The real reason is they thought Vada had gotten pretty persnickety and she couldn't be bothered with them. Looking at her now, she sure would hurt her feelings if she had told her the real reason.

"Let's forget about you two leaving. Mother you and dad will visit every now and then, won't you?"

"Now daughter, you's doing some good thinking. We will visit. Let me tell you this last story why we can't leave this place. You see, Baby, my folks was in slavery on this plantation. My fore-parents picked cotton on this place and we did too. Pursa's family came a bit later. With the vegetables, we have seen some hard times farming. The summers with not, no rain. Old man Duncan called me and some of the other farmhands together. Looked like we had to eat syrup, cornbread, side-back and wild greens for a while. You kids ate a lot of that stuff. Liz sure could make good cornbread. You kids not only liked cornbread, but you kids were hungry. Thanks to be God, he showed us many great ideas about farming." Vada always thought the reason they ate so much cornbread was because they liked it. Now she knew, it was hunger.

"Mother, I believe I'll take a walk down to the house", Vada said getting bored with so much talk of the past which she had heard time and time again. She also longed for her husband and friends.

"Baby, sit and talk with your folks. It's been a long time since we seen each other."

"I'm sorry Mother. I didn't mean any harm. I just wanted to see the old place just one more time."

"The old place is still the same, the same old path, same old things in the house except for the curtains you sent not too long ago. You looked at the place when you first came home. It will be sitting like that til the day we die. When you and your husband come back this spring, you can look and talk til your heart is content."

"Daughter, me and some of the farmhands been getting some big catches at the lake. Remember the days we used to fish at the lake, we got some big catches then too."

"Do I remember. Some were a foot long." They laughed. "What I like to know is how do you keep the grass so green?" Vada said trying to keep the conversation from going flat.

"Well I tell you. I use—I think I hear Trout at the door." Sam got up and let the dog in. "Daughter look at that dog, skinny, dirty, wet, cold— he must have swimmed the lake to get back home. He's been gone a month this time. Musta gone all over Mississippi looking for a gal. Dog, you know what? I's going to buy you a wife for your Christmas present."

"Alright Dad. Maybe he likes running around the country looking for a gal", Vada said kind of laughing at her father.

"He might be a long distance man, but I doubt it. He needs a wife. I thought he would be around for me to talk to when your mother got her tail-feathers up and he would take back to me. All that dog wants is a gal", Sam said giving Trout two cans of dog food. Look at that dog, he's too tired to say thank you. He will sleep around for three or four days, then off he go. They say a dog is man's best friend, but this dog is his own. We will go right tomorrow and get him a wife."

"Think that will suit him just fine", Pursa said smiling.

Vada turned her head and had a good silent laugh at her father and mother talking about a dog needing a wife. Trout had stretched along the other fireplace in the kitchen and had gone dead to sleep.

Just then, Terence stumbled into the kitchen holding her stomach. Pursa shouted with excitement, "What wrong with you child? Sit down here child." Pursa and Vada helped Terence to one of the chairs. "How long has this been going on?" Pursa wanted to know.

"Oh, I had the first attack the other day. It seems to be happening every morning. I spoke to Auntie about this. She said I might have a bug of some kind. If I get sick like this again, I'm going to the doctor. I can't be getting sick like this all the time."

"I don't know if you won't keep getting sick or no", Pursa said. "Let me look at you child." Pursa pulled down Terence' eyes, looked at them, then she looked at the dip in her throat. "You got a bug alright; you's going to have a baby", Pursa said with a smile in her voice.

"I'll be a duck with side-pockets", Sam said jumping up and down.

"I am so happy for you", Vada said with joy.

"A baby!" Terence said slowly. "Oh my gosh, I hadn't thought of that. Pursa are you sure? I got to tell Andrew right now."

"I'm sure, but you wait til tonight and tell him real loving like. If you wake up in the night and you see him smiling in his sleep, then you know what he's smiling about. Now you run along and help him finish decorating."

"Oh we have finished decorating. Andrew wants you all to come out and see how it looks. We kind of arranged the lights. First I want to show Vada something. Vada, come with me."

Vada followed Terence up the stairs to what used to be the ball room. In the ballroom, Terence went to a closet and opened the door. Staring out at Vada was an oil painting of her mother and father. Terence moved the two paintings out of the closet. Another surprise was a painting of old Mr. and Mrs. Duncan.

"Oh Terence", Vada exclaimed. "Did you do this? How did you get the two to sit down for you. The paintings are so much like them. They look so real." Not letting Terence get a word in, Vada kept commenting, "I like the skin tones. Father is a nice dark brown and mother is not too yellow."

"I did them from memory. I wanted to surprise them for Christmas. I got the antique white frames from the cellar. They really helped bring out the tones in the paintings. I only had a picture of father Duncan."

"All I have to say is you are a genius. If you have time, I would like you to do father and mother for me."

"I will be happy to. I'm glad you like them. This is one of my presents to Andrew. I got him a horse too, but he tricked me into telling him about the horse. We better get the others so we can see what they all think of the decorations."

They all agreed that the decorations were just beautiful and would take top prize if there was one, if old Sam didn't have to decide. The house looked like a picture on a magazine cover.

Chapter 20

They were standing on the porch chatting when two cars drove up. One car came half way up the left side of the drive and the other, right side. The first thing that jumped into their minds was, who is this? From where they were standing, they could see it was trouble. The men wore red bandanas over their nose and mouth. Their hats were pulled down as if to shade their eyes from the sun. They looked like hold-up men, cowboy style. But they all knew this was a lynch mob. The Duncan's, Sam, Pursa and Vada were speechless. Their mouths were locked with fear. Their bodies were frozen where they stood, but their inners were trembling on the inside with fright. The men pulled the bandanas off. There were four men in each car. The men got out of the cars and walked slowly. About twenty feet from the porch, one of the men on the left stepped out about three feet. In his hand was a sixteen-gauge shotgun. The man with the gun cried out in a loud hideous voice, "She's dead, she's dead you hear." The soft cold southern breeze stirred the scent of whiskey in the air. "You heard what I said—she's dead! She was the only one I loved and you had to kill her for your lust for power. You tried to hide your sins from that pretty wife. You wanted people to think you were pure as gold. You son of bitch. My wife knew you were a no good son of a seacock." Doff pulled a bottle from his pocket; he took a swig of whiskey to help him do his mission. His face turned red, his voice furious. "I'll you tell your wife how you used to meet my wife for play. How can you stand there with your niggers, specially with that nigger bitch you had that bastard by? How can you be so bold?"

"Doff, you get off my place. If you don't, I'll have the Sheriff take care of you", Andrew finally blurted out with his eyes having a deadly stare of shock, still frightened from the mob.

"I'd like to see you try to move me, good buddy. I told you I would get the son of a bitch, if she died. You know you sent your nigger Sam to beat my wife trying to keep her from telling that pretty wife what a no-good, low-down son of a bitch you are. I loved her and you are going to pay for her life. Alright men, get Sam."

Sam was standing somewhat in the yard. Doff held the shotgun on the others on the porch as the men went for Sam. Sam stood glued to ground. When Sam did move, two of men grabbed him. The women started

177

screaming loud and piercing and crying. As the men carried Sam off by his feet and arms, fear left Vada. She started beating on the men yelling, "Leave my dad alone. He hasn't done anything, you white bastards." Two of the men grabbed Vada by her arms and twisted them in back of her until she screamed, "You're hurting me." Vada stopped trying to get away from the men. With the men holding her, she looked helpless at the men who carried her father away. Suddenly, Vada cried out, "For God's sake-don't kill my father. He didn't kill your wife." Tears were streaming down her face.

Terence was shouting and pleading for Andrew to do something. Andrew didn't know what to do or say. To Andrew, all of this was a nightmare. Andrew started to make a move toward Doff.

"Andrew, I dare you to make one more step. I'd as soon kill you as Sam", Doff hissed in a loud angry voice, holding the gun in firing position.

Out of fear and shock, Andrew said in a calm and somewhat nervous voice, "Doff you must be a mad man. You know Lee built her own pit and fell in it."

"You are a liar. You and your niggers are the cause of all of this trouble."

Cars stopped on the busy highway to watch the commotion. All who were looking saw it was a lynch mob. Terror stared at them. The excitement of terror made them want to see this gruesome drama of life and death. The men had a time getting Sam to one of the cars. Sam had put up a good fight for his life. The old man had a lot of steam in him. He had gotten loose from the men three times. The people standing around did nothing to stop this awful thing.

All of a sudden, Pursa came down the steps with some of the branches from the decorations. She started beating Doff with them. Trout came out of nowhere to where the men were trying to hold Sam in the car. Trout tugged and pulled at the men's clothing, charging and rearing, biting the men. The men tried to keep Trout off of them and hold on to Sam. At the same time, Doff took the gun and forcefully pushed Pursa off of him. As he pushed Pursa off of him the gun, with his finger on the trigger, went off with a loud boom. One shot and Pursa fell dead, grasping the evergreen in her hand. People ran every which way.

Vada and Terence were crying out of control. Andrew just stood there looking at Pursa's small body—shaking his head in disbelief as the red, red blood spurted from Pursa's body.

With Trout's help, Sam got away from the men. Sam ran back to where Doff was. One man said, "Look out Doff!" Doff turned and in a split second, there was another loud boom. Doff had pulled death again.

Sam said real innocent-like, "You done killed my wife. We ain't done nothing." Sam fell to the ground and gave up the ghost.

People were still standing around looking at this tragedy.

Through all the excitement, Andrew got into the house and got the gun out of the desk drawer. In a loud angry voice, he said, "Doff if you don't drop that gun, I'll be forced to kill you." Andrew shot one bullet at Doff's feet. Andrew was a good shot. He had gone hunting too many times with old Sam. Doff seemed to have lost his power, anger and madness. Without hesitation, Doff dropped the gun. The men drove off in one of the cars. Doff looked from Sam to Pursa. He had killed two people he had known all his life. To his knowledge, he had done no wrong. Doff looked like wilted lettuce in hot sun. He looked again at Sam, Pursa and then at Andrew and at Vada and Terence. Doff had a queer look on his face. That look on his face said—what have I done? By this time, Sheriff Bates and his men had arrived on the scene.

Vada knelt down, took her father in her arms, looking at her mother looking toward Heaven with her tears running down her face, she cried out, "Lord is this the kind of death you wish for my father and mother to die?"

Andrew went from Sam to Pursa, then with dry tears in his eyes said, "They're gone, all gone." Terence was at his side with tears flowing from her eyes, looking at the two people he came to love so dearly. Looking at her husband, she saw in him the love that was as strong as death.

Sheriff Bates had two of his men carry Vada into the house. The Duncan's followed.

The gruesome drama of life and death had passed in review. People started to gather around to view the dead, but Sheriff Bates made them all leave. Someone was nice enough to put sheets over Sam and Pursa. Poor Trout laid by Sam's body, whining in a crying-like manner sounding like a child that had lost his mother.

What will they do to Doff and his men? You know and I know, with Christmas just around the corner, the merry will be taken out of Christmas for many that knew these two people. Not because of these two people died, but because of the way they died and the justice that will never be, because their skin is black. As black folks, we let justice pass and wave good-bye. We demand justice only up to a point. We don't demand justice for black on black. The white man looks down on us and looks off. For this cause, why does the black man look up to the white man for justice, when we don't demand justice from the black folk? Why do we look for justice from the white man? Because he is in authority and because he wrote the books of law. The authorities should exercise the law to the fullest.

What will they do to Doff and his men—that is the question.

There was much mourning for Sam, and Pursa McCloud. Yes tears fell from the white eyes as well as the black. They laid them in the Duncan's burial grounds. I could hear Sam and Pursa singing in sweet harmony 'Swing low sweet chariot coming for to carry me home.'

But Sam's spirit wailed from the grave saying, "Today, this is not the question, shall this nation remain half free, deceive laws for a faithful people or shall we have full rights for all races in this country? Today, the question is—shall this nation be godly or ungodly? For we as a nation have come this far by faith. Our motto 'In God we Trust.' What will we have our children to feed on. Vain thoughts of men or the true way of God. Oh little children of so little faith, our way of life isn't left up to the standards of men, but God. Let us not forget that life is bitter and life is sweet. We are all Americans."

Behold how good and how pleasant it is for brethren to dwell together in unity. Psalm 133.

The black American still seeks after what the great war was so bravely fought for. We go from state to state trying to find this liberty and justice for all from that year 1863 to this year 1963 and beyond.

About the Author

Thelmore McCaine is a native resident of St. Louis, Missouri. Thelmore was blessed with an abundance of talent. She is an artist, working with oils, chalk, acrylic paint, clay, and mud. She is also a seamstress, doing what she calls "upholstery folding." She has designed and built furniture, and she loves to decorate. She writes when she is inspired, having written six books, and hopes to have them all in print. She has truly used her talent.

– Robyn Foster

Printed in the United States
36004LVS00004B/406-417